PETER DRAX

MURDER BY CHANCE

With an introduction
by Curtis Evans

DEAN STREET PRESS

Published by Dean Street Press 2017

Introduction copyright © 2017 Curtis Evans

All Rights Reserved

First published in 1936 by Hutchinson & Co. Ltd.

Cover by DSP

ISBN 978 1 911579 55 7

www.deanstreetpress.co.uk

PETER DRAX
MURDER BY CHANCE

Eric Elrington Addis, aka 'Peter Drax', was born in Edinburgh in 1899, the youngest child of a retired Indian civil servant and the daughter of an officer in the British Indian Army.

Drax attended Edinburgh University, and served in the Royal Navy, retiring in 1929. In the 1930s he began practising as a barrister, but, recalled to the Navy upon the outbreak of the Second World War, he served on HMS *Warspite* and was mentioned in dispatches. When Drax was killed in 1941 he left a wife and two children.

Between 1936 and 1939, Drax published six crime novels: *Murder by Chance* (1936), *He Shot to Kill* (1936), *Murder by Proxy* (1937), *Death by Two Hands* (1937), *Tune to a Corpse* (1938) and *High Seas Murder* (1939). A further novel, *Sing a Song of Murder*, unfinished by Drax on his death, was completed by his wife, Hazel Iris (Wilson) Addis, and published in 1944.

By Peter Drax

Murder by Chance
He Shot to Kill
Death by Two Hands
Tune to a Corpse
High Seas Murder
Sing a Song of Murder

INTRODUCTION

Eric Elrington Addis, aka "Peter Drax," one of the major between-the-wars exponents and practitioners of realism in the British crime novel, was born near the end of the Victorian era in Edinburgh, Scotland on 19 May 1899, the youngest child of David Foulis Addis, a retired Indian civil servant, and Emily Malcolm, daughter of an officer in the British Indian Army. Drax died during the Second World War on 31 August 1941, having been mortally wounded in a German air raid on the British Royal Navy base at Alexandria, Egypt, officially known as HMS *Nile*. During his brief life of 42 years, Drax between the short span from 1936 to 1939 published six crime novels: *Murder by Chance* (1936), *He Shot to Kill* (1936), *Murder by Proxy* (1937), *Death by Two Hands* (1937), *Tune to a Corpse* (1938) and *High Seas Murder* (1939). An additional crime novel, *Sing a Song of Murder*, having been left unfinished by Drax at his death in 1941 and completed by his novelist wife, was published in 1944. Together the Peter Drax novels constitute one of the most important bodies of realistic crime fiction published in the 1930s, part of the period commonly dubbed the "Golden Age of detective fiction." Rather than the artificial and outsize master sleuths and super crooks found in so many classic mysteries from this era, Drax's novels concern, as publicity material for the books put it, "police who are not endowed with supernatural powers and crooks who are also human." In doing so they offered crime fiction fans from those years some of the period's most compelling reading. The reissuing of these gripping tales of criminal mayhem and murder, unaccountably out-of-print for more than seven decades, by Dean Street Press marks a signal event in recent mystery publishing history.

Peter Drax's career background gave the future crime writer constant exposure to the often grim rigors of life, experience which he most effectively incorporated into his fiction. A graduate of Edinburgh Academy, the teenaged Drax served during the First World War as a Midshipman on HMS *Dreadnought* and

Marlborough. (Two of his three brothers died in the war, the elder, David Malcolm Addis, at Ypres, where his body was never found.) After the signing of the armistice and his graduation from the Royal Naval College, Drax remained in the Navy for nearly a decade, retiring in 1929 with the rank of Lieutenant-Commander, in which capacity he supervised training with the New Zealand Navy, residing with his English wife, Hazel Iris (Wilson) Addis, daughter of an electrical engineer, in Auckland. In the 1930s he returned with Hazel to England and began practicing as a barrister, specializing, predictably enough, in the division of Admiralty, as well as that of Divorce. Recalled to the Navy upon the outbreak of the Second World War, Drax served as Commander (second-in-command) on HMS *Warspite* and was mentioned in dispatches at the Second Battle of Narvik, a naval affray which took place during the 1940 Norwegian campaign. At his death in Egypt in 1941 Drax left behind Hazel --herself an accomplished writer, under the pen name Hazel Adair, of so-called middlebrow "women's fiction"--and two children, including Jeremy Cecil Addis, the late editor and founder of *Books Ireland*.

Commuting to his London office daily in the 1930s on the 9.16, Drax's hobby became, according to his own account, the "reading and dissecting of thrillers," ubiquitous in station book stalls. Concluding that the vast majority of them were lamentably unlikely affairs, Drax set out over six months to spin his own tale, "inspired by the desire to tell a story that was credible." (More prosaically the neophyte author also wanted to show his wife, who had recently published her first novel, *Wanted a Son*, that he too could publish a novel.) The result was *Murder by Chance*, the first of the author's seven crime novels. In the United States during the late 1920s and early 1930s, recalled Raymond Chandler in his essay "The Simple Art of Murder" (originally published in 1944), the celebrated American crime writer Dashiell Hammett had given "murder back to the kind of people who commit it for reasons, not just to provide a corpse; and with the means at hand, not with hand-wrought dueling pistols, curare and tropical fish." Drax's debut crime novel, which followed on the heels of Hammett's books, made something of a similar impression in the United Kingdom, with mystery writer and founding Detection Club member Milward Kennedy in the *Sunday Times* pronouncing the novel a "thriller of great merit" that was "extremely convincing" and the influential *Observer* crime fiction critic Torquemada avowing, "I have not for a good many months enjoyed a thriller as much as I have enjoyed *Murder by Chance.*"

What so impressed these and other critics about *Murder by Chance* and Drax's successive novels was their simultaneous plausibility and readability, a combination seen as a tough feat to pull off in an era of colorful though not always entirely credible crime writers like S. S. Van Dine, Edgar Wallace and John Dickson Carr. Certainly in the 1930s the crime novelists Dorothy L. Sayers, Margery Allingham and Anthony Berkeley, among others (including Milward Kennedy himself), had elevated the presence of psychological realism in the crime novel; yet the criminal milieus that these authors presented to readers were mostly resolutely occupied by the respectable middle and upper classes. Drax offered British readers what was then an especially bracing change of atmosphere (one wherein mean streets replaced country mansions and quips were exchanged for coshes, if you will)—as indicated in this resoundingly positive Milward Kennedy review of Drax's fifth crime novel, *Tune to a Corpse* (1938):

> I have the highest opinion of Peter Drax's murder stories.... Mainly his picture is of low life in London, where crime and poverty meet and merge. He draws characters who shift uneasily from shabby to disreputable associations.... and he can win our sudden liking, almost our respect, for creatures in whom little virtue is to be found. To show how a drab crime was committed and then to show the slow detection of the truth, and to keep the reader absorbed all the time—this is a real achievement. The secret of Peter Drax's success is his ability to make the circumstances as plausible as the characters are real....

Two of Peter Drax's crime novels, the superb *Death by Two Hands* and *Tune to a Corpse*, were published in the United States, under the titles, respectively, *Crime within Crime* and *Crime to Music*, to very strong notices. The *Saturday Review of Literature*, for example, pronounced of *Crime within Crime* that "as a straightforward eventful yarn of little people in [the] grip of tragic destiny it's brilliantly done" and of *Crime to Music* that "London underworld life is described with color and realism. The steps in the weakling killer's descent to Avernus [see Virgil] are thrillingly traced." That the country which gave the world Dashiell Hammett could be so impressed with the crime fiction of Peter Drax surely is strong recommendation indeed. Today seedily realistic urban British crime fiction of the 1930s is perhaps most strongly associated with two authors who dabbled in crime fiction: Graham Greene (*Brighton Rock*, 1938, and others) and Gerald Kersh (*Night and the City*, 1938). If not belonging on quite that exalted level, the novels of Peter Drax nevertheless grace this gritty roster, one that forever changed the face of British crime fiction.

Curtis Evans

CHAPTER I

JOHANNIS KUDORFER was a native of an eastern Mediterranean state. By profession he was a master mariner, and he might have made a success of it had not greed led him into certain ventures which even the most charitable had characterized as shady. The agents of a certain firm of underwriters had suggested to Johannis that it might be in the interests of all concerned, and most certainly of the underwriters, if he were to transfer his energies to some other profession.

Ships which Johannis commanded acquired a most unfortunate tendency to leave their natural element and try conclusions with rocks. Sometimes the accident was attributed to the presence of fog and at other times to malevolent and hitherto unknown currents. But whatever the reason might be the result was usually the same, and the owners of the vessel concerned experienced the pleasure of learning that she had become a total loss. The crews, it may have been supposed, were invariably gifted with second sight, for they never failed to leave the sinking ship clad in their newest suits and carrying their belongings in waterproof bags.

The true value of the ship and the amount for which she had been insured could never under any circumstances be made to agree. The difference was invariably in favour of the owners, who profited by the disaster to the tune of several thousands of pounds. Johannis was cunning. He had never actually been bowled out. Occasionally the underwriters fought the claims in the English courts and in that event Johannis and his brother wreckers attended. The story they recounted had been carefully rehearsed and the ship's log had been written up in accordance with this prearranged version.

Now you may wreck a ship once and get away with it. You may even be successful at the second attempt, but to make a habit of such a dangerous pastime is to ask for trouble. People are apt to become suspicious. The brokers and underwriters concerned became more than suspicious. They were morally certain that Johannis was a thorough bad lot, and, in order to protect their interest, those who had suffered through the vagaries of the ships which Johannis had commanded called a meeting. At that gathering it was decided that not one of those present would underwrite any risk to a ship which had the doubtful honour of carrying Captain Johannis Kudorfer.

This was very unfortunate for that hardy and resourceful mariner, but he, being of a saving disposition as well as of a philosophical turn of mind, had accumulated a sufficient sum of money to purchase the Island of Posnik. There he settled down to the life of a wealthy landed proprietor. He enjoyed collecting rents from the fishermen who constituted almost the entire population of the island, and there were times when he even carried out the duties of bartender in the only public house of which the island boasted. Such shops as there were came under his sole control, and Johannis in the course of time grew fat and, it would appear, lazy and contented. But once a seaman always a rover. He tired of unaccustomed ease and safety, and when a cable addressed to Captain Kudorfer was brought to his house one day by a ragged, bare-footed boy, his heart began to thump. Perhaps it was from one of his old ship-owning, swindling friends who had need of his services? Maybe it was. . . . He slit open the flimsy envelope and read the brief message.

If disengaged and wishing employment cable Hartford Neeles London.

Hartford. Hartford. He was sure he had heard the name somewhere before. It was fortunate for Hartford's chances of receiving a favourable reply from Kudorfer that the latter had not heard of that very private meeting in the City of London at which the confidence of those present had been unreservedly withdrawn from Johannis. Mr. Hartford, in the role of a broker, had been present, and as the story of Kudorfer's life had been laid bare he began to entertain a certain respect for this Levantine scoundrel. Hartford himself was a scoundrel, and was therefore in a position to appraise Johannis' worth at its true valuation.

Sam Hartford should, if appearances went for anything, have been a farmer or a country parson. He was fat and possessed an engaging manner which at one time or another had caused the unwary to repose in Sam a confidence as ill-deserved as it was misplaced. He would, one might have thought, have done very well as a commercial traveller, and in point of fact he had tried his hand at that profession among many others with a monotonous lack of success.

At the age of thirty-five Sam had graduated in the hard school of confidence tricksters, and if there had been such a thing would no doubt have taken an honours degree. The police, unfortunately for Sam and luckily for the public, had suggested that he should really give the West End a rest, and it was in the role of a broker that he transferred his attention to the City, where one fine day he attended the meeting at which Johannis Kudorfer was discussed with such charming candour and complete disregard for the law of libel. A couple of months after this meeting Sam was unlucky enough to be discovered making some totally inaccurate entries in the petty cash book.

Then followed two lean months and Sam had to tighten his belt, while Johannis, in his position as the king of the Island of Posnik, let his belt out at the rate of one hole per week.

A few weeks before the murder of Geoffrey Hunt Sam was riding eastwards on a bus bound for a doss-house in the Mile End Road which, for the time being, he called home. He had spent one penny on a fish-cake and one on an evening paper. Eightpence remained, and the further financial outlook was so unsettled that Sam's usually benign expression had given place to one of rueful despair. Lack of good food and a sufficiency of beer to wash it down had taken all the stuffing out of him. A man sitting behind him leaned forward and clapped Sam on the shoulder.

"What cheer, mate, you don't look so good."

"Why, if it ain't Dusty! Where are you bound, pal?"

"Home, but come on and have a wet first," Dusty suggested. "I'll stand treat. I took thirty bob this morning. How are you fixed, Sam?"

"Cleaned right out, and that would be my luck on the very day that I lit on a job that would make my blooming fortune just as easy as kiss your hand."

At Aldgate station Dusty and Sam got off the bus. Dusty led the way into a saloon bar and ordered two pints of bitter.

"Come over to this table in the corner. We'll be able to chin there without any bloke busting in."

Sam drank deeply from his glass and then set it down with a sigh of content.

"Nothing ain't so bad as beer can't make it better. Wonderful things, hops. Have you ever thought of—"

"I know all about hops," Dusty interrupted. "What I wants to hear about is this swell job of yours. I'm about fed up with jawing my head off at a lot of half-baked mugs and I'm ripe for a little flutter."

"How much dough have you got, Dusty?" asked Sam, but Dusty only winked in reply and laid a finger to his nose.

"You're not trying to con me, are you, Sam? 'Cause if you are, you're out of luck this time, old cock. I've got a little cash for an investment, but none to give away."

"Investment's the word for this little idea of mine, Dusty. And it's watertight. You couldn't help clearing eight thousand quid, but it would have to be cut three ways. You see, there's the bloke what put me on to it. He would want his share The exes won't run to more than a thousand, or say twelve hundred at the outside, so we ought to have more than eight thousand between the three of us."

"Expenses twelve hundred? Look here, Sam, you don't think I can raise that? Twelve hundred pounds! Make it shillings and I might be able to help a bit."

"Now there ain't no need to get excited, Dusty. I know it wouldn't be likely for you to have twelve hundred pounds, but all I should want would be enough to start the show. Something to bait the trap with. I could do it with fifty, but a century would be better. I don't want to take no risks."

"Fifty! Now you're talking! But I don't say I've got it. Anyway, you go on and spill the beans and I'll tell you what I can do."

"Righto. That's fair enough, but it's a long story."

Sam glanced at his empty glass and Dusty took the hint.

"I've been working in the City," Sam began, "in an insurance broker's office, and while I was there I heard a lot about the swindles that are worked by blokes that get a ship insured for double her value and then sink her and collect the insurance money from the underwriters. I palled up with a chap in another office and as soon as I laid eyes on him I knew him for a shyster. He seemed to think I was the same as him, but how he could tell beat me. Anyway, he told me of a job he was hoping to pull off if he could get anybody to put up the dough. He asked me to go in with him and I said I would. His story sounded good to me, so I did a bit of nosying around and I found that what he said was true enough. At least most of it was. His name's Brown, but everyone calls him Alfred. He's a little feller. Not the sort you'd take any notice of if you saw him in the street, but he's as smart as a whip. He's sandy-haired and wears glasses. Doesn't speak much, in fact—"

"All right, I'll take him as read," Dusty interrupted. "Let's get on with the story."

"Well, the way he told it to me was this. He knows a bloke what owns a ship which is about ripe for the ship breakers. She's got a month to run before she comes up for her next Lloyds survey, and from what Alfred tells me she couldn't earn the money that would have to be spent on her if she was run till her screw dropped off. The freight market at the present moment is as rotten as a last year's egg. But—and this is where we come to the interesting part—this ship is insured for a little over twelve thousand pounds against a total loss. Her value for breaking up is somewhere in the region of two thousand, and that's the figure she could be bought for today. There or thereabouts. If we can raise the oodle we'd buy her and get some sort of cargo. We wouldn't need to bother about the freight. We'd just run her to some out of the way spot and sink her."

"Now look here, Sam, all I know about ships is seeing them on pictures. I've never been on the sea and I'm not going."

"That's all right. There won't be no need for either of us to turn into ruddy sailors. I know of a chap who can turn the trick for us. His name's Kudorfer. I sent him a cable and he'll be here by the fifteenth of the month. A month or two back I thought I had a good chance of mizzling a spot of cash from the place I was working at, but before I could bring it off they gave me the push and it was only about a measly five quid I lifted. I was going to take to the dogs. You see how I'm landed, with this bloke turning up next week wanting his passage money and heaven knows what else. I tell you this, Dusty, I've been fair driven wild this last week thinking of thousands of quids going down the drain all for the want of a measly hundred or so."

"Let's get this straight, Sam. I haven't got the hang of it yet. The idea is, as I see it, to buy this ship and sink her, and the man who's going to do it is this bloke Kudorfer. By the way, what nationality is he? A Greek?"

"He calls himself a Lavakian," Sam replied. "Says he belongs to some potty little state somewhere in the Ægean. But that doesn't matter a hang. We haven't any too much time to waste if we want to get that couple of thousand before he turns up. I'll tell you how we'll do it. We'll put an advertisement in one of the morning papers which'll read something like this:

"Exceptional opportunity for young man of sea-going experience to purchase a share in sound progressive concern. Employment guaranteed."

"That sounds O.K. to me," commented Dusty, "and true enough except that there isn't any business as yet. But why do you want to put in the bit about 'seagoing experience'? Kudorfer'll be able to do all the needful in that line, won't he?"

"No, that's the trouble. He's a dago, and we could only get him on board as a passenger or as a supercargo. The sort of bloke I want to get hold of is a merchant-service officer who has got a little cash and is fed up with taking orders from someone else. We'll offer him the post of skipper, and after that there won't be any trouble getting the money out of him."

CHAPTER II

International Developments Ltd. was a child of the brain of Sam Hartford. It had taken him quite a long time to fill up all the forms required by the various Company Acts, and when he had finished and stuck on the last stamp he examined the various documents with excusable pride. It was true that the company did not boast any assets in the way of real property or office furniture. It was also true that the nominal capital was £100, of which £1 had been paid up. The particular business in which the company was to deal failed to materialize, and Sam regretfully placed the papers in an old tin box and tried to forget about them.

Now that he had fallen in with Dusty and there seemed a chance of raising the wind he decided to revive the moribund company, and in an extra-ordinarily short space of time the words "International Developments Ltd." were painted in large black letters on a glazed door in an office building in Chancery Lane. Before the paint was dry a van arrived bringing carpets, furniture, and a typewriter, and Sam and Dusty spent a happy afternoon trying to make the rather dingy room look like the office of a successful and progressive business concern. At four o'clock Alfred arrived.

"Here's the bloke that put me on to this biz," Sam announced. "He's going to give us a hand."

"Pleased to meet you." Dusty looked at the little man with interest tinged with contempt. "Proper little runt," he muttered to himself; "but he can do the dirty work."

Alfred, after shaking hands with Dusty, peeled off his gloves and examined the office.

"Yes, it'll do," he said at last. "But what we haven't got is books. You know, ledgers, cash books and files. I'll see to that. I know a place where I can get some cheap. When does the balloon go up?"

"The advert was in this morning's paper," Sam replied. "We've just got to wait now till the fish begin to bite. Where d'you want your desk, Alfred?"

"I'll sit here in this room. And you can stop in the other. I'll give 'em the once over and if I think they're any good I'll send 'em in to you. But before we start on the game, what's it going to be worth to me? That's what I want to know."

Dusty and Sam exchanged a look which Alfred noted but ignored. Sam coughed and fiddled with his tie.

"Well, of course, Alfred, Mr. Miller here is putting up the cash and I'm going to do most of the work so to speak, so I thought—I mean we thought—that if you were to take £500 that would be fair. You see," he added quickly, noting a dangerous gleam in Alfred's cold grey eyes, "it's not as if you're risking anything, and all you've got to do is to sort of dress the place. Bang away at the typewriter and make out you're busy as hell."

"I'm treasurer and secretary of this company," Alfred announced quietly; "and if you don't like it the whole thing's off. One word from me to the brokers and you're sunk. This was my idea from the start and I'll only let the business go on if I get a one-third share. I'm going to get some tea now, but I'll be back in an hour and you can let me know what you've decided."

"'Strewth!" said Dusty as the door closed behind Alfred. "He's got teeth, that blasted little rabbit. You didn't put me wise to this, Sam. I thought we were going to cut fifty-fifty."

"Secretary and treasurer!" Sam lay back in his chair and mopped his brow. "Of all the flaming little twisters! And me thinking the same as you that he couldn't say boo to a goose. Honest, Dusty, I never thought he'd turn nasty like this, and after me offering him five hundred. It's not as if he had anything to do or anything to lose, but it's always the way when you think you've got a thing all set, some bloke comes along and chucks a spanner in the works."

"There's no good going up in the air about it," said Dusty quietly. "Not at this stage, at any rate. When he comes back you tell him we agree to his condition, but don't make it look as though you're giving in too easy. Have a bit of an argument about it first. When we get the money'll be time enough to start worrying."

"I've got an idea," announced Sam. He had regained his accustomed placidity and was puffing away at a pipe. "What I'll do is this. Tomorrow I'll take young Alfred round to the Consolidated Bank and we'll open an account there in the name of the company and arrange it so that all cheques have got to be signed by the three of us. Then, when I can get rid of him, you and me'll go to the Empire Bank and open another account in the company's name—but this time it'll only be me and you that'll sign the cheques. Twig?"

A smile spread over Dusty's face.

"That's the idea, mate, and I don't mind admitting I wouldn't have thought of that way out. This is a bit out of my line."

Next morning there were six callers at the offices of International Developments. Five had no money, so they didn't stay long. The sixth Alfred thought might do, and he sent him in to Sam who was seated at a desk in the inner office surrounded with papers.

"Ah, good morning, Mr.—" he glanced at the card which Alfred had given him. "Mr. Crane, or I should say Lieutenant Crane. What can I do for you?"

Maurice Crane was about thirty years of age but looked no more than twenty-five. In the eyes of Sam Hartford he was ripe for plucking—ingenuous and inexperienced in the ways of business men. For twelve years Maurice's pay had arrived each month in a little envelope. About half of it went to the mess-man, one quarter or less to his tailor, and the remainder was spent with no thought for the morrow. The idea of saving his money or investing it was never considered, and when one day he had taken it into his head to retire from the Royal Navy and had received the sum of twelve hundred pounds, he hadn't the slightest idea what to do with it. Henry Crane, his brother and senior by fifteen years, had given voice to a strong disapproval of his younger brother's action. Rather snuffily he suggested that the gratuity of twelve hundred pounds should be invested in 3½ per cent Conversion Stock. With the obstinacy of the completely ignorant, Maurice stuck his toes in at this point and said that he was perfectly capable of looking after his own affairs and money. This statement was quite untrue, but Henry, having had a certain experience of men in his career at the Bar, withdrew from the discussion. If Maurice wanted his advice he could damn' well ask for it.

Their parents both having died a few years before, Henry gave his brother a room in his flat in 25 Hilberry Mansions. In due course a collection of packing-cases and tin trunks arrived, which contained, in addition to a varied collection of other people's clothes, a bundle of curios which Maurice had picked up during three years on the China Station. There were silken sarongs, woven with gold and silver threads, models of native canoes, a few parangs and a kris which Maurice had bought in Sarawak. He was rather proud of the kris.

His uniforms were sold to a second-hand clothes dealer in Ludgate Circus, and it was then that Maurice first began to realize the joys of complete idleness. When he woke in the morning his first thought was that he needn't get up. He had no watch to keep. No one could send for him and ask why the devil he hadn't done this or that, and ask him what he thought he was doing.

This blissful state lasted exactly fourteen days, by which time his small stock of ready cash had run out, and, though he wouldn't have admitted it, he began to feel bored. He studied the advertisements in the morning papers of "Appointments Vacant", but it seemed that if you did not hold a University degree there wasn't much left for a man of his age, except a job as traveller in soft goods, whatever they were, or selling vacuum cleaners on commission, "car essential". It was only when he discovered the "Businesses for Sale" column that he felt there was some hope. Some of the advertisements sounded too good to be true.

Investment £500. Salary as Assistant Managing Director £750. Previous experience desirable but not essential.

Of what the experience should consist was never stated. The advertisement which Sam Hartford had inserted, however, took

Maurice's fancy. It looked as though it might suit. Anyway, he'd give it a go.

In answer to Hartford's question, Maurice replied that he had come about the job mentioned in the advertisement.

"Yes, I see," said Sam, and brought out a large blue print of the *Karnoc*, which he unrolled and placed on a table in the window. "Perhaps I had better explain quite briefly the nature of this business. Primarily I am a ship broker, but now and again I run a ship myself when I see a chance of good freights. A few days ago I learnt that the ship, the S.S. *Karnoc*, was for sale cheap. The man who had her went broke and the mortgagee was anxious to realize. As you know, prices have never been worse, and when it was suggested that if I made an offer of ten-and-six a ton it might be accepted, I went into the matter rather thoroughly. She is an old vessel, as you can see from the particulars on the plan. She was actually built in 1878, but she passed her last survey all right and was classed 100 AI. I have had a man look over her engines and hull. Here's his report."

It was Alfred who had drafted this imposing-looking document and indeed he had only just finished typing a fair copy when Maurice had arrived. It had got nothing to do whatever with the S.S. *Karnoc*, but was, in fact, taken from a report on another ship, which report Alfred had, with considerable foresight, taken from his employer's office.

Maurice skimmed through the typewritten sheets until he came to the last paragraph which read: "In my opinion this vessel is worth at least £3200 sterling."

"That works out at a little over twelve shillings a ton," Sam explained. "So you see she's a bargain, but I don't know why I'm bothering you about these figures. You see, I'm really looking for someone to go as skipper of her. The pay would be at the minimum Board of Trade rates with a bonus of 1 per cent on gross profits. Perhaps I ought to explain that it is the invariable practice of this company to insist on the captain having a small share in the venture. The reason is obvious. It ensures that he does everything in his power to make a good trip and waste as little time as possible in loading and unloading. Of course, the captain's investment is necessarily limited, as there are several members of the firm who are entitled to take a share."

"It sounds a darned good show," Maurice replied, "but I'm afraid I can't fill the bill. I haven't got a master's ticket, but I know a fellow who has. His name is Hunt, Geoffrey Hunt. I'll suggest it to him. Perhaps it would be as well if you could give me all particulars."

"Well, I don't think there's much more I can tell you," Sam replied. "I know where we can get a cargo at a good rate of freight, so a profit is assured. If necessary we can always sell the ship for at least £1000 more than the present owner is asking. It's a pity you can't take the skipper's job, but there it is."

Alfred, who had been listening to this conversation, entered the room at this juncture and placed a basketful of letters on Sam's desk. Sam effected the introduction between Alfred and Maurice and explained the state of affairs. Alfred studied Maurice for a moment in silence, and then:

"But you shouldn't have much trouble getting a ticket," he said. "I dare say you've got the necessary sea time in, and a week or two at a crammer's will be enough to get you through the exam. We want people on board whom we can trust," he added.

Maurice flushed. "That's very nice of you to put it like that and it's rather a good idea about a crammer's. I must say I should like to be in on this show. It's just the sort of job I should like."

When Maurice had left the office Dusty came out of his hiding-place behind a tall cupboard in the corner and followed the others into the inner office.

"Well, what luck? He looked like a sucker, as much of him as I could see, but the question is, Sam me lad, has he the dough?"

"Yes, I think he's got some all right," Sam replied. "But I didn't want to force the pace. He's keen, but I want to see him much keener before I touch him for a cheque, 'cause then he won't be so eager to make inquiries. If there's one thing we don't want it's people nosing round asking questions. I'd like to shoot every solicitor, then I'd be driving me own Rolls-Royce."

"It's all very well going slow at the first," Alfred agreed, "but we can't afford to wait over long. Then someone else'll buy that blinking ship and all the cash we've laid out'll be wasted."

"My cash, that was," Dusty put in. "Don't forget that." He crossed over to the window and leaned over the plan of the *Karnoc*. "She's a tidy size, ain't she, Sam?" he asked, and then read: "'5105 tons gross register'. Does that mean she'd carry that amount?"

"Add a third to it and you'll get about her capacity," said Alfred. "With some cargoes she'll take more than that even."

"Ships is a mystery to me, I don't mind admitting, but what I'd like to know is, how you're going to make her do the disappearing act? If you run her ashore on to rocks, isn't there a chance of some interfering swine coming along and pulling her off?"

"There's ways of doing it," said Alfred.

"I dare say there is, but I want to know what they are."

Alfred pointed to the engine-room marked on the plan.

"There's a valve there on a pipe which runs through the bottom of the ship. Yes, there it is, you can see it marked 'Kingston valve'. You open that, blow off the steam from the boilers and then hop into the boats. It takes anything from five to six hours to sink a ship that way, so there's plenty of time to get clear."

"And what happens if another ship comes along and sends someone on board and tows her ashore?" asked Dusty.

"That's Kudorfer's job," Sam replied. "As Alfred and me know, he's never been caught out yet. He's an artist at this sort of job."

CHAPTER III

ALFRED WAS SO abstracted when he left the office of International Developments that he gave a newsboy sixpence for a paper and did not wait for the change. He was worried. Somewhere, some time, he had heard the name of Geoffrey Hunt, but in what connection he was unable to recall. It was something sticky, he was pretty certain, but Alfred's various little adventures were usually sticky. He was a go-between. When a robbery had been committed the owners of the stolen property reported the matter to the police and to their insurance company. Sometimes the police were successful, but there were occasions when they had to own themselves beaten. It was then that the company which carried the risk of the stolen property sent out a hurry call for Alfred, and when he arrived they put the matter to him quite simply. They wanted the property back. Could he help them? Alfred's invariable reply was that he didn't think he could, but that if he did hear anything he would give them a ring.

It was very seldom indeed that the "ring" did not materialize, and then Alfred would hazard a guess that if so and so were done it might be that the goods would be discovered, say, in a litter basket on the Victoria Embankment. There were times when Alfred was employed by the police to effect the return of stolen goods. There was no question of compounding a felony, for no promise was ever given or even suggested that the thief would not receive his proper punishment were he caught.

It was in connection with one of these transactions, Alfred felt sure, that he had either met or been told of Geoffrey Hunt. He turned over the question in his mind as he walked down Norfolk Street to the Embankment, and before he had crossed the road and gained the tram stop he had made up his mind to go and see his Uncle Thomas. He would know Hunt if anyone did.

Uncle Thomas in his younger days had had sufficient experience of crime and prisons to be convinced that honesty, though quite a good policy for them who could afford to follow it, didn't butter his bread or fill his pint pot. When, after the expiration of his second stay at Dartmoor Prison, Uncle Thomas was escorted to Prince-town Station by a warder and handed a third-class ticket and directions for finding the office of the Prisoners' Aid Society, he decided that all this nonsense must stop. Prison life might be all right for some, but he liked his beer. The result of this resolution was that he hired a barrow and went in for hawking. His total capital was one pound one and ninepence, and his first stock was a lot of bananas which were just on the turn. He took care to halt his barrow at a respectable distance from a street light, with the gratifying result that he was able to pay the man from whom he had hired the barrow and go to bed with the comforting feeling that he had earned a profit and drunk half of it.

The desire for beer and yet more beer prevented Uncle Thomas from achieving the position of even a minor captain of industry, and it was quite on the cards that he might have descended to selling matches outside a tea-shop, had he not fallen in with an old friend with whom he had spent many dreary years at Dartmoor. It was almost with the feeling of one old Harrovian meeting another old Harrovian in the heart of darkest Africa that Uncle Thomas sighted his friend of the mail-bag and oakum-picking days in the public saloon of the "Dog and Duck".

The net result of this reunion was that Uncle Thomas agreed to receive and dispose of a packet of jewellery that his friend had "picked up" in the country. He was so successful in executing this commission that in the course of time Uncle Thomas became known to a certain section of the community of crime as the best fence in the Borough of Southwark.

He took a little shop and filled it with junk, which he bought at auction sales and carried home in a basket on four perambulator wheels. The basket bore the words "Pearl Laundry, Ltd.", and Uncle Thomas could see nothing out of place in his pushing this contraption through the streets while attired in a rusty frock coat and greenish top hat. He was never one to put much value on appearances. As his balance in the post office savings bank mounted up and in the course of time reached double figures, he became dissatisfied with the fare doled out by a grudging landlady. He decided to marry a lady who would do his cooking and clean his house, in return for seven-and-sixpence a week. That was Uncle Thomas's solution of the servant problem, and it worked most successfully.

The house he rented was No. 96 Graves Crescent. It was a thin little house with only a couple of rooms on each floor, but after a bed-sitting-room with a quarter share of a bathroom it was quite a good substitute for a suite at the Grosvenor Hotel. The wife he chose was a hard-working woman who preferred working for Uncle Thomas to toiling eight hours a day in the back room of a Jewish tailor in Whitechapel, and, in order to augment the weekly seven-and-sixpence she received from her lord and master, she took in washing. The Pearl Laundry basket came into its own again, and when Uncle Thomas was feeling unusually good-natured he would collect or deliver the washing. Besides, this perfectly legitimate business was a convenient cloak to Uncle Thomas's real business. A roll of silk could be wrapped in a dirty towel, and who would look for the results of the Notting Hill "smash" among a bundle of socks or handkerchiefs?

By tram and bus Alfred reached Graves Crescent, and in response to his knock the face of Uncle Thomas appeared above the casement curtains of the dining-room window. It was one of the old man's rules, never departed from, that the front door was not to be opened unless the person opening it knew the one outside.

"Come in, Alfred. How's things?"

"Not so bad."

"You look posh enough. What's the new lay you're on?"

Alfred swung round on Uncle Thomas and grasped him by the shoulder.

"What d'you mean—new lay? Who's been squawking?"

The old man laughed wheezily and took a pinch of snuff.

"Not like you to get rattled so easy, Alfred. Come along into the room and have a drop of something to settle your nerves. The old woman's gone to dish up the supper. It's tripe. There'll be plenty for you."

He poured a tot of whisky into a broad rummer and handed it to his nephew: "The siphon's on the side if you want it."

Alfred took a sip of his drink and then set down his glass and turned in his chair.

"Sorry I sort of flew off the handle just now, but I'm on a job that's going to take some doing if it's to be pulled off. If people start talking I'll have to chuck it up and that means losing a packet. They can jug you for fraud, can't they?"

"Obtaining money by false pretences is a misdemeanour punishable by seven years' penal servitude," said Uncle Thomas in the manner of a park orator. "I know. I did five years and two months out of my seven, and I haven't forgotten a single solitary day of that stretch, neither. It was being locked up in the winter for sixteen hours a day that got me. I remember once—"

Alfred had had experience of Uncle Thomas in reminiscent vein and interrupted the threatened story.

"Do you know a man named Hunt, Uncle? Geoffrey Hunt? I've heard of him but I can't place him."

"Hunt? Geoffrey Hunt? Yes, I know the man, I think. He's a little rat of a fellow, isn't he?"

"I don't know. I never saw him to my knowledge. He's a twister, isn't he?"

"Yes, he is that," Uncle Thomas agreed dryly. "He thought he was a gentleman. Why, I dunno, except he once owned a dinner jacket and a boiled shirt. Last time I saw him was at the Old Bailey when the Snicker was put away. They used to work together, them two. Hunt did the window-dressing while the Snicker did the work—and got jugged—and Gentleman Geoffrey slid off with the oodle. The busies were on to him, but he was too smart for 'em. Besides, he had the sense to come to me. I put the stuff where nobody could find it, and after a year or two I broke it up and realized eight hundred quid. I gave Hunt a couple of hundred out of it, which was as much as he deserved. The cheap skate!"

"Where's your hiding-hole, Uncle?" Alfred asked.

The old man wagged his head and laid a finger to his nose.

"You see this house, Alfred? The furniture, and the drink you're pouring down your throat? Well, there'd be none of that if I didn't keep that little bit of information under me hat. It's made my fortune and has kept me out of stir for the last twenty years."

"I wasn't trying to pump you," Alfred hastened to reassure the old man. "I was only wondering . . ."

"Well, if you keep on wondering till I'm under the sod pushing up the daisies, that'll suit me," replied Uncle Thomas. "Now what else was you wanting to know about our pal Geoffrey?"

"Where does he hang out? Has he any dough? And is he a double-crosser?"

"At present he's working up West from a flat in Clark Street. I've forgotten the number, but I could get it for you."

"That part doesn't matter much. Tell me anything else you know about him."

"He's got some cash," Uncle Thomas replied, "and is a member of one of them Service Clubs. He was in the R.N.R. during the war, that's how he got in. After the war he went to sea in the Merchant Service, but work didn't suit me lad of wax and he took up the crooked lay. He found it easier, seemingly. As to his being a double-crosser or not, I can't say. I've never heard anything against him in that way, but, then, his line don't often cross mine. He goes for hard cash."

Mrs. Honeypenny entered the room and caught her husband's eye.

"All ready, dear. Shall I get the beer up?"

Uncle Thomas threw a bunch of keys down on the table.

"Yes, two bottles. I'm dry."

Alfred glanced at the keys as Mrs. Honeypenny leaned over the table to pick them up.

"That's a funny sort of a one, ain't it?" he said. "That flat one. I've only seen one like it before, but I can't mind where it was."

Uncle Thomas looked up from the pipe he was lighting and a frown wrinkled his forehead.

"That key? Why, that belongs to the shop," he explained after a short pause.

Alfred knew that he lied but forbore to press the matter. It would come to him in time—the kind of lock that key fitted.

When supper was finished and cleared away Uncle Thomas took Alfred into the sitting-room.

"Sit down, Alfred. We'll be quieter here while that woman's messing about. I want to hear what sort of job you've got on with Geoffrey Hunt. Will there be any pickings?"

"I'm afraid there'll be nothing for you, Uncle," Alfred replied. "It's going to be hard cash this time and no 'busting' or 'smashing'."

Uncle Thomas nodded. "I see. You're going in for the long firm racket?"

"No, nothing like that. This is on the level. At least there isn't a dog's chance of being bowled out. The worst that can happen is that we won't get what we're after."

"Well, what's it all about?" asked the old man impatiently.

"You wouldn't understand if I told you. It's got to do with a ship."

"Which means you're not spilling any beans. Maybe you're right. Ship, you said? So that's why you're taking in Gentleman Geoffrey. But he's forgot all he ever knew about them. Besides, he goes on the booze and he's losing his nerve, they tell me. You know, Alfred, you ought to keep out of this. You say it's safe, but you know less than my cat about ships, and if you don't know your job inside out it'll come unstuck. You see if it don't."

"Oh, for God's sake don't start croaking. We haven't got it going yet and it's going to be queasy work the next few days. There's Sam—you know him?"

"He hasn't got the guts of a louse."

"That's part of the trouble. He thinks he's running the show, but he'll never carry it, and I damned near told him so. And then there's Dusty Miller. He's all right in his way, but too flash for my way of thinking."

"Yes," agreed Uncle Thomas. "He's a good 'barker' and he does a bit of pitching in the markets, but that kind never stick at anything for two days together."

"He's put all his dough in this job."

"Of course that makes a difference. He's a clever bloke in his way." Uncle Thomas rubbed his chin ruminatively. "I've watched him selling stuff and he's a wizard at that game. He could sell a box of plants to a bloke what hadn't got a garden. He'd make him feel that the one thing he did need was a dozen mixed wallflower, and like as not they'd turn out to be Canterbury Bells or Sweet William."

When Uncle Thomas had seen Alfred off at the front door he sought his wife out in the kitchen.

"That young fellar's going to get into trouble one of these days if he's not careful," he said.

CHAPTER IV

Maurice Crane drove to his club on leaving the offices of International Developments and looked up Hunt's name in the Quarterly Navy List. His memory of Hunt was a bit hazy after ten years, but his impression was that he was the man for the job. He had a bit of money. Of course that was some time ago, and he had probably lost it by now, but still it might be worth getting on to him. Crane scribbled a note, addressed it "c/o the Admiralty", and sent it off by a District Messenger. It would be fun to meet Hunt again. He was so different from the rest of the men he knew. In what way it was difficult to say exactly, but he had drive, abundant spirits, and a useful knack of overcoming any difficulty which might arise in a manner quite his own. That he wasn't straight was a fact which Crane had quite failed to perceive, and if anyone had said a word against his friend he would have resented the suggestion.

The note which Crane had despatched was delivered to Geoffrey Hunt on the following morning while he was deciding how far a couple of shillings would go towards buying a breakfast to fit his appetite. Lunch was too far distant to worry about, and as for the rent due at the end of the week—well, if he, Geoffrey, didn't have a bit of luck by then his landlord would be out of luck too.

It was not easy to make out from Crane's scrawl what exactly was meant, but at least it wasn't a dun, and Crane, if he remembered rightly, was a fair example of the genus "Mug". He would sting him for lunch and probably a fiver.

They met in the hall of Crane's club, and over a cocktail exchanged memories of the old days. "I saw old Simpson the other day at the 'Goat'. You remember him, he was our purser." And. "Do you know what happened to Cox? He got tied up with a barmaid at Plymouth. He's got a job at Elstree doing crowd work."

Hunt stood it for a time, but when coffee was reached and Crane showed no sign of coming to the point, he broached the subject of the "job" mentioned in Crane's letter.

"Stiffen the Dutch! Of course. I knew there was something frightfully important I wanted to see you about," exclaimed Crane.

He explained in a muddled sort of way the gist of his talk with Sam Hartford.

"They want a fellow to skipper this old tub. It seems there's a packet of money to be made out of her, and they're willing, in fact they insist, that you take a share. Hartford is an awfully decent sort of bloke and absolutely straight, I'm sure. He's got an office in Chancery Lane."

"Why don't you take the job?" Hunt queried.

"Haven't got a master's ticket, old man. You have, and I thought you were the sort of bloke who'd jump at this job. It's in your line and there's a chance of clearing quite a little bit."

"What were they asking you to put into it?"

"Round about two thousand."

Hunt laughed.

"You can count me out. I'm—well, not exactly broke, but as near it as no matter."

Crane ordered two liqueur brandies.

When Geoffrey Hunt left the club he took with him a five-pound note—"Let you have it back at the end of the week, old man"—and the address of International Developments Ltd. He spent an hour at Somerset House, and later paid a visit to a Public Library, where he consulted Lloyds' Register of Steam and Motor Vessels. Armed with the information he had gained regarding the company and the S.S. *Karnoc*, he took a bus to Chancery Lane and in due course reached the office of International Developments. He turned the handle quietly and entered the outer office. There was no one there. He took down a ledger, the entries in which apparently related to the business of a corn dealer. Another had apparently been used by a draper. "As I thought," he said to himself. "It's a plant. I wonder now . . ."

He tiptoed across to a door marked "Private" and opened it.

A cut off the joint and two veg, washed down with a pint and a half of bitter, are not conducive to a wakeful afternoon, and Sam, on his return to the office, had settled down in the armchair in his room with a newspaper over his head.

"Good afternoon."

The newspaper slipped to the floor as Sam wakened with a jerk, to see a stranger standing before his desk, smiling.

"I'm sorry if I startled you. I didn't get any answer to my knock, so I thought I'd better walk in and see if there was any-one about."

Sam rubbed his eyes, then pulled down his waistcoat and straightened his tie.

"What do you want?" he asked abruptly, with the peevish-ness of a newly awakened man.

"I'm awfully sorry if I've done anything wrong. A fellow called Crane sent me along here. He said there was a skipper's job going, and as I'm at a loose end I thought I'd give you a call."

"Crane? Of course; yes, I remember now. He said something about a friend of his—Hunt?"

"That's my name and these are my qualifications."

Hunt took a paper from his pocket and laid it before Sam.

"Foreign going extra-master's ticket. That ought to be good enough for you. Now what's the proposition? Crane wasn't any too clear about it."

Sam repeated the explanation he had given the day before.

"Just an ordinary trading venture," he concluded. "With perhaps less risk of loss than the usual trip of its kind. The ship is cheap."

"And old," commented Hunt. "Due for her survey in the au-tumn, and what d'you think that's going to cost you? She's bound to need a lot doing to her, and if you don't repair her she won't be classed at Lloyds and you won't get anyone to carry the risk."

"But you haven't seen the ship, have you, Captain Hunt?"

"No."

"Then may I ask where you got your information?"

Hunt parried the question with another.

"Have you inspected her?"

"No, of course not. What would be the use of that? I'm a busi-ness man, not a marine surveyor. As a matter of fact I have a report on the ship furnished by an excellent firm. Perhaps you'd like to read it?"

At the end of his perusal, Hunt handed back the papers.

"Yes, that's all right as far as it goes, but the question of the survey for re-classification hasn't been dealt with. It's a most important point, as I understand you will require the man taking on the skipper's job to put up some cash."

"Yes, that is so. That is merely an ordinary business precaution. It is really in the nature of a fidelity bond."

"With one important difference," Hunt pointed out; "which is that, as I understood it from Crane, your firm holds the money. You would have your hold on me, but what guarantee have I got that I even get my pay, let alone my share of the profits?"

"You will have your shares in the company, and if by any chance you had a grievance later on you could always proceed against the company in the ordinary manner."

"And if the company went bankrupt, where would I be?"

"Well, you can take it or leave it," snapped Sam. He was getting tired of this inquisitive young man. His experience had been that the people who gave the most trouble and asked searching questions were ever loth to part with their cash. "I don't mind betting there's dozens of chaps who'd jump at a chance like this."

"Perhaps you're right," said Hunt, and picked up his hat. "I'll be getting along."

Geoffrey Hunt had been a twister himself too long not to recognize a man who was playing the same game as himself. It was fairly clear that Crane and himself were the pigeons to be plucked, and at first he was inclined to throw up the whole business. Crane had money, though. A couple of thousand at least, and at that particular moment Hunt was ready to do quite a lot for two hundred pounds, let alone two thousand. He stepped into a telephone-booth, rang up Crane, and fixed up a dinner for that night at a quiet restaurant in Greek Street. He knew the proprietor and could rely on obtaining a quiet table where they could talk without risk of being overheard.

As soon as they had given their order and the waiter had withdrawn, Hunt broached the subject of the S.S. *Karnoc*.

"I've been round to see your pals of the International Developments this afternoon," he announced, "and I must say I'm rather interested."

"Do you think it's a sound idea?" Crane interrupted.

"Oh, I couldn't say one way or the other. It seems all right on the surface, but there may be snags. Don't you think it would be better if you were to consult your solicitor and let him make the preliminary investigations?"

Crane laughed. "I haven't got a solicitor worth calling one. A snuffy old man in Gray's Inn thinks he manages my affairs, but he's dead from the neck up."

"You want to change him?" suggested Hunt. "Get on to a younger man who's not old enough to be hidebound. I did know of a man, but unfortunately he's gone abroad." He might have gone farther and explained that his friend had left the country about a month before the police got on to his tracks, and that several of his clients had been rendered penniless by his unconventional way of handling their money.

"I'm not saying anything against this company, of course," Hunt continued. "But you have to be very careful in going into any business on the investment-cum-employment basis. A great number of them are barefaced swindles. They take your money, pay you a salary for six months, and then go into liquidation if it's a company, or bankruptcy if it's an individual trading on his own; the assets having been transferred by some fictitious transaction to a third person who doesn't exist."

"I say, but don't the police get on to blokes that do that? I mean to say, it's fraud or embezzlement or something, isn't it?"

"Scotland Yard would like to get them if they could, but it's usually devilish difficult and expensive. That's why you hear of so few prosecutions, and yet there are advertisements of dud concerns in the papers every day. As I said, I've no reason for supposing that this particular business isn't absolutely sound, but it's only common sense to take precautions and to make a few inquiries."

"Yes, but how? I've never done anything like this before. I mean, investing my own money. When my pater died the money was invested by old Porlock, the family solicitor, the man I told you about. Look here, Hunt, I've got a brain-wave. Why shouldn't you look into this for me? You seem to know what to do. If it turns out to be O.K. I'll put up the cash and you take the skipper's job. What d'you think about that?"

This was going to be easier than he had thought, and Hunt repressed the smile of satisfaction which rose to his lips.

"I don't mind doing it, but of course I couldn't take anything. Just to oblige you, old man."

"Well, it's awfully good of you, Hunt. Are you sure you don't mind?"

"You're forgetting I'm to get a job out of this if it comes off. If it doesn't—well it's only a day or two wasted. And now, what about going along to the Palladium for the second house? There's usually quite a good show on there."

At Scotland Yard there is a department known as the Central Branch which knows no bounds to the territory which it covers within the Metropolitan Area. On occasions it operates farther afield at the invitation of Chief Constables in the provinces, and in the course of time the men who make up the personnel of this division have accumulated a wide knowledge of the class of criminal whose particular foible it is to change their area of operations as soon as they have made a successful coup. A special room in the Records Department has been given over to the life histories of such of the "con" men who have made the acquaintance of the inside of a cell. The name of Geoffrey Hunt was unknown to the men who were in charge of the stacks of steel files. Up to date he had been lucky, but Detective-Sergeant Woods was living in hopes that one day he would have a watertight case against Hunt.

As luck would have it, at the very moment that Crane and Hunt left their restaurant, Woods was strolling along Great Compton Street on his way from the station to his home. He had spent eight solid hours that day "keeping observation" on a certain house, and he was tired and in need of a drink, but the sight of Hunt with a mug in tow was sufficient to make him shelve thoughts of rest and refreshment for the time being.

Hunt, Woods suspected, was broke and had been for some time. It might be worth his while to follow him and his friend. The detective spent an uneventful but enjoyable evening in a stall a row or two behind his quarry, and at the end of the performance he watched Hunt take leave of his friend. Crane jumped into a taxi and, as it swung out of sight round the corner into Oxford Street, Woods walked up to Hunt.

"'Evenin', Mr. Hunt. Who's your pal?"

"I wondered when you were going to beetle up and ask me that," Hunt replied with a laugh. "That's why I waited here for you."

"You didn't want me to spoil your game, I suppose?"

"Game? I'm on the level, Woody. Come and have a drink and I'll tell you. We can get one in the 'Comito' in Glasshouse Street."

Over a glass of lager and a smoked salmon sandwich, Hunt explained his business with Crane with such an unexpected candour that Woods did not believe one word of the story.

"It's like this, Woody. This man—er—Simpson's his moniker—is an old shipmate of mine. We were in the same destroyer at the latter end of the war. He was Sub-Lieutenant R.N. and I was an R.N.R. Loot. We met in the 'Coach and Horses' in Bruton Street a couple of days ago and we fixed up this show tonight. There's no crooked stuff in it, I swear that."

Wood sniffed.

"Dammit, man, I wouldn't twist an old pal like Simmy! Give me credit for some decency."

"I wouldn't trust you an inch, Hunt. I'm sorry, but there it is. You haven't been pulled yet, but your time'll come if you don't lay off this 'con' game."

Hunt walked home alone to his flat in a thoughtful mood. It was annoying having been spotted, but forewarned was forearmed. Woods wasn't a fool. Hunt realized that he would have to watch his step, but that was nothing new. The question he had now to decide was how to act. Whether to go in with the International Development crowd and share the haul, or play a lone hand? Naturally enough, they wouldn't want him to come in. It would be another mouth to feed. But if he managed to screw the cash out of Crane and stick to it himself, there wouldn't be a dog's chance of putting the blame on anyone else. The question was how? He had little doubt in his own mind that the money which Crane might be induced to put into the company would go straight into the pockets of the promoters, and that the steamship *Karnoc* would remain in the possession of her present owners. If this wasn't the crookedest scheme he'd struck he'd eat his hat. Tomorrow he would make another call at the office in Chancery Lane and find out if there were any others in the swindle before he decided what line to take.

Alfred Brown was waiting at the Cranes' flat when Maurice returned.

"I'm sorry to disturb you at this hour," he said. "I wanted to have a word about this *Karnoc* business, and time is pressing."

Maurice threw down his hat and coat and led the way into the sitting-room.

"Well, let's have a drink first. Whisky-and-soda?"

Alfred took in the contents of the room in one rapid glance.

"You've got a nice little place here," he said as he took his glass and drew a chair up to the fire.

"Yes, it's not so bad," replied Maurice casually. "But I must say I prefer the country. The trouble is that our house in Norfolk is miles from anywhere."

"In Norfolk?"

"Yes. Right up on the north coast near a place called Starring. My father died last year, and what with all these confounded taxes we can't afford to live there. We had to sell out a lot of stuff, just to keep it going."

"You mean land?" asked Alfred.

"No. My pater's collection. He had quite a nice lot of silver. Sheffield plate. But as a matter of fact we've managed to hold on to the best of it."

"Sheffield, eh? You can always get a price for that, can't you?"

"Yes, I believe so. Fill up your glass."

"Well, if you want a buyer for any more, let me know. I know a man who does quite a bit in that line."

"Thanks, but I don't think I need trouble you. We have a man up in Norwich we usually deal with."

"You'd get better prices in town," Alfred persisted.

"I dare say, but that's all in my brother's hands. He's a bit sticky about the whole show and talks of shoving what's left in a bank, but what good that's going to do anyone I don't know. He wants me to go up there and collect it, but it's a deuce of a fag and I dare say it's safe enough where it is. We've got a damned good caretaker who lives in the house."

A packing-case standing in one corner of the room attracted Alfred's attention.

"Are you moving house?" he asked.

Maurice heaved himself out of his chair and lifted the lid of the case.

"Oh no. This is just a lot of junk I brought home from abroad. There's no room in the flat for it all, so I'm sending it up to the Grange tomorrow."

Alfred picked up a long knife which was lying on the top of the case.

"That's nice work," he commented, and ran his finger over the inlaid silver work on the knife sheath.

Maurice nodded carelessly.

"Yes, it's not bad. I had half a mind to take it along to the British Museum, but I couldn't be bothered. It's a kris, and that hair fastened to the hilt, I believe, is human. I bet a few people have been laid out by it."

When Alfred took his departure half an hour later Maurice realized that not a word had been spoken about the *Karnoc* venture and wondered vaguely what had been the object of Alfred's visit. Thoughts of bed, however, were uppermost in his mind and he dismissed the question as not being worth bothering about and went to bed.

CHAPTER V

Johannis Kudorfer arrived in the River Thames on board a small Greek vessel. He and his daughter Lena were the only passengers, and Sam had no difficulty in finding him. Practically speaking, Johannis was the only man who wasn't working. His luggage consisted of a small tin trunk lashed with rope.

"So you have come. You are Mr. Hartford, yes?"

"That's me," was Sam's cheery reply. "I'm glad you were able to come, Mr. Kudorfer."

"You have work for me, yes?"

"A job after your own heart, Mr. Kudorfer, and there's not another man I could trust to pull it off."

If Kudorfer was pleased at this flattery he concealed his feelings. Not a shade of expression did he permit to interrupt his steady stare. He was taking Sam in in his own way. Greeks he knew, and Turks. Once he had done a job for a man who said he was a German. But an Englishman! Could he trust this fat, red-faced man who laughed and smiled for no reason that he could see? He would have to be careful.

He turned and beckoned to a girl who was standing alone by the rail, smoking a yellow cigarette in a long black holder.

"Lena! Come here."

She straightened herself with languid grace and advanced. She was tall, yet slightly made, with unusually small hands and feet. Her features too were small and regular. But it was the eyes that held Sam's attention: black, compelling eyes that glittered with lazy humour behind the long black lashes. She seemed to glide across the deck without effort towards the two men.

"This is my daughter, Lena," Johannis explained, and Sam stammered a greeting.

"A pleasure, I'm sure," he added, and then looked about him vaguely.

"Are we to stay here all day?" Lena asked as she slowly tapped the ash off her cigarette. "I have already been too long in this ship."

Sam grinned. "Not too posh, is she?" he said. "Well, we'd better be moving. Is that all you've got?"

Kudorfer grunted in reply and shouldered his tin trunk.

•••••

"When do I start work?"

Lena had retired to her room in the cheap hotel which Sam had chosen. Sam and Johannis were seated on hard plush chairs at a glass-topped table in the dreary lounge.

"Glad to see you're so keen," replied Sam. "I'll explain what I want you to do."

When he had finished Kudorfer asked:

"And this man, Hunt. Can he be trusted?"

"Yes, but he knows nothing. What I thought was that you make for Posnik—you know the locality—and I shall arrange with Hunt that when you get near to it you will act as a sort of pilot. Take the wheel and advise him the course to steer."

"But he has eyes, this Hunt. When we close the land he will stay on the bridge all the time, and if I steer for a rock—well, what do you think? That he will stand there and say 'Bravo, my son, that is the way?' No! He will—"

"I was present at the inquiry into the sinking of the *Barnia*," Sam interrupted. "There was some trouble with the compass, I think, or was it the tides or fog which caused that little accident?"

Kudorfer grinned for the first time since he had landed in England.

"It was the compass, yes. Somebody had removed the Flinders Bar and in its place had put a piece of wood. The magnets inside the binnacle too, they were —how do you say it?—a little *dérangé*."

"Couldn't you do that again, Mr. Kudorfer?"

"It is possible, yes; but you know how things happen. One time all right. Second time I do not get the chance, and then all is wasted and we have to try again."

"That's the devil of it," Sam replied. "There won't be a second time. The ship is due for her survey in August and her insurance policy expires on the 1st of September."

"So? That is not good. Let me think. Today is Saturday, is it not? The 15th of June? In the week commencing the 5th of July there is spring tides and if God is good there will be fogs. If we arrive at Posnik then maybe I can do what is needed. You will arrange it so that we arrive at night time. There is but one light on the island and the keeper of that light is my son. It may be that I could tell him that on a certain night his light must fail: that he shall go to his house, which is two miles away, and arrange for a light to be shown from there. It is done sometimes to assist the fishermen. The lights have been mistaken before. Perhaps Mr. Hunt will also be so unfortunate. Who knows? And now Mr. Hartford, to business. The money. I shall want two thousand English pounds. One thousand before I start and the other on the day the insurance money is paid. How and where the payment is to be made we can agree later. Is that not so?"

Sam was not prepared for such a demand, and decided wisely enough that food and drink would assist him in his bargaining.

"I think we'd better have lunch."

"No. We stop here till we have arranged everything. Not till then will I eat nor will I drink. Understand?"

Sam nodded dumbly. This was a tougher sort of customer than he had bargained for. He called over a waiter.

"If you won't have a drink, I will. A double Scotch and Schweppes, waiter."

"Perhaps I will change my mind. Whisky for me too, if you please. No soda. No water."

When the drinks arrived Sam fortified himself with a good draught and began to feel better. He'd show this stinking little dago where he got off.

"I think you've got a wrong idea of this job, Mr. Kudorfer," he said, with an ingratiating smile. "You see, I'm putting up the cash and arranging the whole affair, and besides, I have a partner, a Mr. Miller, who you'll meet later. The insurance money I have calculated can't be much over six thousand and the expenses will be very heavy. We've got to put down the money for the ship."

"How so? You have not bought her yet? And you send for me to come here as quick as I can. How long do you think that I shall wait in this place? It is only fit to house dead bodies."

"The deal goes through next week. The bill of sale is made out and notice sent to the Underwriters and to the Registrar. When we hand over the money the ship is ours, and you can sail, I hope, before the end of the week, or at the latest next Wednesday. You'll want time to settle in on board and you'll have cables to send about the lighthouse. For the love of Mike don't forget to do that. If you don't bring it off this journey we're finished."

"But the ship. Is she ready? What about the crew, coal, stores, everything?"

"Mr. Hunt is busy seeing to that now. You will meet him later and be able to fix up all the details then. Alfred will be there too."

"Alfred? Is there another of them?"

"Yes, yes; but he's not in on this show really. He thinks he is, but Mr. Miller and myself are the only two that count."

"What does he know, this Alfred?"

"Nothing really. All the arrangements are in my hands."

Kudorfer finished his drink and set down the glass.

"We have forgotten the money you shall pay me. Two thousand English pounds. That is all right, is it not?"

"I'm afraid not, Mr. Kudorfer. I couldn't possibly go to that figure. You see, I'm not a free agent in this matter. There is my partner to consider and he wants his share. As I said, the expenses will be heavy. I'm trying to arrange for a cargo out, and unless we can get an advance of freight that won't bring us in a cent if the ship becomes a total loss. Five hundred is as much as I can promise you, and that won't leave much for Miller or myself. Two-fifty down. To be paid in cash before you leave, and the other half when we have a satisfactory settlement with the brokers."

"Fife hundred pounds! You have the impertinence to offer me that? Me, that has received never less than fife times that figure, and then I was captain and it was easier. Oh, so very much easier."

"I would have put you in command if I could have managed it, Mr. Kudorfer. But you know what the regulations are in this country?"

"No, I do not know them nor do I care. Why could you not sail this ship under the flag of my country? Then all would have been simple. My uncle would be chief engineer. My cousin Karloff the chief mate. Yes, there would then be no difficulty."

"There are two reasons why I couldn't do that, Mr. Kudorfer," Sam replied. "First of all, there wasn't time to do as you suggest, and secondly, I very much doubt if the underwriters would have permitted the transfer of the policy to my name if you were to be captain. You are almost as well known in the City of London as in your own Island of Posnik. It is as unfortunate for you as it is for me."

"I don't care what they say about me. It is lies. All lies, and I want two thousand English—"

"Now look here, Mr. Kudorfer, be reasonable. If I haven't got it how can I pay it you? I might be able to come up a little on my figure of five hundred, but not much. Say seven-fifty. Two-fifty down and—"

"No."

Two hours later Sam walked into the office of International Developments Ltd. Dusty was sitting in the one and only easy chair reading an evening paper.

"Have you seen the dago?" he asked.

"Yes, and I've had hell's own time fixing it up with him. He stood out for a couple of thou., but I said to him, 'Now look here, old chap—'"

"Cut it short, Sam. What did you have to promise him?"

"A thousand, and if I hadn't got half a bottle of Scotch into him on an empty stomach I wouldn't have done that."

"That's not bad going, chum. It looks as if we're all set."

"Yes, but we may have a spot of trouble with Alfred. He's a wrong 'un."

"He doesn't look it."

"I know. He's as smart as they're made and has never been inside. Of course I wouldn't mind his being a crook, but I heard this morning from a bloke I know that he once shopped one of his pals. We'll have to keep our eyes open. If he once got his hands on this couple of thousand of Crane's he'd be off like a lamplighter."

"What! And not go through with the deal?" asked Dusty.

"Well, his share wouldn't come to so very much more than that," Sam replied. "I don't know, of course, what he'd do, but he's the sort that would go for the bird in the hand even if it meant leaving us flat. Besides, if he had the cash he could carry through the deal on his own. Don't forget that."

"But he doesn't know Kudorfer," Dusty objected.

"He knows his name and where he's living. If he offered Kudorfer a few hundreds more than I did he'd have him in his pocket."

"You're not getting windy, are you, Sam?"

"Garn. Windy? I'm looking ahead, that's all. Taking a line along the jumps, in a manner of speaking. Whatever happens, there's one thing we can always do if Alfred tries the double-crossing game. We can put the black on him."

"That's right," Dusty agreed, and then asked doubtfully: "But he could do the same to us, couldn't he? It stands to reason."

"No, no exactly. If Alfred tried to blow the gaff on us what could he prove? Nothing. It would only be his word against ours. But it would be different the other way round. You know that old geezer what lives down in Southwark? Uncle Thomas they call him."

"I've heard of him. He's a downy bird, ain't he?"

"As they make them. The rozzers have been trying to get their claws on to him for years, but he's too fly. Alfred does most of his dirty work. Never mind how I know, but I do, and we've got that against him. If we worked it right the cops'd be able to find all the proof they need to put Alfred and his blinking Uncle Thomas where they belong. Alfred's got some game on at this very moment. I'm not sure what it is, but I'm going to find out."

At eight o'clock that evening Sam called for Johannis in order to take him down to the *Karnoc*, which was lying moored head and stern to buoys in Blackwall Reach. It was a long and annoying journey, but whether in bus or tube or while forcing their way along the crowded pavements of Limehouse, Johannis preserved a complete silence. He was turning the whole business over in his mind. Sam he had assessed as a man who might be trusted to keep his word, but whether he had the guts to carry out a dangerous project Johannis doubted very much. He smiled too easily and talked too much. What sort of a man would he be if things went wrong? And this man Alfred . . . Sam was afraid of him, that was clear enough.

The man who interested Johannis more directly was Geoffrey Hunt, for Hunt would be shipmates with him for three weeks. Was he a man who could be easily fooled—or made drunk? It was much the same thing. Instinctively Johannis felt for the phial he always carried sewn into a seam of his waistcoat. In it was the essence of a herb which the women in his country used to quiet a restless child. He had distilled it himself, and to make sure of its efficacy had given a dose to his maternal uncle. The result had been better than he had dared to hope for. His uncle had slept for three days and had then awakened not much the worse. On being told of his lengthy sleep, he had sworn an oath never to drink with his nephew Johannis again.

The sun had set and lights were beginning to wink out on the river when Sam, with the silent Johannis by his side, reached the corner of the dock street from whence led an alleyway between two giant warehouses to a flight of rotting wooden steps. The water of the river washed oilily against the staging, making a gurgling and sucking sound as the level rose above the supporting timbers.

"That's her!"

Sam pointed to a dark shape lying a hundred yards downstream.

"Yes, I see, and how do we go on board? Swim?"

"We'll get hold of a waterman in a minute. We'll go in here and wait."

Sam pointed to a door in the wall where a yellow light showed through a glass pane in the door. Above Kudorfer could just make out a low roof and a couple of dormer windows.

"What is this?"

Sam grinned.

"You wouldn't expect to find a pub in a place like this, would you? I was surprised myself when I first found it."

"In England, yes, I would be surprised," replied Johannis. "But in my country, no. Every house sells wine—not that stinking beer. Beer is your religion."

Sam opened the door and disclosed a low room. Blackened oak beams made a chequer-board of the white plaster ceiling. Oak panelling covered the walls. In one corner there was a bar which Sam made for like a homing pigeon. A man turned as he approached, and Sam stopped as he saw the face of Geoffrey Hunt in the light of the swinging oil-lamp.

"Gee, I never thought to see you here!" he exclaimed.

"Why not?" replied Hunt coolly. "Not very odd that I should want to have a look at my new command, is it? Besides, if you want me to get away next week. I'll need a crew. It's usual, you know, to have one. Have you seen the *bateau*?"

"We're going off tonight," Sam replied, "if we can find someone to put us on board."

"George here'll fix that for you. Won't you, George?"

The barman looked doubtful.

"It's getting late, mate, but if you don't mind waiting I expect I'll be able to get something for you."

Sam nudged Johannis, who was standing back in the shadow.

"Meet your captain, Mr. Kudorfer. This is the man I told you about, Mr. Hunt. Your supercargo."

"Oh yes."

Hunt surveyed the squat figure by Sam's side for a moment and then thrust out a hand.

"Glad to know you, Mr. Kudorfer. If we're to be shipmates, let's have a drink on it. What's yours?"

It was pitch dark by the time George found an obliging waterman, and Sam, with a full cargo of beer on board, negotiated the slimy, weed-grown steps with difficulty. Johannis, on the other hand, stepped on board the skiff with the poise of a man well accustomed to such difficult manœuvres.

The accommodation-ladder of the *Karnoc* was triced up a couple of feet above the water level, but Johannis leapt on to it like a cat and pulled Sam up after him. The night watchman met them at the gangway with a hurricane lamp in his hand and Sam explained his business.

"Come to 'ave a look round, 'ave yer? Well, you won't see much. Better take my lamp."

Johannis led the way up a steep iron ladder to the bridge.

"All I want to see is the compass," said Johannis as they emerged on to the bridge, where a torn canvas dodger was flapping in the wind. He walked over to the steering compass and pulled the cover off the binnacle.

"Yes, I know this make. I shall manage all right—if I get a chance." He bent down and opened a door in the binnacle casing. "Show a light here, please."

Sam held the lamp while Johannis thrust his hand into the opening and manipulated the pulley which supported the correcting magnets.

"You see," he said after a few minutes' silence, "the needle, he go to the East. To the right. Now watch! He go to the West. If I arranged them just so, it will mean that the ship will be steered to the westward of her course. It is very simple, is it not? But not everybody knows how to arrange it as I can. One point. Two points. What you like."

He replaced the magnets in the position in which he had found them, and looked round for the charthouse. At the sliding door he felt for the switch and clicked it.

"Of course, I forgot. There is no power on. Never mind, this lamp will do."

He searched through a deep drawer in the chart-table and then with a grunt of satisfaction drew out a chart and unfolded it.

"You see, my friend, here is Posnik. Before we get there we must pass through this Strait. It is narrow. At the most two hundred metres wide, and there are rocks, plenty of them. Enough to sink a battleship, let alone this old washing-tub. At the end of the Straits is the harbour and above it the lighthouse. That light is what we sailors call a leading light. One keeps it on a certain bearing East by North and thus one keeps clear of these rocks. Now, you see this little black square on the chart? That is the house of my son. If with this ruler I lay off that bearing of East by North, do you see where it would lead us?"

Johannis rolled a parallel ruler across the chart and drew a line in pencil.

"It goes into that bay, doesn't it?" asked Sam.

"Yes, that is right. You have the idea. But before one gets there, what would one find? One rock. Two rocks. Dozens of rocks. One could not miss them. We should be going at full speed. What chance would the ship have of remaining afloat more than, say, half an hour? And the water is deep. You see the soundings. Fifteen fathoms is the least. That is ninety feet."

"Something would be showing, wouldn't it?" asked Sam.

"Yes, her masts—but that is all. You are thinking of salvage, but you forget the tides and the hole the ship would have in her. Take my word for it, of all the ships in which I have sailed and which unfortunately sank in such a place as this—not one of them was salved. And who, I ask you, would want to save a ship which is as old as this one? The work would cost three times what she is worth. I tell you all this. I show you what I can do. There need be no more talk. I shall bring my baggage on board here and stay. I shall be more comfortable. Tell the man, please."

"You can't do that very well, Mr. Kudorfer. You see, the ship isn't ours yet. Not until we hand over the money. I want you to come to the office next week and see the papers signed. I want you to meet my partner, Mr. Miller."

"Will Captain Hunt be there?"

"No, I haven't told him about it, but if you wish to see him I can arrange for you to meet him."

"I do not like Captain Hunt, and he does not like me. It will be difficult if he comes. Can you not get some other man to take his place. One who is a fool?"

"It would be difficult," replied Sam. "There's not much time, and besides, if he does not come we may not get the money. It is a friend of his who is going to supply it."

"But once you get the money can you not tell Captain Hunt to go to the devil?"

"I could, of course, but if he starts any trouble it might queer the whole show. Once we get the ship started all will be well."

"I repeat I do not like this Captain Hunt."

· · · · ·

The encounter with Sam and Johannis Kudorfer at the "Seven Seas" in Limehouse had confirmed Geoffrey Hunt in his suspicion that there was some business on foot in connection with the *Karnoc* of which he had not been told. It was the first he had heard of Kudorfer taking a passage in the ship. If he were going as an ordinary member of the crew or even as a passenger, what reason could there be for him to visit the *Karnoc* at that hour of the night? He waited until Sam and Johannis came ashore and then he himself went back on board. The watchman was in the galley making himself a pot of tea when Hunt walked up the ladder.

"Gor' lumme, if it ain't the capting back agin! What's going on ternight, anyway?"

"I've brought you a bottle of beer," said Hunt. "I thought you might be thirsty."

The watchman grinned.

"I'm allus thirsty—for beer. Let's have it."

He opened the bottle and poured the contents into a tin mug.

"'Ere's good 'ealth an' a good trip. Is them two what was aboard 'ere ternight going with you?"

"One of them is. Why do you ask?"

"They're a funny pair, ain't they? That red-faced bloke looks more like a barman ter me, an' I couldn't make out the other bloke. Furriner, wasn't 'e?"

"Yes. He's the one that's coming."

"Well, Captain, I've sailed wiv a few dagoes in my time, an' Dutchies. I've never trusted any of 'em. 'E looked worse than most, an' if I knows anything 'e'd be a 'andy lad wiv a knife if 'e was be'ind you. There was a mate in one ship I was in fell foul of just such a feller an' 'e didn't 'arf cop it right between the shoulder-blades. The old man give 'im a lovely funeral. We was lying off Surabaya at the time an'—"

"Where did they go when they came on board?" Hunt interrupted.

"Go? Why, up on the bridge. I watched 'em. The red-faced feller says could I give 'em a lamp an' they took this 'ere one of mine."

"What did you do?"

"I stayed by the gangway, but I saw them stop outside the wheel-'ouse alongside the standard compass. They talked there for a bit and then moved over to the wheel where the steering-compass is. I listened careful, but I couldn't catch a word they said."

"What happened after that?"

"They went into the chartroom an' it wasn't long afore they come down the ladder an' called to me to take me lamp, an' not as much as a blasted bob for me trouble."

Hunt picked up the lamp.

"I think I'll go up top and have a look around. Here! You have a swig of this. It'll keep the cold out."

Hunt laid a whisky-flask on the galley stove.

An examination of the bridge failed to disclose what the business of Sam and Johannis might have been, and Hunt turned into the chartroom. He set down the lamp on the table and at that moment noticed that a drawer had not been pushed right home and the corner of a chart was sticking out of its folio. He drew it out and unfolded it.

"Posnik!" he muttered.

The pencil line which Johannis had drawn had not been rubbed out, and Hunt noted its direction running from the deep-water channel through a maze of rocks and shoals and terminating in a house on the cliff overlooking the Strait. He ran the parallel ruler over the chart, noted the compass bearing of the line, and wrote it down on a slip of paper. What the significance of such a line was he could not think at the moment, but he made up his mind to purchase a duplicate chart and, in conjunction with the sailing directions of the locality, discover what it meant.

• • • • •

The night porter had come on duty and the lounge of the Hotel Wareham with most of its lights extinguished was looking more than usually depressing when Alfred arrived at 11 p.m. A call to Kudorfer's room produced no result and he settled down to wait.

Half an hour later the porter's voice roused Alfred from an uneasy doze. "This is the gentleman you wished to see, sir." Alfred rose, blinking and shivering slightly, to see Kudorfer's eyes fixed upon him. The porter withdrew and Alfred indicated a chair.

"I'm sorry to have called on you at such an hour, but it was absolutely necessary that I should speak to you tonight."

"I am very tired and would like to go to bed. I have talked too much today."

"You've been seeing Mr. Hartford, I suppose? Well, it's about that business that I came here tonight. If you would spare me ten minutes I should be very grateful."

"Does Mr. Hartford know that you were coming here tonight?"

"No. And now let me ask you a question, Mr. Kudorfer. Has Mr. Hartford given you the money he promised to pay?"

"What business is it of yours may I ask, Mr.—er—"

"You can call me Brown. I am a partner with Mr. Hartford and Mr. Miller, so you see it is as much my business as anyone's to discuss the matter with you."

"You a partner? Mr. Hartford told me nothing of this. He said there was only one other in it with him."

"Yes, he would, curse him. It's lucky I came tonight. I think I shall be able to give you some very interesting information, but first of all may I ask for an answer to my question? Has Mr. Hartford paid you any money?"

"No, he has not. Tomorrow he will pay. He gave me his word."

"He will not pay you tomorrow or on any other day. He hasn't got the cash, and the man he's going to get it from is a crook."

Kudorfer pulled up a chair and sat down.

"You interest me, Mr. Brown. Please go on."

"The man who is putting up the money is called—well, never mind his name, he doesn't count. The important part of it is this—and it's something which Mr. Hartford does not realize—the money is being obtained through a man named Hunt who is a well-known swindler."

"Hunt? Not Captain Hunt?"

"I believe he calls himself a captain. His first name is Geoffrey."

"Yes, yes. That is the man Mr. Hartford introduced me to. So he has got a hand in the money business? This is indeed interesting. Continue, please."

"There's nothing much more to tell you, Mr. Kudorfer. Mr. Hunt has not been told of the real reason for this venture, and he only stands to get his pay as captain of the ship as his share. He would very much rather have the £2000 in his pocket. He is a man who likes to get money without working for it."

"I do not like Captain Hunt. I have said so to Mr. Hartford, but apparently he could not or would not do anything. It was my wish that Captain Hunt should not be employed and surely I am more important than that man?"

"There's no doubt about that," Alfred agreed. "It is a pity that Mr. Hartford is so unreasonable."

"You said Hunt was a swindler, did you not?"

"Yes, he is known to the police. He is what is known as a confidence trickster."

"So? This is going to be very difficult, Mr. Brown. This Captain Hunt, if we can't get rid of him, will make trouble. I know his kind. Have you anything to suggest?"

"Yes, Mr. Kudorfer. I think I can show you a way out of the difficulty. If I buy the *Karnoc*, I should get a skipper of whom you approved—"

"A fool. A damn' fool," Kudorfer interrupted.

"Any sort of fool you like," Alfred continued. "But the point is that you and I would be the only two interested in the affair at all. The others would be completely and utterly out of it. I would provide the capital. You would do the work and we could split fifty-fifty."

"Fifty-fifty?"

"Yes, you know. Half each after deducting expenses."

"This is more like business as I understand it. I am glad to have met you, Mr. Brown. I think if we work together we make a *grand coup*. I should like to see Captain Hunt then. Ha, ha! Yes, that would be good. But—" He held up a stubby forefinger.

"Can you produce the cash, Mr. Brown?"

"Yes. I shall have the money very shortly. Our agreement shall be that we halve the net profits and I pay to you the sum of £100 to cover your expenses. How does that appeal to you, Mr. Kudorfer?"

"It is very fair. Do you know that Mr. Hartford promised me but £1000? But wait a moment, the net profits. What will they be?"

"The ship is insured against total loss for twelve thousand. Allowing for the purchase money and bunkers, stores, et cetera, I can't see that we'll clear less than nine thousand."

"And that robber, that swindler Hartford, told me the insurance was for but six thousand. Again let me say that I am indeed fortunate to have met you, Mr. Brown."

"Good evening."

Alfred looked up with a start and saw standing behind Johannis a girl clad in a shimmering frock.

"This is my daughter, Mr. Brown. She can be trusted. Lena dear, come and sit down. We have been talking about the *Karnoc*."

Lena slipped into a chair.

"And all is going well?" she asked, with a slow smile.

"Of course, my dear. Mr. Brown is going to provide the money."

"But what about the other one—Mr. Hartford?"

Alfred laughed.

"I'm afraid you must count him out."

"Oh!"

Lena fitted a yellow cigarette into her holder and leaned forward to take the light which Alfred offered her.

"What exactly does this mean? It was Mr. Hartford who asked you to come to England, was it not?"

Johannis nodded.

"I think I ought to explain, Miss Kudorfer," said Alfred. "The original idea of buying the *Karnoc* was mine. Sam Hartford, or rather his friend Miller, put up a small sum of money for the preliminary expenses. Hartford would be no good in a tight corner."

"A tight cornaire?"

"Yes, you know, if there was trouble. I think he'd be better out of it."

"Mr. Brown is going to provide the money we need, my dear," said Johannis as he pulled stolidly at his black cigar. "That is so, is it not?"

"Yes. I'll have it by Thursday of next week at the latest," Alfred replied, and silently prayed that it would be so. He had a plan by which he might be able to raise the money by a certain method, but it would necessarily take a bit of working and he would have to rely on at least one other man besides himself. It would be safer to have a second string if it were feasible. This girl now, could she not assist? Maurice Crane looked the sort who was susceptible to the wiles of a pretty woman, and he had money. Sam was after it, but if he, Alfred, worked fast he could collar the lot before Sam got wind of any double-crossing. Alfred called for drinks and before they arrived he had decided what to say.

"Mr. Kudorfer, there is a man who is interested in our business. He has money. His name is Maurice Crane. Sam Hartford tried to rope him in but didn't have any luck."

Alfred paused while the waiter set down the drinks, and when he had gone continued:

"We shall need at least £2000, and I can get that amount all right, but there are certain to be other expenses which we haven't allowed for. Anything we could get out of Crane would be useful and provide against accidents."

"Well, that is your business is it not, Mr. Brown? I do not know this Mr. Crane. It is you who must talk to him."

"Yes, I know that, but I don't fancy my chances much. I saw him last night, and though he was pleasant enough and a fool, yet I felt that he did not like me."

Lena looked up at that moment and found Alfred gazing at her. She understood his meaning in a flash.

"And so you want a girl to help you to obtain that money, *n'est-ce-pas*?"

"Well—er—"

"Oh, what is the good of quibbling. Is that so? Or is it not?"

"Be quiet, Lena." Johannis stubbed his cigar savagely into an ash-tray and turned to Alfred. "Cannot you do your own work, Mr. Brown?"

"This is rather a special kind of job, Mr. Kudorfer, but of course if you don't want your daughter mixed up in it I shall say no more about it."

"I did not say that. Tell me more about this man Crane. Has he plenty of money?"

"I think he could raise a thousand or two," Alfred replied.

"And Lena, what would she have to do?"

"Make herself pleasant and have a good time. This man Crane would, I think, be susceptible to the charms of such a very pretty girl."

"That may well be so, my friend," responded Johannis dryly. "But should I not rely on Mr. Hartford? He has made promises as well as you and has not asked for the assistance of my daughter in fulfilling them."

"I'm sorry, but I'm afraid I did not make myself clear," replied Alfred. "I shall provide the purchase price of the *Karnoc*; that is understood. But, as I said, there will be no harm in having a little extra cash in case of accidents. If your daughter fails, or even if she does not care to undertake the job, well, no harm will be done, and don't forget, if you come in with me, you will have no Captain Hunt to deal with."

"Yes, that would be all right, Mr. Brown. I do not like Captain Hunt." Kudorfer thought for a minute and then leaned forward and laid a hand on Alfred's knee. "If Lena does what you suggest, any money that she may obtain I will keep. That is to be understood, and until you show to me the cash with which to buy the ship, I will not break with Mr. Hartford. It would not be wise."

"As you will." Alfred accepted the conditions with as good a grace as he could muster.

Lena meanwhile had been leaning back in her chair watching the two men with every appearance of quiet enjoyment. She neither flinched nor blushed at the bargaining, but her black eyes glittered as they rested first on the mask-like face of her father, then on the more eager countenance of Alfred. Catching her glance and noting her long, lithe lines as she lay back in her chair, Alfred had no doubt that she would be able to execute her share of the contract.

"Now you must have another whisky-and-soda," he said, "to seal this bargain and drink success to this venture. Miss Kudorfer?"

Lena smiled at him through her long, black lashes. "Thank you," she said. "I think I deserve a drink too."

They drank deeply and then shook hands on what Alfred was pleased to call their gentlemen's agreement.

CHAPTER VI

ALFRED'S MOTTO was: "If you want a dirty job well done get someone else to pull it off for you." By these means one cut out the risk, and if the profit was reduced—well, that was a minor consideration. The job he had in mind on the Saturday morning following his visit to Maurice Crane was the theft of the collection of Sheffield plate from the Grange at Starring. Alfred had realized during his short talk with Maurice that the chance of screwing the purchase price out of the latter was about a hundred to six against and no takers. But whatever came of that, whether he won or lost, it would do no harm to lift the silver. At any rate it would realize a certain amount of ready cash.

Nick Wheeler, known to Scotland Yard as a practised burglar, was drinking his morning half-and-half when Alfred stepped into the public bar of the "Goat and Compasses", Southwark. The two men exchanged a meaning glance and Alfred passed into the private bar. Nick joined him a moment later.

"Well, mate, how does she go?"

"Rotten," replied Nick. "And you?"

"Not so bad. Want something to do?"

Nick spat on to the sanded floor.

"I don't mind," he said slowly. "But it mustn't be anywhere round here. You know Truscott?"

Alfred nodded and Nick went on:

"He's been tailing me for the last week. Whatever it is'll have to be a country job. Things is too hot here."

"Let's take a walk," Alfred replied. "Keep a hundred yards behind me and don't join up till I give you the sign."

It was in a dirty little eating-house that Alfred and Nick came together again half an hour later. A child who could barely stagger, but had already achieved that invaluable ability to spot a plain-clothes man a mile off, was posted as a look-out. A blowsy woman engaged in scratching her head nodded as they entered. Alfred led the way to a curtained recess and broached his plan.

Later in the day Nick sought out Uncle Thomas in his shop in the Borough High Street.

"I've got wind of a likely crib," Nick began. "It's down in the country."

"You know my terms," was Uncle Thomas's reply. "Fifty-fifty of what I clear. You get the stuff and I'll do the rest."

But Nick was not satisfied.

"The crib's near a couple of hundred miles from here," he explained.

"All right. You can have an advance for your train fare, if that's what's eating you."

"Yes," sneered the other, "can't you damn' well see me with a couple of cases of white stuff getting off the train at Liverpool Street. What I wants is a motorcar. What about that old shandrydan of yours? You never use it, hardly."

It was not a tactful way of negotiating a loan for the ancient, round-nosed Morris which was Uncle Thomas's pride and joy.

When he had nothing better to do he polished its battered body and patched the hood until it looked like a crazy quilt. The engine to him was a complete mystery, and except when he put in oil or petrol he was never known to open the bonnet.

"Lend you my car!" snorted Uncle Thomas. "I'd as soon drive it into the river, 'cause that's where it'd be sooner or later if you tried to drive it."

"Oh, all right," replied Nick. "Then you won't see the stuff. Genuine Sheffield plate they tell me it is, and you can unload that sort of stuff better than anyone else I know of. In fact, you're the only one I could trust, and it do seem a damn' shame not to lift it. The people are all away except an old geezer of a gardener."

But Uncle Thomas was proof against flattery. He knew he was one of the few reliable fences in the trade and he liked to hear people tell him so. Still, he wouldn't lend his car.

"Here, I'll tell you what, old man," said Nick. "I'll go by train and get the stuff an' you come up with your car and take it over. You could do the run easy in a couple of days."

"How far did you say it was?" asked Uncle Thomas.

"Two hundred miles. There or thereabouts."

"I could do that in a day easy," boasted the proud owner of the car. "Two days! Why I could get to Edinburgh in that time."

"'Course you could," replied Nick. "Now then, what about it?"

"I'll think it over," replied Uncle Thomas. "There's my business. It won't run itself while I'm away."

The next morning after breakfast Uncle Thomas sought out a young man of whom it was said by his father that his only trouble was that he was honest. By noon he was installed in the shop with strict orders as to what he was and was not to do. If parcels arrived they were to be placed in a hole in the wall by the fire-place, and all callers were to be informed that Uncle Thomas had gone to the seaside for his health. With half a dozen last-minute injunctions Uncle Thomas drove away with his wife, leaving his house locked and shuttered, and with Hector Brown in charge of the shop.

At a steady speed of twenty-five miles an hour Uncle Thomas rattled through the suburbs of Finchley and Hendon on to the

Great North Road. His wife at a sign from her master blew the horn, for Uncle Thomas needed all his attention on keeping a comparatively steady course. There was half a turn of back lash in his steering-gear.

In the course of time and not without a few stops for the refreshment of the car and its passengers, Uncle Thomas reached his destination, a tiny village on the north coast of Norfolk, and there he took rooms and prepared to wait. During the day he pottered along the marshes and smoked his pipe. His top hat had been replaced by a rakish straw and his rusty frock coat by a ready-made tweed suit. He looked very odd. So odd, indeed, that the village policeman, a man of few ideas, left his digging for an hour to have a talk with the stranger. Uncle Thomas was expansive.

He was, he said, a retired tradesman from Blackpool. His wife was delicate, and where else would he come but to the East Coast? Two doctors had advised it. The policeman agreed that it was a wise choice and, feeling that he had now discharged his duty, returned to the more pressing business of trenching his garden.

Uncle Thomas was having his morning pint of mild and bitter at the "Blue Boar" when he heard the news of the burglary at the Grange. There being no other customers, the landlord gave Uncle Thomas his version of the affair. Apparently the gardener who acted as caretaker had not heard anything during the night, but that very morning as he was going to feed his chickens what did he see but a ladder against an upper window.

"Damn' fool," said Uncle Thomas to himself. "What the hell did he want to leave it there for?"

To his informant he raised a face of well-simulated surprise from his tankard and wiped his mouth with a voluminous silk handkerchief, an involuntary gift from Mr. Selfridge.

"Well, well, fancy that now," he said aloud; and then added fatuously:—"Who'd have thought it?"

"That's right," replied the landlord. "That's what I said to Bob Hackle. Him that's our policeman. I says to him I says—"

"Was there much taken?" interrupted Uncle Thomas. "Though I don't suppose anybody knows yet."

"Indeed they do. At least Goodbody the gardener says he knows, but he won't say."

"Very annoying," commented Uncle Thomas.

"What's that?"

"I mean the whole affair is most distressing. Disturbing to the village."

On his way back to his rooms Uncle Thomas passed P.C. Bob Hackle pushing his bicycle up the hill. He stopped and mopped his face.

"Fine goings on, I must say," he said. "Burglary, no less. Have you seen anything of any strangers about? Any cars? "

"No," replied Uncle Thomas. "I haven't. Where are you off to?"

"Back to the Grange. The Chief Constable'll be there waiting for me, I don't doubt. 'Why 'ave you done this?' he'll ask. And 'Why 'aven't you gone there?' and me with only a bike. If I did all as was expected I'd have to have a pair of wings."

Uncle Thomas quickened his pace when he left P.C. Hackle to continue his journey. The Chief Constable here already and no doubt a dozen assorted police inspectors, sergeants. . . . It was time to be moving.

Before the Chief Constable had really got going with his investigations Uncle Thomas and his wife were chugging steadily along southward and westward. The Morris seemed to have benefited from her visit to the sea more than Mrs. Honeypenny, for though the old car didn't exactly romp up the hills she pulled quite steadily. By lunch-time the party reached its objective, an extensive stretch of common land. Uncle Thomas stopped the car and took out a map.

· · · · ·

At about the time when Uncle Thomas learnt the news of the sacking of the Grange, Maurice Crane was awakened by his brother, who waved a telegraph-form in his face.

"Here! Read this."

"No. You can," Maurice replied. "I've had a thick night."

"The Grange has been broken into. That's the sum total of it."

"But there wasn't anything worth taking, was there?" asked Maurice sleepily.

"Only about a £1000 worth of silver," replied Henry dryly. "The police want someone to go down and check over the inventory. I've got it here."

"All right. Well, old Porlock can go or send one of his clerks. A day in the country would do them a world of good."

"The trouble with you, Maurice, is you're bone lazy. You don't seem to realize that we're not rolling in cash. The whole income from the estate barely covers the repair and maintenance account, and things are quite tight enough with me. I don't want to go chucking a fiver away if it isn't necessary."

"Oh, all right. I'll go." Maurice flung back the bedclothes. "But it's a damn' nuisance. I've got to see a bloke on business either today or tomorrow."

"I'll lend you my car," Henry replied. "And you can get back by tea-time tomorrow at the latest."

Maurice, at the wheel of his brother's Lagonda, followed the trail blazed two days earlier by Uncle Thomas at a speed which would have shocked that old gentleman had he been there. At Dereham Maurice left the main road and struck across country. A signpost told him he had but another thirty miles to go, but the road was narrow and steeply cambered. He slowed down to forty. It was not easy to keep the car on the road with all these twists and turns and wobbling cyclists and lumbering farm-carts. He swung round a blind corner blaring his horn. An ancient Morris going the same way was occupying the exact centre of the road. It was too late to pull up and Maurice took a chance that the ditch on the right was not as deep as it looked. He was wrong. It was much deeper. The Lagonda heeled over and drove her off side wheel into a tangle of briars. Uncle Thomas drove on. Maurice sounded his electric horn once more to attract attention to his plight. Uncle Thomas pulled up his car and looked back.

"Are you hurt?" he called out.

"No. I'm all right, but the car—" The remainder of the sentence was drowned by the roar of Uncle Thomas's engine and crash of gears. In less than a minute he was out of sight. Maurice crawled out of his seat and swore. Of all the unprincipled old ruffians! Forced him into a ditch and then drove calmly away. At that point Maurice remembered that he had forgotten to take the number of Uncle Thomas's car, and he swore again.

Uncle Thomas was not good at reading maps and he had wasted a considerable amount of time in his search for a particular track which ran across the common land. Twice he had had to turn the car by backing into gateways, and on each occasion his near sidewing had suffered. It was after the second attempt that he had caused Maurice to take to the ditch. His wife suggested that they should go back, but Uncle Thomas refused.

"The fewer people I see or that sees me the better it'll be," he said, and on receiving Maurice's assurance that no bones had been broken he drove away as quickly as he could. He even exceeded his self-imposed limit of twenty-five miles an hour for half a mile. Then a disused chalk pit caught his eye.

"We're nearly there, old woman. Hold tight, and for God's sake don't fall out!"

Walking is a very pleasant form of exercise if you like it. Maurice Crane was out of luck. He hated walking. The road was excessively hard and stony, there was no wind, and the sky was cloudless. However, despite these handicaps, he reached a house with a telephone by two o'clock and summoned a breakdown car from Dereham.

"She don't look too bad, do she, Bill?"

Bill, who had started life as a blacksmith and now called himself a mechanic, merely grunted and picked up his trusty friend, a seven-pound hammer.

"All she wants is a tap here." He pointed to a spot on the dumb iron of the Lagonda now standing four square on the road.

"No, you don't!" said Maurice. "I'll try her as she is."

The engine broke into life and he let in the clutch carefully.

"There's not so much the matter with her," commented Bill's mate.

"Just a tap there with the sledge, that's all she wants. You can see that angle iron's bent. Can't ye now?"

Maurice settled the question of whether to hammer or not to hammer by calling for his bill, settling it, and driving away. The car certainly made a very odd noise when negotiating right-hand corners, but otherwise she appeared to be none the worse for her dive into the ditch, and Maurice arrived at the Grange without further incident.

An inspector of police was sitting on the steps of the front door smoking a pipe when Maurice arrived, and he explained that the Chief Constable had left him in charge.

"We've been round the house, sir. I got the keys from the gardener, but I can't see that there's much been taken nor damage done."

Maurice handed over a bundle of typewritten sheets.

"That's the inventory. Perhaps you'd like to get on with it while I look for a bite of lunch in the village."

When Maurice returned, the Inspector was in the butler's pantry counting knives and forks.

"Well, how goes it?"

"All present and correct, sir, excepting a black tin box which should have been in the library." He consulted the list in his hand. "Nothing said here about what was in it."

"Black tin box? Yes, I seem to remember something about that. I have an idea there was some silver packed in such a box."

"Was it a valuable collection, sir? Do you happen to know?" queried the Inspector.

"Yes, it was worth quite a bit," Maurice replied. "But I shouldn't like to put a figure on it. It was valued for Probate at £1000, but whether it would fetch that in the open market is quite another matter."

The Inspector locked up the house.

"Well, that's all we can do here, sir. I wonder if you'd mind coming with me to see Colonel Sharp. He's at the station and I know he wants to have a talk with you."

Maurice found the Chief Constable looking tired and worried when he entered the charge-room. A sergeant and police-constable were standing near the door.

"Oh, it's you, Mr. Crane. We expected you earlier. I waited at the Grange until one o'clock, but—"

"I'm sorry about that," Maurice replied, "but I had a little bother on the road with my car. As a matter of fact, I suppose I ought to report it." He explained what had occurred, and as he finished P.C. Hackle stepped forward.

"You'll excuse me, sir," he said, addressing the Chief Constable, "but I think I have an idea who the old man in the car might have been. Of course, I can't be certain, but there was a man corresponding to the description which Mr. Crane has given who has been staying at Mrs. Higginbottom's in the village for the last two days. His wife was with him."

"Was there a woman in the car you saw?" the Chief Constable asked Maurice, who nodded.

"Yes, she was wearing a black hat—that was all I could see of her."

"Inspector! Why wasn't I told of this before? I asked if any strangers had been seen in the district within the last twenty-four hours and you told me none had been observed."

"That was what the constable told me, sir. You see, I live over at Hinton and only come round here twice a week,"

"Well, Hackle, what have you got to say for yourself?"

"Well, sir, when the Inspector put the question I thought naturally enough that what he wanted to know was had I seen any suspicious characters. Mr. Honeypenny was all right, sir, that I'll swear. He answered my questions without any trouble. Shopkeeper, he said he was—from Blackpool, I think it was."

"When did you see him last, this Mr. Honeypenny?" snapped the Chief Constable.

"This morning, sir, at about twelve o'clock. I was on my way back to the Grange after putting through a call to the Inspector. He was coming down the hill from the 'Blue Boar' and going in the direction of his lodgings."

"Did he say anything to you?"

"No, sir. Nothing to signify. I told him about this here burglary."

"You would," commented the Chief Constable dryly.

•••••

Alfred waited in his rooms on Wednesday, expecting to hear from Uncle Thomas or Nick Wheeler that the job at the Grange had been successful, but by nine o'clock there had been no message. Feeling vaguely uneasy he set out on foot for the Borough and made his way down Graves Crescent to No. 96. The windows were shuttered and there was no response to his ringing of the bell. He could hear it jangling in the basement. Alfred glanced at his watch. It was a quarter to ten. He would go round to the shop. It was possible that Uncle Thomas was there, for there were occasions when the old man used the bed-sitting-room on the first floor. The house in Graves Crescent he felt sometimes was too large for him, and too lonely when his wife paid her infrequent visits to her mother.

It was a large, double-fronted shop in Southwark High Street, built in the days when small-paned windows were the fashion. Uncle Thomas, since he had taken over the tenancy twenty years ago, had never had the windows cleaned. Not that that mattered much, for the inside of the shop was stacked with furniture. Most of it was junk, but there were some bits and pieces which Uncle Thomas had picked up at country sales for a few shillings and which were eagerly sought for by rich old gentlemen in shabby clothes.

There was a light in the upper window when Alfred arrived outside the shop and he turned the handle of the outer door. It was locked. He knocked and rattled the handle and a moment later the window overhead was thrust up and Hector called out that the shop was shut.

"Yes, I've found that out myself," Alfred replied dryly.

"Oh, it's you, is it?"

The head withdrew and a minute later Alfred heard the bolts being shot back and the rattle of the chain as it was unhooked.

"Expecting burglars?" he asked as he slipped past Hector into the shop.

Hector re-fastened the door and followed him up the steep flight of stairs to the room above.

"No," he said in reply to Alfred's question. "But there's a lot of stuff in the shop and I can't be too careful. I'm expecting the old man back any time now."

"Yes, so am I," said Alfred as he lit a cigarette and threw himself into the only comfortable arm-chair.

"I thought he'd be here before this. I was wanting to go out tonight," said Hector.

"Well, what's stopping you?"

"The old man told me particular I was to stay on the premises till he got back."

"How long do you want to stop out?" asked Alfred. "I can wait here till eleven, if that's any good to you."

Hector accepted the invitation gratefully and Alfred let him out and locked the door after him. When he had gone Alfred switched on the lights in the back shop and pulled a sideboard away from its position where it was masking the fire-place. A few minutes' work with a screwdriver revealed a hole in the wall. Alfred shone a flash-light into the cavity. It was empty. He replaced the bricks and returned to the upper room to wait.

Half an hour later his patience was rewarded. There was a sharp double knock on the outer door, followed by three single blows at longer intervals. It was Nick Wheeler.

"I was kind of expecting you," said Alfred. "When did you get back?"

"Only this afternoon. I got into the wrong train at Norwich and had to change twice, and when I stepped on to the platform at Liverpool Street, blimey, if my old pal Detective-Sergeant Clark wasn't there to meet me! He had a car and all, and he took me to Marlborough Street. There was nothing he didn't want to know. Where I'd been. How long I'd bin there and what I was up to. I stuffed him with a yarn he didn't swallow. I never expected he would, but it didn't matter. I hadn't got nothing on me but a packet of fags and a *Daily Mail*. I'd planted me tools with the loot, and it was lucky for me I had."

"Where was that?" asked Alfred eagerly.

"In an old chalk quarry not very far from the Grange. I went there on me bike and then went on to Dereham and caught a train. Where's Uncle Thomas?"

"You ought to know. You saw him last, didn't you?"

"Never put a peeper on the old geezer since I left the Smoke yesterday. He fixed up where I was to put the stuff and said that he'd lift it the same day I put it there. He must be on his way back now. He went in that old box of iron he calls his car, didn't he?"

"Yes, and if he hasn't run into anything he should be back any minute. I've sent the lad out. He's not in on this."

"Who's that?" asked Nick.

"Hector, they call him. He's a sort of a cousin of mine. I think he's half barmy, but the old man employs him in the shop sometimes."

"Barmy? He looked all right the last time I seen him," said Nick.

"Oh, you know. Soft. His dad tried to bring him up in the right way, but the kid's gone straight in spite of him. He thinks Uncle Thomas is the cat's whiskers. Had any chow since you got back?"

"A snack, that's all. Is there anything here we could have?"

"I'll have a look."

Five minutes later Alfred returned with a loaf of bread and a tin of sardines.

"Can you make do with that, son? There doesn't seem to be anything else except a bit of pie the mice have been at."

"That'll do me a treat, Alfred."

"All right, get on with it while I make a pot of tea."

Alfred waited until the last sardine had disappeared and then asked:

"How did the job go? No snags, were there?"

"No, mate. It was as you said. As easy a crib to bust as ever I've seen. No one in the house except the gardener, and he was right over in another wing."

"Well, tell us all about it. Gosh, you're a dumb one, Nick. But you are a worker, I'll say that for you."

"There weren't nothing to it, as you might say. The box you wanted was in an old wall-safe that had been made in the year dot. No combination. Just ordinary lift-and-slide lock. There used to be a lot of 'em about a few years back, but they've gone out o' fashion, worse luck. After that I went back to the first floor, where I'd got in by a ladder to the bath-room window. I always makes for a bath-room window. It's the last one anyone thinks of bolting or putting on a catch. I don't know why it is, but that is what I've found. I shinned down the ladder and on to my bike. It was getting light before I got to the common the old man had fixed on, which was lucky, as I had hell's own business in finding the place."

"No doubt it was the right one?" queried Alfred.

"No. I found the place all right. No need to bother about that."

Hector returned to the shop on the stroke of eleven o'clock and Alfred reported that there had been no news or sign of the old man.

"I'll be getting along. Coming, Nick?"

While they were waiting for a bus Alfred asked:

"I suppose you didn't see anything else in the house worth pinching, did you?"

"No, nothing worth money. There was a nice lot of curios though, and I brought one away. I thought you might like it as something to remember the job by. It might come in useful to you too, if you were in a tight corner."

"What is it, Nick?"

"You wait. I sent it off by post this morning from Dereham, addressed to Mr. Alfred Brown, care of an accommodation address in Kennington. I thought that would be the safest way of getting it home."

"Thanks, Nick. I'll tell Hector to call for it tomorrow. It won't arrive much before then, I shouldn't think. He can bring it to me at the office. I shall be there about four o'clock, I expect. There's a conference on."

• • • • •

It was not until nearly one o'clock on the Thursday afternoon that Maurice Crane got the repairs to his Lagonda completed and was able to set out for London. He knew that Hartford was anxious to push on with the purchase of the *Karnoc*, for he had received on the previous morning a note from Sam in which he had stated that he had obtained an option on the *Karnoc* which was due to expire at midnight on this very day. Consequently he pushed the car at a steady fifty-five along the Newmarket road and reached Baldock at two o'clock, where he stopped for half an hour for a sandwich and a glass of beer.

Between Baldock and Stevenage he passed through the small village of Warbuck. It was market day and a row of stalls lined each side of the roadway, compelling the traffic to slow down to a walking pace.

"Dammit, if that isn't the old scoundrel who forced me off the road!" Maurice said to himself as he caught sight of Uncle Thomas in the Morris a hundred yards ahead of him. When he got on to the open road again, Maurice stood on his accelerator and, passing the Morris, forced Uncle Thomas to stop.

"You're the fellow I've been looking for!" he shouted as he jumped out into the road.

Uncle Thomas looked pained and surprised.

"My dear young man. Do you mind telling me what is the matter with you? To my certain knowledge I've never seen you before. You know, you mustn't do this sort of thing. You have upset my wife. Would you mind removing your car and allowing me to proceed on my journey?"

"You were on the Dereham-Starring road yesterday, weren't you?"

"I may have been, but is that any business of yours?"

"And you forced me into the ditch and drove on as though nothing had happened. You're a public danger and I've a darned good mind to run you in."

A policeman who was passing on a bicycle heard the dispute and dismounted.

"Well, what's the trouble?" he asked, and Maurice explained.

"But, look here, officer, I don't want to kick up a fuss about it, I've got an appointment in London which I don't want to miss."

"Driving away after an accident!" said the policeman. "That's a serious offence. I'm afraid I'll have to ask you two gentlemen to come along to the station with me."

Uncle Thomas had a short, whispered conversation with his wife, who, during the altercation, had been sitting quite motionless with her eyes fixed on the road in front of her. She had learnt by bitter experience that it was better for the peace of the home if she showed no interest in Uncle Thomas's affairs.

"I presume the presence of my wife will not be necessary," said Uncle Thomas as he clambered out of his seat. "But if it should prove to be so, you can send for her. Stay there, dear, till I return," and then added in a whisper: "remember what I told you. We'll meet at the shop."

Maurice gave his version of the events leading up to the ditching of the Lagonda, which the sergeant on duty at the Warbuck police-station wrote out laboriously, and as he blotted the last word he turned to Uncle Thomas.

"What is your name?" he asked.

"Thomas Honeypenny," Uncle Thomas replied. "And I should like to make a protest. This young man's story is—"

"Just a minute, if you please," the sergeant interrupted, and turning on his stool consulted a printed notice pinned to the wall behind him.

"Honeypenny's your name, is it? Well, the Norfolk police want to see you about a little business in their county. No. Don't say anything now. Time enough when you see them. You will be detained. I now formally charge you with being concerned in the breaking in and entering of the Grange, Starring, in the County of Norfolk. Anything you may say will be taken down and may be used in evidence. Do you wish to make a statement?"

"No. Not at present, except that the charge is absurd and I deny it."

"If you wish to communicate with a solicitor, you will be given the usual facilities. Meanwhile, will you follow the constable. Cell No. 3, Willcocks, and search the prisoner."

"What about the car, sir?" said the constable who had brought Uncle Thomas to the station. "Shall I bring it round here? There's a woman in it."

"Yes. Put it in the yard," the sergeant replied. "And bring the woman in here."

"I say, sergeant, that was a bit of luck my running up against the old blighter like that, and the queer thing is that it was my brother's house that was burgled."

"You don't say, sir? Well, if that ain't a queer coincidence, but it's not the first time I've seen a go like this. When I was a young constable—"

"I'm awfully sorry to interrupt, sergeant, but I really must be buzzing off. I must get to town tonight."

The sergeant looked doubtful.

"I'll have to get on to my Inspector, sir, and report this affair, and he'll be sure to want to have a word with you. I'm afraid I must ask you to wait here until he arrives. He's only ten miles away and will be over within half an hour."

"It's past two o'clock now," said Maurice, "and I suppose I'll have to tell my story to him all over again. It is damned annoying. Do you think I could get away by three o'clock?"

"Oh, before then, sir, I hope. I'll get through on the 'phone right away."

Five minutes later the constable who had gone out to bring in Uncle Thomas's car returned with the news that the woman who had been with Uncle Thomas had disappeared.

"There weren't a sign of her nowhere, sir. Of course, she may have got a lift from another car on the road; I can't say."

"Right, give me her description," the sergeant replied.

· · · · ·

It was perfectly true, as Sam had pointed out to Dusty Miller, that the police would be well pleased if they could obtain a conviction against Uncle Thomas. They had his photograph full face and side. Each one of his fingers had produced a print which was filed at Scotland Yard. Detective-Sergeant Truscott knew him well and he often dropped into the shop for a chat. He even read a book on old furniture with the idea of drawing the old fossil out, and of late he had been making some headway, or so he imagined.

Uncle Thomas, who knew rather less about antiques than a salesman of a hire-purchase furniture firm, smiled to himself when Truscott was not looking. When he was young, Uncle Thomas had fallen into the indiscretion of opening his mouth too wide to a member of the Force. The result had been a short visit to the Old Bailey and a somewhat protracted stay in the wilds of Dartmoor. He had learnt his lesson, but though the old man had given nothing away up to date, Truscott had hopes, and on the morning after the visit of Nick Wheeler and Alfred he called at the shop. There was no response to the bell set ringing by his opening of the door, and he sidled down the narrow lane, flanked high with stacks of tables and chairs, to the door leading into the back shop. A fire was burning in a little stove and there was a smell of varnish and beeswax in the air. Hector, who was lifting a pot of glue off the fire, looked round.

"Hullo, Bill!" he said in surprise. "What are you doing round here?"

The detective threw his hat down on the table and perched on a high stool.

"That's what I should like to ask you, old man," he replied. "I didn't know you worked here."

"It's only temporary," Hector replied. "My uncle had to go down to the country somewhere and wanted someone to come in and look after this place while he was away, though why he should worry I don't know. There's only been one customer in during the two days I've been here, and all he wanted was a leg of a chair mended."

"Perhaps the old man thought there might be a burglary," suggested the detective.

Hector laughed.

"Oh, he's got some quite nice bits of stuff, if you can only find them," said Truscott.

The two men had met a year before at one of the socials at the local church hall, when the detective had induced Hector to join him in running the working lads' club. The acquaintance had developed into a very real friendship and the detective was perturbed to find that Hector was working for such a man as Uncle Thomas. Sooner or later he felt the boy would be drawn into one of the old man's nefarious schemes, and if things went wrong he would be left to hold the baby.

"Where's the old man off to?" Truscott asked.

"I dunno. He went off on Monday with his missus in the car. He said he'd be back yesterday, but he didn't turn up. Alfred was in last night waiting for him."

"Alfred?"

"Yes, he's a nephew of Uncle Thomas and my first cousin."

"Do you know him well?" Truscott asked carelessly.

"No. I can't say I do," replied Hector. "He's not my sort really. I don't know what he does for a living, and I don't think his people know either. He doesn't talk about himself."

The detective walked over to the bench where Hector was scraping off the old glue from the broken chair leg. He watched him in silence for a minute and then:

"I should give this job a miss if I were you, Hector," he said. "It won't do you any good, and I shouldn't like to see you get into any trouble."

The other laughed.

"Someone's been telling you fairy stories, Bill. I've heard them myself but I don't pay any heed. It's only bar-room chat. I suppose being a policeman makes you suspect everyone."

"To the pure all things are pure," said the detective dryly. "You're too blamed charitable; that's what's the matter with you, my lad."

"Oh, I know the old man was in trouble one time, but that was years ago. He's been straight ever since, but that's a thing you as a policeman are incapable of understanding. If once a man's convicted, he's finished."

"That is the popular idea of the police point of view, I agree, but it's not true. If a man wants to keep out of trouble the police won't stop him. They'll give him a helping hand if they can."

"What have you got against Uncle Thomas?" asked Hector sharply. "I mean anything definite?"

"Now, Hector, for heaven's sake don't let us quarrel about your Uncle Thomas. You know me well enough surely to realize that I don't talk merely for the sake of saying something. I admit I only suspect your uncle at the present moment, but I have several very good reasons for my suspicion. One of these days I hope to lay him by the heels, and I don't want you mixed up in it."

The shop bell rang at that moment and Hector laid down his work and went to attend to his customer, leaving the door ajar. Truscott shifted his position and was able to catch a glimpse of a man dressed in a seedy tweed suit and cloth cap, pulled down over his eyes.

"Looks like someone I know," thought Truscott, and waited to hear the man's voice. It was Nick Wheeler. This was interesting. Nick had been arrested in connection with that country burglary up in Norfolk and subsequently released. He strained his ears to catch the conversation, but Nick was whispering into Hector's ear and Truscott could not make out a word.

"That's another man I must warn you against," he remarked when Hector came back. "He is a convicted house-breaker and a petty larcenist. If you tell me that he's turned over a new leaf and is keeping chickens, you can save your breath, for I won't believe you."

"That's only the second time I've seen him," replied Hector, nettled at the detective's jeering tone.

"And if you've any sense it'll be your last. What did he want?"

"Nothing in your line, Bill." Hector smiled. "Sorry to get wild, just now. I know you're a good scout, but I'm rather fond of Uncle Thomas. He's been very good to me, you know. Gave me pennies and sweets when I was a kid and now he's giving me thirty bob a week for this job and there's practically nothing to do."

"He's not a philanthropist, kid. Don't run away with that idea."

"Oh, don't start that business all over again. Wicked old man lures innocent boy into crime. Sobbing white-haired mother and stern judge. Life ruined. Suicide . . . It's like a penny novelette, except there's no blue-eyed heroine to rescue me."

"I won't say any more about it, Hector. The incident is closed, as the politicians say. Have a 'bine?"

Bill Truscott was in a thoughtful mood when he left Uncle Thomas's shop. He had tried to find out what Nick Wheeler had said to Hector, but without success. There had been a report at the station about the burglary in Norfolk when he had reported for duty, and a Printed Information had given particulars of Nick's arrival at Liverpool Street and his arrest.

Nothing incriminating nor of a suspicious nature was found on the man, but it is believed that he was connected with the breaking and entering of the Grange, Starring. The method of entering the house was that employed by Wheeler on several previous occasions. The probability is that the stolen property was hidden in the vicinity of the village of Starring, and will be removed by either Wheeler himself or one of his associates. The Metropolitan Police will work in close conjunction with the County Authorities, to whom every assistance is to be given in accordance with regular practice.

Truscott knew Southwark. Not only the busy High Street with its ceaseless stream of traffic, but the odd corners, the coffee shops, the public houses, and the doss houses which the criminal population of the district were known to frequent.

Detective-Sergeant Truscott ran through in his mind the places of call to which Nick Wheeler was likely to go, and proceeded to search each one in turn. If he had wished, he could, of course, have walked out of his hiding-place in Uncle Thomas's back shop and met Nick there and then, but he had thought at the time that this course would be unwise. If it were realized by Nick that he, Truscott, was a friend of Hector's, he would lose what advantage he had gained by having the entrée to the shop when the owner was absent.

The public houses were filling up with labourers in for their morning wet when Truscott began his round. At the "Fox and Grapes" he drew a blank. It was the same at the "Ring of Bells" and "Leg of Mutton", and he was beginning to wonder if he had been wise in not tackling Nick at the shop.

The "Brewery" in Southwark is known to few. It was not a brewery but a shed. Who the owner was nobody who went there knew or cared. Most of them were past caring about anything, and Old Smoky, the bearded, self-appointed caretaker and steward of this very queer club, could not have told you the origin of the name if you had asked him. In point of fact, in the past someone had brewed beer in the shed from hops and malt and yeast bought in packets from the grocer in Thin Street. The formality of a licence had been dispensed with, and the crowd of assorted lags who congregated there daily had profited from the omission. The stuff looked like beer, and to those gifted with a vivid imagination it tasted a little like beer. The important part to them was that the price was one penny for half a pint served in an old fruit tin.

Old Smoky, however, when he took over, either did not know or could not be bothered to learn how to brew the liquid known as beer, and depended for his supplies on the enterprise of the barman at the "Ring of Bells". Swipes, the leavings of countless glasses and tankards, found their way into an enamelled jug beneath the counter of the public bar, and from thence to the empty tins of the "Brewery" and the throats of its members. Besides beer of a kind, there were beds of a sort beneath a neighbouring railway arch, where the thunder of trains overhead and the rustling of rats among the refuse underfoot failed to disturb those who paid tuppence for the luxury of a hammock made of sacking.

Truscott pushed open the door of a burnt-out factory, of which only the walls were standing, and threaded his way through piles of debris and wrecked machinery, down a flight of brick steps and through an archway into the "Brewery".

There were ten members of the club present when the detective made his appearance, and they each regarded him much as a bishop would view the intrusion of a racing tipster into the silence room at the Athenaeum. They moved uneasily. Those who were standing sat down, while those who were sitting stood up. Old Smoky, ensconced in the only chair, alone did not move. He was accustomed to Truscott's informal visits and had not got anything on his conscience. Nothing, at least, which fourteen days or forty shillings would not settle. He even had the temerity to offer the detective half a pint in a rusty tin can.

"What's the matter with you? Ain't you thirsty?" he asked the detective, who waved it aside.

"No, I've had all I want this morning, thanks," he replied, and cast his eyes over the men around him.

"Any of you boys seen Nick lately? No, I suppose you haven't," he continued after a short pause in which, in their several ways, each member denied all knowledge of Nick.

"'E ain't bin getting into trouble, 'as 'e?" queried Old Smoky in shocked tones. "I allus thought as 'ow 'e was a decent lad."

Truscott smiled. By no stretch of imagination could he have described Nick Wheeler as a "decent lad". A man who knew warders in three convict establishments a great deal better than the governors did themselves; knew which of them "came the rough stuff" if you so much as winked an eye, and which might respond to judicious "oiling". Nick was quite a decent burglar, but certainly not a decent lad.

The detective sat down on an orange box and filled his pipe.

"No, I wouldn't go as far as to say he's been getting into trouble," he said in answer to Smoky's question. "But he's been doing his best. Are you sure you haven't seen him?"

"As God is my judge—" Old Smoky began.

"All right. All right," Truscott interrupted. "I'll take your word for it," and added to himself, "not that it's worth twopennyworth of bad winkles."

Half an hour of the undiluted company of the "Brewery" club was enough for Truscott, and when one o'clock struck he thought he'd take a stroll. The river was not far off, and a broken board in a fence let him through on to a deserted quay. This he knew, from his intimate knowledge of the geography of Southwark, to be Spender's Draw Dock, a cut made into the land at right angles to the river, a hundred yards long and not more than two hundred feet in width. There was a time when sailing ships, towed all the way from the Nore, had lain in that berth to discharge their cargo, but with the growth of the great docks farther downstream, with their network of roads and railway lines, Spender's dock had not been much in request.

It was low water when Truscott walked along the quay-side and, except for a great trough-shaped depression filled with dirty water, the mud was uncovered. A man in long thigh boots and equipped with a wooden rake was walking to and fro in the mud, pushing his rake before him. When it came upon an obstruction he bent down to pull it out. Up against the wall there was a collection of bits of old iron and stones.

"Anything coming in here?" Truscott called out, and the man straightened himself.

"Yes, there be some talk of it, but it's not the first time I've bin sent to clean the berth and then nothing came of it."

He pointed to a jagged lump of concrete which he had just pulled to one side.

"That's not the sort of stuff you want a ship to sit on. If it got her under the turn of her bilge it would buckle her plates and I'd lose my job. Can you tell me the time, please, mister?"

"Gone one o'clock," Truscott replied.

"Blimey, I didn't know it was as late as that. I must 'a' missed the hooter."

He clambered up the vertical ladder on to the wharf and began to pull off his long boots.

"What's the name of the ship coming up?" Truscott asked.

"The *Karnoc* I believe it is," the man replied. "Going to lay up for a spell, so they say, though there was some talk of her being sold, but I don't know."

"Is she going to discharge here?"

"No, she's light. And she can't get in except right at the top o' Springs. Besides, there ain't no railway within a quarter of a mile. This 'ere dock's finished, that's what it is, except for them that wants a lay-by berth."

The detective's return to the "Brewery" coincided with the arrival of Nick Wheeler. Old Smoky gave a warning whistle, but Truscott called out as Nick was about to turn back through the archway.

"It's all right, Nick! I don't want you except for a little talk, that's all. No need to get windy."

Nick grinned sheepishly and edged over to where old Smoky was cooking something over a fire.

"I know you ain't got nothing on me, mister," he replied. "And I can't tell ye anythin' neither, for there's nothin' I got to tell."

"All the same, I'd be glad if you would come for a walk with me as far as the High Street. Maybe your memory'll improve as we go along—"

CHAPTER VII

ALFRED WAS the first to arrive at the office on Thursday afternoon. He employed the time while waiting for Sam and Dusty in examining the papers relating to the *Karnoc*, which were piled on a desk in the inner office. He took the bill of sale together with the option issued by the owners of the ship and put them in his breast pocket. While there was any chance of his obtaining the necessary sum to complete the purchase on his own, he would stick to these papers. If Uncle Thomas had failed in his part of the Norfolk burglary, he, Alfred, would give the papers back to Sam and let him get on with it. Not that there was much chance of the old man letting him down. He had never failed him yet, but Alfred felt vaguely uneasy. Despite its age and failings there should have been no reason why the Morris had not brought Uncle Thomas back to Town the previous evening. There was no mention of any arrests connected with the Grange affair in the morning papers, and if the old man had been caught with the goods the Press would doubtless have regarded such news as "good copy".

Kudorfer and Lena were the next arrivals. Johannis' eyes lit up with pleasure when he saw Alfred there alone.

"How does it go, my friend?" he asked. "You have the money, yes?"

Alfred touched his breast pocket.

"Yes, I've got a certified cheque here," he replied, and held out his hand to Lena. "I wasn't expecting to meet you here," he said, and Lena gave him her slow smile.

"You are not very polite, Mr. Brown. I am sorry if I am in the way, but my father is nervous of your London traffic when he is alone."

"I'm sorry, Miss Kudorfer. I didn't mean to appear discourteous, but you know this is to be a purely business meeting, and—"

"You think I had better go. Is that it?" Lena interrupted, and then pointed to the door leading to the inner office. "Can I wait in there? I shall be—oh, so very quiet."

As the door closed behind her Johannis turned to Alfred.

"Would it not be possible, my friend, to fix this business up between us two? I do not trust this Captain Hunt, and as for Mr. Hartford—I think he is a fool."

The sound of footsteps in the passage outside saved Alfred the trouble of explaining why exactly he could not fall in with such a scheme. Such an explanation would not have been easy, for he had lied when he said he had the necessary cash.

The newcomers were Sam and Dusty Miller, and when the latter had been introduced to Johannis the talk became general. Alfred pretended to have just met Johannis for the first time, questioned him about his trip from Posnik, and asked him how he liked London, while Sam smoked cigarette after cigarette and stared at the door in nervous expectation. He and Dusty were at the end of their slender resources, and if further supplies of cash were not forthcoming things would become distinctly difficult. There was Kudorfer's hotel bill and passage money, the repayment of which he had demanded in addition to the thousand pounds promised for his future services on board the *Karnoc*. Cables also would have to be sent to Johannis' son so that the little matter of extinguishing the light at Posnik harbour should be suitably arranged.

At a quarter to four Sam interrupted the conversation between Alfred and Johannis with a suggestion that they should get down to business. Maurice Crane was due at four o'clock, he explained.

"And I suppose Hunt will be coming along too?" said Alfred; but Sam shook his head.

"I thought it would be better to keep him out of it until we had got everything fixed up," he explained.

"That is good," said Johannis, and took the chair indicated by Sam. Sam himself faced the door with Dusty by his side opposite Johannis. Alfred sat at the other end of the table next to the door.

When they were all seated Sam proceeded to give a brief outline of what remained to be done in order to get the *Karnoc* ready for sea, and he assured the other two that Johannis was the right man for the work he had to do.

"Captain Hunt, I feel, can also be relied upon. Of course, he has been told nothing of the real purpose of our venture, but—"

There was a knock, and in response to Alfred's cry of "Come in", the door opened and Hector sidled in. He was carrying a parcel under his arm.

"What do you want?" asked Sam sharply, angry with the nervousness of a weak man. "You've come to the wrong place. This is—"

"That's all right; this is a friend of mine," interrupted Alfred, who slipped from his chair and drew Hector into a corner. "What's up? Anything wrong?" he asked in a whisper, his thoughts flying to what might have happened to Uncle Thomas.

"No. Everything's O.K.," Hector replied. "Nick told me to collect this and bring it to you. There was a wire from Uncle Thomas at lunch-time which I thought you'd like to see, so I brought the parcel along at the same time. Nick told me you'd be here."

Alfred snatched the telegram from Hector's hand and read it hurriedly.

"Thank God. The old man is on his way. He'll be back tonight," he muttered. "I'd half thought that—but never mind. Let's have the parcel."

Alfred cut the string and stripped off the paper, revealing a black wood sheath carved and ornamented with inlaid silver. He recognized it for the one he had seen in Crane's flat. He withdrew the knife it contained and, laying the sheath aside, he felt the double-edged blade with his thumb.

"You'd better be going, Hector. We're busy," and as Hector closed the door behind him Alfred turned to the others.

"What do you think of that?" he asked. "A pretty bit of work, and as sharp as the day it was forged, I'll bet."

Dusty took up the sheath which Alfred had put on the table.

"Malayan," he said after a careful examination. "Or possibly it came from Borneo."

"What's it worth?" asked Alfred. He was toying with the naked blade and did not notice that Kudorfer had his eye fixed upon the glittering steel.

"Worth?" said Dusty. "That depends on who wants it and what he wants it for. As a curio I should say you might get a quid for it if you were lucky. There's some people might give you a bit more, but it wouldn't be to put in a glass case that they'd buy it, if you understand what I mean."

"For the love of Mike shut up," said Sam peevishly. "Can't you talk about your blinking knife some other time?"

Dusty took the knife from Alfred and ran the tips of his fingers over the carving of the haft. It was black as pitch and had been rubbed smooth by countless hands.

"Go on with what you were going to say," Dusty urged. "Don't mind me."

But before Sam could collect his thoughts there was another knock at the door. Johannis, with his eyes on the knife which Dusty had laid aside, alone did not look up.

"Captain Hunt!" Sam half rose from his chair.

"Yes. You weren't expecting me to call, were you? But I'm here, representing Mr. Maurice Crane."

"Isn't he coming?" asked Sam.

"Search me. I haven't seen him all day, but whether he turns up or not, I'm the man who's going to put the O.K. on this business before any dough changes hands."

He pulled out the chair beside Johannis, sat down, and crossed his legs.

"You thought this was going to be a walk over, didn't you?" he asked Sam with a sneer.

Alfred from his end of the table leaned forward.

"Now, Captain, don't let us have any unpleasantness, please. Mr. Hartford is very much worried about this business and he, and in fact all of us, are anxious to settle it on a friendly basis."

"I bet you are. You don't want trouble, but you want money. Well, I'll tell you something. I've been down to have a look at that muck barge you call a ship. Yes, it's the blinking *Karnoc* I'm talking about, and you needn't look so pained about it. You've seen her too, and you know she's only fit for the breaker's yard."

"She's got a seaworthy certificate," Sam objected. "And she's not due for survey until September. However, if there's anything you think needs doing before you sail, you've only to say the word and it'll be done."

"I dare say," replied Hunt, slightly mollified. "But there's nothing that can be done which could turn her into a profit-earning proposition. All the engines, especially the high pressure, require to be opened up, the bearings re-bushed, and as for the boilers—well, you couldn't keep enough steam in them to run at more than five knots. The condenser's leaking at practically every tube."

"Do you mind telling me where you obtained this very interesting but entirely inaccurate information, Captain Hunt?" It was Alfred who put the question, and there was something in his voice which caused the others to turn in his direction. "We have had a report from a very competent firm of surveyors which was entirely satisfactory. I cannot think that any cursory examination you may have made can carry much weight in the face of such a report. Besides, you have no qualifications as an engineer, I believe."

The colour began to mount in the cheeks of Hunt and he thumped his fist on the table.

"I've certain information. It doesn't matter a toss where I got it, but I know it's right. To buy that ship would be like chucking your money into the sea, and I'm damned if I'm going to let Mr.

Crane invest one penny unless, of course . . ." He looked at Sam questioningly. Then at Dusty and lastly at Alfred.

Sam dropped his eyes. Dusty took out his cigarette-case and fiddled with the catch. Alfred alone met Hunt's mute inquiry with level gaze.

"Go on, Captain," he prompted. "You were going to make some suggestion, weren't you? Let's have it."

"All right. I'll come out of the wood. This show of yours is crooked. It stands to reason it must be. With the present rates of freight it's taking some of the best-found ships afloat all their time to make their expenses. What chance in hell has a tub like the *Karnoc* of making anything but a thumping dead loss? That is, of course, if she's run square. What you've got up your sleeves I don't know, but I don't go as skipper and I won't let Crane give you a bob till I know what the game is."

"Oh, well, I dare say we can find someone else who would be willing to lend the necessary amount," said Alfred quietly. "There's more fish in the sea—"

"Yes, I know," put in Hunt, "and there's a mug born every minute, which is lucky for some of us. But I'm not finished. Here's another thing. I'm going to keep an eye on you blokes, and if you get another pigeon to pluck I'll be there, and if I don't get my rake off I'll queer your pitch. But I've got to know everything, and the first thing you've got to tell me is what is the idea of sending this damned dago in the ship?"

"Look out!" screamed Sam.

Alfred flung himself across the table one split second too late. The knife which Hector had brought a few minutes before, the knife with the carved sheath inlaid with silver, had been driven up to its haft between the shoulders of Captain Geoffrey Hunt.

After his first shout of alarm, Sam sat motionless, staring so that one might have thought his eyes would drop out of his head. He stared as the body slumped over the table with a terrible unwinking gaze. Then:

"It's not true! It's not—"

Alfred elbowed his way past Dusty, knocking over a chair in his passage, and thrust a hand over Sam's mouth.

"A handkerchief. Quick!"

He crumpled it up into a ball and thrust it between Sam's teeth.

The door to the inner room was flung open and Lena appeared in the opening. Her eyes were large with fear and her hands were working feverishly. "Father!" she called, and Johannis looked up with a scowl.

"Be quiet, you fool!"

"Fool?"

Lena took in the scene with one swift glance: the body slumped across the table; Dusty's scared, white face; Alfred stifling the cries of Sam, who writhed in his chair, beating the air feebly with his pudgy hands.

"Fool?" she repeated. "It is not I who am a fool."

She turned and pointed to the room behind her.

"You must take him in there and keep him quiet!"

"Take his legs," ordered Alfred, and Dusty leapt forward to obey. Between them they half dragged, half carried Sam into the inner office and laid him in the arm-chair by the desk.

"Go and lock the outer door."

Dusty sped to carry out the order. When he came back Sam was sobbing like a girl. Hiccoughing, racking sobs which seemed to shake the very room. Alfred had withdrawn the handkerchief and was gripping Sam's wrist.

"I'll quiet him down in a minute," he muttered. "Can you get a glass of water? There's whisky in my flask in my hip pocket. Take it out and mix a strong peg. Half and half."

Dusty did as he was told and Alfred took the glass and held it to Sam's lips.

"Good, he's taking it. You're all right, Sam. You're all right."

Sam's head fell forward on his chest.

"I must wake up. I must wake up. Take him away. Dusty, did you put the blotting-paper out and the pens? It's like a board meeting. What a lovely knife. I wonder where—I wonder . . . Oh, my God! . . ."

Alfred put a hand under Sam's chin, jerked up his head, then slapped him on the cheek. Sam shrank back.

"Alfred! Yes, it's Alfred. You'll look after me, won't you, Alfred?"

"Here, drink this up and have a cigarette, and you'll feel better."

Lena was leaning on the desk, smoking a cigarette and watching Alfred. A moment later a head appeared round the door. It was Johannis. He looked first at Alfred and then at Lena, who in answer to his mute inquiry nodded slowly.

"It is the only way," Johannis muttered, and felt for the phial in his waistcoat. Then he tore at the lining and pulled out the tiny bottle. The cork was stuck in tightly, but he pulled it out with his teeth.

"Give him ten drops. That is all. He will sleep."

Dusty held the glass while Kudorfer, with a hand as steady as a rock, allowed the drops of the viscous fluid to fall into the glass. They were crimson like blood, but they spread and disappeared as they sank in the whisky. Alfred took the glass.

"Now finish this up, Sam, old man, and you'll feel fine."

In less than a minute the drug began to take effect, and the three men, Alfred, Dusty, and Kudorfer watched with relief as Sam's head began to nod. They settled him down in the chair with a cushion behind his head, but not until the sound of his deep breathing broke the silence did they move.

It was typical of Alfred that he did not burst into recriminations and abuse of Kudorfer. He accepted the inevitable. For a moment he thought of dashing out into the street, running anywhere as long as he got away from that room. Then he thought of calling the police. Of locking Kudorfer in with his victim. Then thought of the questions which would inevitably follow. Whose is the knife? How did it get into the room? Dusty would say it was brought to him, Alfred. Sam would confirm the story. He would be charged as an accessory before the fact. The evidence as far as it went was dead against him. If he told who had brought it and they questioned Hector, that damn' fool might say anything. Perhaps that Alfred had told him to bring it there.

When two men set out to commit a crime and one of them intends to commit an act of violence and the other man is cognizant of this intention, and if, furthermore, an act of violence is committed by one man, the result of which is the death of a third person, both men may be found guilty of murder.

Alfred had read these words somewhere and remembered them now with strange vividness. Yes, he remembered now, it was the summing-up of a judge in a murder trial in which two men had been found guilty of murder and had been sentenced to death. He had read about it in an evening paper one night on the top of a bus. If the whole truth came out all would be well, but it was too big a risk to take.

Kudorfer, who had returned to the outer office, was sitting at the table rolling a cigarette as Alfred came through the door. Dusty had thrown up the window and was staring down into the street forty feet below. He was trembling and his hands were clutching the sill. Alfred closed the window and took him by the shoulders.

"For God's sake, man, pull yourself together. You and I have got to work this so that nothing is discovered. Sam's quiet for the time being, but when he wakes we'll have our work cut out to make him keep his mouth shut. Meanwhile, there's a hell of a lot to be done. Kudorfer, go and sit by the door. Your daughter must stay with Sam."

Alfred satisfied himself that the door was locked and then put the key in his pocket. There were footsteps in the passage outside, but they passed by. He could see shadows through the glazed top part of the door. If Crane should turn up at this moment? Alfred turned back to where the dead man was lying still sprawled across the table. A rivulet of blood was trickling slowly across the polished surface and dropping on to the floor. He picked up a sheet of blotting-paper and dammed the stream. The paper crimsoned slowly until it could absorb no more, and then the stream began again.

"There's a curtain in the other room. Bring it in here," he ordered Dusty, who was still standing dazed before the window.

Dusty stared, and it was not until Alfred had repeated the command that he walked to the inner room as a man in a dream. Alfred tore the curtain into strips and plugged the hole in the back of the dead man in which the knife had been. At last the blood ceased to flow.

"What have you done with the knife, Kudorfer?"

"It is here. Look! I have cleaned it on the carpet."

He slipped it back into its sheath as he spoke and then went on:

"Truly this is a good knife. What did our friend say? It was not valuable except to somebody who wanted it. I want it. I shall keep it."

Alfred shuddered, and for the first time since the blow had been struck he was assailed by a feeling of nausea.

"No, you don't. I'll look after that." He pulled out his flask and took a swig of the neat spirit, then handed it to Dusty.

"Go on, man. Take it. Drink it. Finish it if you like. I'll be all right now."

He waited until Dusty had given back the flask empty; then he took a step across the room.

"Give me a hand, Dusty. We'll lay him down in the corner here."

Together they lifted the inert body of the murdered man. His arms hung down limply and caught in a chair.

"You must lift him right up, Dusty. Now, one, two, three, lift! That's the way."

"Let's get out," Dusty muttered. "Out of this. We can't do anything."

"Yes," said Alfred. "And what then? The body'll be found. We'll be traced to this room. The man who brought the knife saw us all here not a quarter of an hour before it happened."

"We can get away," muttered Dusty. "I know where we can lie up and then get a boat out of the country."

"No, I've thought of all that," Alfred replied. "We couldn't make it. No man has ever got away with it like that."

Dusty shuddered and clutched at the table. His fingers touched something warm and sticky. He raised his hand and stared at the blood which smeared it.

"Here, wipe it off with this."

Alfred held out a strip of the curtain.

"No, it's no good, Dusty. You and I and Sam and Kudorfer are all in this. I've thought it out and if we keep our heads we'll get away with it. The trouble will be to get rid of the body, and we must think out some way to do it; but first of all we've got to clean out this room. We must strip every scrap of stuff which has blood on it. You mop up all the blood you can see while I look round."

At the end of a quarter of an hour the room was beginning to look more tidy. On the bare boards by the door Alfred had accumulated a pile of blood-soaked cloth and blotting-paper. The chairs which had been knocked over had been set on their legs again.

"Take off your coat and examine it for bloodstains," Alfred said to Dusty, and stripped off his own. "Is your shirt all right? And your cuffs? Yes, I think you're O.K., but I've got some on one of my sleeves."

He took the knife which Kudorfer was holding in his hand and gave it to Dusty.

"Here, rip my sleeve off up at the shoulder."

He added it to the pile and then stood in front of Kudorfer.

"Listen here, you damn' swine. You've got to help too. Do you understand? You've got to do what you're told or you'll be hanged as sure as God made little apples. If any one of us makes a false step we're finished, and get it out of your head once and for all that all the money in the world could help you in an English court."

"Yes, I understand. I do what you say and I go where you tell me. But the ship! Now that Captain Hunt is dead, can we not get her? You have a cheque—money. You tell me so. We will sail away on her to Posnik and there we will be quite safe. No one comes to Posnik if I do not wish it."

"We can do nothing until we get rid of the body," Alfred replied. "It must not be found and nothing must be left in this room which has one drop of blood on it."

He dragged the table to one side and surveyed the great crimson stain on the dun-coloured carpet. It was wet and soggy to the touch.

"That'll have to go. We'll get a new one. Dusty, get some water and wash down the boards. No, wait a minute. I've got an idea."

Alfred picked up an ink-pot and deliberately poured the contents over the blood stain.

"We'll send it to be dyed black. That ought to do the trick. Do you think you can find some place near here?"

"Yes, I think so, but what about the underfelt?"

He had ripped up a corner of the carpet and turned it back. The blood had soaked through, and even the boards were stained in patches a dark purple. The carpet was rolled up and the tell-tale parts of the felt were cut out and put on the pile by the door. Dusty was washing down the boards and skirting when he called to Alfred, who had gone to see how Sam was faring.

"Come and look at this!"

He pointed to a string of spots on the wall. They ranged from the size of a sixpence to that of a five-shilling piece. Dusty rubbed at one tentatively with his wet duster, but the only effect was to spread the half-dried blood over the wall-paper.

"That's no good. You're only making it worse," said Alfred. He called to Kudorfer. "How did this happen?" he asked.

"That? I do not know unless perhaps when I withdrew the knife like this." Johannis gave a quick flick of his wrist to demonstrate his meaning. "Yes, he was sitting there and I was sitting by his left hand here. Yes, that is how it happened."

Alfred grunted in disgust.

"Well, what are we going to do? We can never get that blood right off the paper, and we can't take the walls away."

"Why not paint them out?" Dusty suggested. "Get 'em off with soap and water as well as we can first and then give it a good coat of paint."

"Yes, that might do, but paint would look odd, wouldn't it? Why not distemper? Lots of rooms are done that way. I'll go out and get some. You wait here."

Dusty cast a frightened glance at the body in the corner and shuddered violently.

"For God's sake pull yourself together, man."

Alfred took him by his arm and forced him into a chair.

"I thought you were going to be all right. If you crumple up now we're landed. He's no blooming good." Alfred pointed to Kudorfer, who was sitting smoking a cigarette as though nothing had happened. "He doesn't know his way about Town. That's the trouble," he explained. "One of us'll have to go with him everywhere."

"I'm feeling sick again," Dusty muttered. He clutched hold of Alfred's coat. "Let's get out of here. I can't stand it."

Alfred paced up and down the room for a minute or two deep in thought, then he took the key from his pocket and unlocked the door.

"We'll both go," he said at last. "Kudorfer, you will stay here. I will lock the door behind me, and if anyone knocks you must keep absolutely quiet. Understand? And if the man in there"— he pointed to the inner office—"if he wakes up, give him another shot of that dope of yours."

As Dusty pulled himself out of his chair his knees trembled so that he staggered and had to clutch at the mantelpiece for support.

"I'll be better outside. Can I have a cigarette?"

Alfred held out his case and then struck a match.

"That's the way, Dusty. You'll be grand."

He opened the door of the inner room and beckoned to Lena.

"Is he all right?"

"He is sleeping and will not wake for yet another hour. Why?"

"I've got to go out I won't be long but I must get a few things in order to clean the place up. We can't leave it like this. Now, if Maurice comes here you must not let him in. You understand?"

Lena looked at him lazily from under her heavy lids.

"You mean that I shall keep this door locked?"

"Yes, of course. If he comes in, we're done for."

"And if he doesn't what will happen? I ask you. He will make a noise and perhaps send for the janitor. He is young and likes his own way." Lena smiled contemptuously. "It is just like a man to suggest such a thing. You have no sense. Suppose now, my friend, that Maurice goes away when he finds the door locked. All will be well you think, but for how long?"

"What do you mean?" Alfred shot out.

"Just this. Listen to me. It is difficult to make a body disappear—"

"Now you leave that to me!"

"Of course, of course. You will know what to do," Lena replied pacifically. "But the police in this country have a certain reputation for finding things. Supposing they were successful in this case. Not perhaps today or tomorrow, but in a few days' time, before we can sail in the *Karnoc*. In every newspaper there will be the news that Geoffrey Hunt has been murdered. Without a doubt Maurice will read the announcement, and if he goes to the police and says 'I knew this man Hunt. He was known also to Mr. Hartford, to Mr. Brown, and to Mr. Miller', that would be very awkward for all these three gentlemen."

Alfred paced up and down the room with quick nervous steps while Lena was talking. When she had finished he halted before her and lit a cigarette with nervous fingers.

"I've figured it all out and my plan can't go wrong, but still it might be as well to keep Crane out of the way. At least for a day or two. Could you get him away?"

"I could do—anything with him. I danced with him last night."

"Where can you go?"

"I shall leave that to Maurice. He will know. When we arrive I shall write to you."

"Righto. Come along, Dusty. We haven't too much time."

At an ironmonger's shop Alfred bought a seven-pound tin of distemper and a brush. Then they walked up to Sole Street, which was nearly deserted, and there they picked up a roll of American cloth and a basket. Five o'clock chimed from a church in Fleet Street when Alfred turned and began to lead the way back to the office. Then a thought struck him.

"We'd better not get back for half an hour yet," he said to Dusty, who had benefited from the walk and was almost himself again. "You see, all the typists and clerks'll be leaving their offices and we don't want to meet more people in the building than we can help. One looks so damned conspicuous carrying this basket, but we must have it in order to get rid of the curtains and those pieces of felt."

At Holborn Circus the two men boarded an eastward-bound bus and rode as far as Aldgate East. Then they changed to another bus and arrived back at the office shortly before six. The staircase was almost empty. Two girls passed them engrossed in conversation. Then Alfred grabbed Dusty by the arm.

"Follow me. Run!"

Alfred dashed along a short passage and had reached the end before he realized that it was a dead end. Dusty was close on his heels. He turned the handle of the last door in the passage. Thank God! It wasn't locked. An astonished typist looked up from her machine at the intrusion. Alfred closed the door behind him and, still panting slightly, asked if Mr. Robinson was in. The typist disclaimed all knowledge of the gentleman. She was angry and alarmed, but Alfred managed to engage her in conversation for several minutes until the danger was past.

"So sorry to have troubled you," he said, and opened the door an inch and looked along the passage. It was all clear. "It was a stupid mistake to have made. I'm afraid we've interrupted your work."

The girl watched them go with relief.

As soon as they were outside the room with the door closed behind them, Dusty asked:

"What the hell was it all about?"

"Didn't you see him? It was Maurice Crane. I don't think he saw us. If he had he would have followed us. It was a narrow squeak."

Alfred picked up the basket and roll of cloth he had dropped outside the typist's door.

"It wouldn't have done to have met Crane. He was a pal of Hunt's and would have been sure to have asked all sorts of awkward questions."

Kudorfer, as imperturbable as ever, let them into the office.

"Lena has gone," he said, "I think, with Maurice."

· · · · ·

Nearly an hour after Alfred and Dusty had left the office there had been sounds of footsteps in the corridor outside. Lena had turned to her father.

"Quick. Get inside that room and keep quiet. That is the step of Maurice Crane."

There was a knock at the outer door. Lena gave a swift look around the room to make sure that all was in order and then opened the door. She gazed at Maurice in silence for a moment, and then:

"You are late. Oh, why could you not have come sooner?"

Maurice took a pace forward, but she barred his way.

"No, no. We cannot stay here. We must go before he returns."

"Who? What the devil's up? You look scared."

Lena laid a hand on his sleeve and drew him into the passage.

"I cannot tell you here. At any moment he may return and then! *Héla!* You would never see me again."

As Maurice and Lena made their way down the stairs, Johannis crept out of the inner room on tiptoe and turned the key in the office door.

The Lagonda settled down to a steady, effortless fifty miles an hour along the Great West Road before Maurice quite realized what he was in for. Lena had given up trying to smoke, for the wind was blowing the ash into her eyes.

"Is it necessary to go so fast, Maureece?"

"Scared?"

"Of course not, but just look at my hair."

"It looks fine like that."

Lena shrugged her shoulders and returned the comb to her bag.

"Where are we going?" she asked.

"Bothered if I know," Maurice replied. He paused, and then went on: "I say, what is your trouble? I mean shoving off like this into the blue? Of course, I'll do anything for you, but I should rather like to know, if it's all the same to you."

"Not now, my Maureece. Let us get out into the country. Then I will tell you, but I promise that my danger is very real."

By the time they reached Birton Mead it was time for dinner, and Maurice swung the car under the arch of an old, half-timbered inn into a cobbled, grass-grown yard.

"By Jove, they've got rather a jolly garden! We'll have drinks sent out there before we feed."

Lena nodded agreement, and they sat side by side on a rough wooden bench, and when cigarettes were lit, Lena began:

"Maureece, I think you are wonderful. A short time ago I had no hope, but now—now I feel like a bird set free from its cage. This evening my fiancé arrived in London."

"But, Lena, you never told me you were engaged. I thought—"

"Have patience, my friend. He is my fiancé in name only. Never would I consent to marry him. In my country a girl is betrothed to the man selected for her by her father when she is but fifteen years old. She has no choice unless . . ." She paused.

"Go on," Maurice urged. "Unless what?"

"Unless she runs away. I could not have left Posnik unknown to my father. Two or three weeks ago a cable came for my father asking that he should go to England. I saw my chance. I pretended to be ill and required a change of air. We talked and talked. Oh, how we talked! But at last I persuaded my father to allow me to accompany him. When we landed in England I made a vow that never would I return to Posnik. Before the *Karnoc* sails I shall run away. My father will be busy with the ship and he will not be able to search for me. That was my plan, and all seemed to be going well when this very afternoon my father told me that my fiancé had followed us on the next ship. If we had met I should have been lost. He is jealous and I knew he would never let me out of his sight." She took a glass from her bag and combed back the curls which had been teased out by the wind. "Tonio would kill me if he thought that I did not intend to marry him," she concluded as calmly as though she were talking of the weather.

Maurice sipped his cocktail, and as he set down the glass he turned towards her.

"You know, you are a most extraordinary girl, Lena. You sit there as cool as a cucumber and tell me things that would scare any English girl into a thousand fits."

"I am not frightened—now. I shall remain hidden until Tonio has left the country, and then . . ."

"Yes, what's going to happen then?" asked Maurice, "Have you any money?"

"No, but I will find some way to live. I can dance. I have a good figure. I can even sing a little. Surely I will be able to find some employment somewhere. In a dance-hall or a theatre. But I do not worry. Today is ours and I am hungry. Come, my Maureece. Please do not look so solemn!" She stretched out her hands and pulled him to his feet. "Throw away your cigarette. Smile! Ah, that is better." She drew him gently to her and raised her eyes to his.

"Lena, you are a little witch!" He slipped his arms around her slender shoulders. "Tell me. Do you—er—love Tonio?"

"Love? That is a strong word. I like him a little."

"But you were to have married him?"

"If I had stayed in Posnik, yes. But now things are different. I do not know why, but they are."

"Do you mean . . ." Maurice tightened his grip on her two shoulders and held her in a vice facing him, so that he could look down into her dark eyes that always seemed half mocking, half encouraging. "Do you mean that *I* have made a difference?"

She tried to shrug her shoulders in his grasp, veiling her eyes with their long lashes.

"Per—haps. New places—new friends. . . ."

"No one particular friend?" he insisted.

"You are being very fierce with me, Maureece."

"I'm sorry. Won't you answer me?"

"Won't you let me go?"

"Won't you let me kiss you?"

Lena put a hand on his chest and held him off, still laughing, teasing, enticing. "Really—you Englishmen are so very—"

He shook her. "Be serious."

"Be patient then—and one day—when I know you so much better—perhaps."

She ducked under his arm, flipped his cheek with her forefinger and, turning, ran quickly into the hotel.

The waiter had set their table in a wide bow-window overlooking the quiet village street. Maurice ordered sherry and, when the waiter had retired, Lena raised her glass.

"Let us drink success to the *Karnoc*," she said.

"The *Karnoc*?" replied Maurice doubtfully. "You know, I don't think I'll go on with that show. I have an idea the blokes in it aren't on the level."

Lena set down her wine untasted.

"Not on the level? I do not understand. You are not suggesting that my father—"

"No, of course not. It's the others I'm not sure about. That chap Hartford, for instance, and the one they call Alfred."

Lena laid down her knife and fork.

"Would you tell me, Maureece, what has made you suspicious?"

"I'm afraid I don't really know unless it was something Hunt told me about them."

"Hunt!" Lena murmured, and the colour drained from her face. The hand which reached out for her glass was trembling.

"I say, what's the matter?" asked Maurice, alarmed at her agitation.

Lena drank off a glass of water before replying.

"It is nothing," she assured him. "I am a little tired, that is all. You were quite right. Mr. Hartford is not one to be trusted. My father has also discovered that. Today, as you know, there was to have been a meeting at the office, but Mr. Hartford did not arrive."

"Then the whole show is off?" queried Maurice.

"No, no. Not so fast. This Mr. Alfred Brown has arranged to buy the ship and my father will sail in her to assist in the navigation when she arrives at Posnik. There are many rocks in the harbour and without him there would be a very grave risk."

"I'd like to have met your father, Lena. Has he met Hunt yet?"

"No, I do not think so. Why should he? But please do not talk about Mr. Hunt. I do not like him. You understand, don't you, Maureece?"

"I'm afraid I don't, but still, what does it matter? Now tell me. Is this *Karnoc* business really coming off?"

"How can I tell? Mr. Brown told my father that he would supply the necessary money but he has not yet done so."

"Then there's still a chance for me to come in on it?" Lena smiled provokingly.

"I thought, Maureece, that you were suspicious."

"Yes, I was, but if Hartford's out of it, and you can assure me it's all right, I'd like to have a share, especially if I can get a passage on the ship. I'm sick of being ashore."

Lena's brain worked quickly. If Alfred's promise of the necessary cash failed to materialize, her father might find it difficult to return to Posnik, and if the body was discovered his life would be in danger. With Maurice's money the way of escape would be opened.

"I can make no promises, my Maureece, but it may be that you can still get your share, and then we could sail together."

"But you're forgetting this blighter Tonio, your fiancé."

Lena cursed herself for the slip she had made, but passed it off with a laugh.

"I shall rely on you, Maureece, to protect me."

Maurice glanced at the loud-ticking grandfather clock in the corner.

"Gosh, it's eight o'clock already. What are we going to do? Stay here or journey on? I know a ripping little pub in Dorset. We could get there by midnight."

"Very well. Let us go to your ripping little pub, whatever that means. I am quite recovered."

"Well, if you'll get ready I'll pay the bill and send a wire." He looked at Lena doubtfully. "I think you'd better be my sister. People are awfully proper in the country."

As a matter of fact it was nearly one o'clock in the morning when Maurice pulled up before the door of the Linden Hotel and a sleepy porter showed them to their respective rooms.

CHAPTER VIII

Uncle Thomas's house was still locked and apparently untenanted when Alfred reached it at seven o'clock. He knocked on the door and rang the bell, but there was no response. The area gate was locked, but he opened it by the simple expedient of lifting the latch clear. The laundry basket, looking rather the worse for wear, stood in its accustomed place on an extension of the top step. Alfred gave a swift glance up and down the street. There was no one in sight.

"The old man'll be back tonight," he informed Dusty, who had accompanied him on the expedition. Alfred had not dared to leave him alone after that scene at the open window when Dusty had stared down at the street below with that strange look in his eyes.

"We'll take his basket back with us. You push it and I'll follow along."

They re-crossed the river by Blackfriars Bridge and turned left up Fleet Street and into Fetter Lane. An alleyway at the back of St. Dunstan's Church led to the block of offices of which International Developments was but one unit. Alfred produced a spanner, took the basket off its chassis and with Dusty's aid put it on to a lift which ran up the back of the building. The janitor who had rooms in the basement let them into the building and Alfred explained to him that they had a load of books and ledgers to move out of their office. In return for a shilling, the janitor manned the winch-handle of the operating mechanism and hoisted the lift with its burden up to the third floor.

"Thanks very much," said Alfred. "We'll let her down ourselves, so you needn't wait up if you'll leave the door unbolted."

"Well, I was thinkin' of takin' the missus to the flicks, and if you're sure you can manage on your own . . ."

"Of course we can," Alfred assured him. "We'll be a little time loading up and I don't want to keep you waiting about."

The floor of the office was littered with ash and the air was thick with the pungent odour of Kudorfer's cigars and of the newly distempered walls when Alfred led the way in.

"I want a drink," said the custodian of the door.

"I bet you do," Dusty replied, "and so say all of us, but we've got a job ahead."

"That's right," Alfred agreed. "We've got to get him out of the way and all this stuff has got to go."

He kicked at the heap of rags and then walked into the inner office. Sam turned uneasily as Alfred laid a hand on his shoulder, and Kudorfer, who had followed him into the room, examined the sleeping man with critical gaze.

"He will wake soon now. I know the signs. If we had some cold water—"

"Time enough for that later," replied Alfred, and asked: "He won't wake on his own account, will he?"

"No, he will drop into a natural sleep. That is all. He is quite safe."

"Good. Dusty, bring in the basket and lock the door behind you. We can't take any risks."

He picked up the American cloth and unrolled it on the table. When Dusty staggered in with the basket Alfred started to slit up the cloth to make a lining for it.

"We don't want any blood dropping out of it," he explained.

"Blood?" said Kudorfer. "He won't bleed any more now. Besides, there is something in the wound. The piece of curtain, is there not?"

"Still, I'm not taking any risks, and before we put him in, there's something we've got to do," Alfred replied.

He took a pair of folding nail-scissors from his pocket and snipped out the laundry-marks from the dead man's underclothing and socks. He even removed the tailor's tab inside the breast-pocket of the jacket, then he threw the scraps of cloth on to the heap by the door. When he had finished, Alfred motioned to Kudorfer to help him lift the body into the basket. The rags and felt were thrust in on top and the lid was fastened down.

"You won't need the other basket which you bought?" asked Dusty.

"No. We'll leave it here for the time being. Now then, Kudorfer, take one end. Dusty, you take the other end and we'll get it along to the lift."

Alfred looked out into the passage and up and down the stairs.

"Yes, it's all clear," he announced. "Come along."

The basket was loaded on to the lift and was lowered to the street level, where Alfred secured it once more to its chassis. Dusty pushed the basket through the streets southwards to Southwark, while Alfred, with the stolid Kudorfer by his side, kept pace a few yards in the rear. As the little procession turned into Graves Crescent Alfred looked ahead anxiously towards No. 96, and, on catching sight of the house, he swore.

"The old blighter's not back yet, curse him," he said to Kudorfer. "But he can't be long now. Run her in here, Dusty."

Alfred opened the area gate and the basket was pushed inside and the gate re-fastened.

"We'll have to come back later," said Alfred. "And then . . ." he paused, deep in thought.

"Yes, what's the next move after that?" Dusty queried.

"The cellar," replied Alfred. "We'll put it in there. Dig a hole and put some quicklime on top. Cover it with coal dust and finish off with cement. No one would think of looking there."

"Crippen did that and he was caught," commented Dusty gloomily.

"Well, have you got any better idea?" asked Alfred irritably. He was beginning to feel the strain of the last few hours. "It was different with Crippen. All his pals knew his wife had disappeared and that started the trouble."

"Well, won't it be the same in this case?" Dusty replied. "Hunt's bound to have some friends who'll start asking questions. Why, there's young Crane. You haven't forgotten him, have you?"

"That's all fixed up. Don't you fret."

"And then there's Sam. He's a twister."

"He hasn't got the guts to do any double-crossing," Alfred replied.

"That's all you know. A day or two ago he planned to run this show on his own."

"The devil he did!"

Alfred felt at the knife, which he had fastened inside his waistcoat under his arm in such a way that no one could notice its presence. That would have to be disposed of where it would never be found. If anything went wrong and he were arrested and searched and the knife was found on him! Alfred broke out into a muck sweat at the very thought of such a catastrophe, and quickened his pace. They were walking westwards now, and when they eventually turned north along Waterloo Road and reached the bridge, Alfred halted and looked down at the water below. He felt for the knife and then remembered that its sheath was made of wood. It would be too risky to throw it into the river. It might float and be picked up. A police boat was chugging its way up-stream against the ebb tide.

"Come on, Alfred," urged Dusty. "What's the good of hanging about here? We've got to get back to Sam. God knows what he'll do if he wakes up in that room alone."

Sam was awake when the three men trooped into the room, but he was still feeling the effects of the drug and smiled foolishly as Alfred walked over to where he was seated, puffing at a cigarette.

"I've been asleep, Alfred. What's the time?"

Alfred told him.

"Eight o'clock?" Sam looked up in amazement. "Then what the hell are we all doing here?" He looked at Kudorfer, at first blankly, and then as memory came flooding back a look of horror overspread his features. His eyes goggled, his jaw dropped and the colour drained from his flabby cheeks. Alfred laughed, while Kudorfer stood as though turned to stone.

"Been having a nightmare," Alfred chaffed. "That's the worst of sleeping on your back in the afternoon."

"Nightmare?" whispered Sam, his eyes still riveted on Kudorfer.

"Yes, you look as if you were seeing a ghost," Alfred replied, and poked Kudorfer in the ribs. "He's real enough. Come on, Sam. Pull yourself together. We want to be moving."

"A dream, was it? Are you sure? I could swear I saw Kudorfer . . ."

"Well, I don't know what you dreamed, you silly old fool, but when we came in here after lunch you were slumped down in that chair snoring like a pig. We thought you'd been on the booze so we left you here to sleep it off, and you don't seem to have done it yet. You're all muzzy."

"Do you mean it didn't happen? That it was—a dream?"

"I tell you nothing's happened. I don't know what the hell you're talking about," Alfred replied curtly.

"Where—where's Hunt? He was here, I'll swear it."

"Keep him talking," Alfred whispered to Dusty. "I'll be back in a minute."

Alfred passed into the outer office and took from his pocket the telegram he had received a few hours earlier from Uncle Thomas. It was the work of but a minute to erase the message it bore and write in another which read: *Sorry shall not be able to attend meeting. Hunt.*

"There you are." Alfred strode back into the inner room and held the telegraph form before Sam's eyes.

"You're not so blotto you can't read, are you?"

Sam spelled out the message and then raised his eyes to Alfred, who was smiling down at him.

"Then it's true. It didn't happen. Oh, thank God for that! Alfred!" Sam clutched his arm. "I had the hell of a dream. I saw him"—he pointed at Kudorfer— "pick up a knife, and—"

"You tell me another time, Sam," Alfred interrupted. "It's getting late."

Sam clutched at the telegram.

"Let me read that again to make sure. Yes, that's right."

"And you see when it was handed in," Alfred pointed out. "At 12.25 at Royston." Then he took the paper and crumpled it into a ball. "Feeling better now?"

"Yes, I'm all right," Sam replied. "But you know that dream didn't half give me a jolt. It was as real as real. We were all sitting round the table. There was you and Hunt and—"

"For God's sake shut him up," Dusty hissed. "I can't stand any more of this."

"Righto. We'll move. Get on your pins, Sam. Say, Dusty, when he goes through the office keep on his left side. I don't want him to see the carpet. I'll follow on and lock up behind you."

At the corner of Carey Street Alfred motioned to Dusty to walk with him and let Sam go on ahead with Kudorfer, and in this fashion the quartet reached Kingsway, by which time Alfred had given Dusty his orders for the night.

"Kudorfer must go back to his hotel and wait there till he hears from me. He'll be as safe there as anywhere, and I think we can trust him to keep his trap shut. I'm not happy about Sam, though. If he ever tumbles to it that what he saw wasn't a nightmare, we'll be in a fix, all of us. He's the one weak link and I'll have to take care of him myself."

At the corner of Kingsway, opposite the Stoll Theatre, Dusty and Kudorfer turned northward.

"Come along, Sam," said Alfred. "You'd better come home with me."

"I'm all right," Sam replied. "My legs were a bit groggy to start with, but I'm feeling fine now."

"I dare say you are, but there's something I want to tell you. Something important. We'll go to Uncle Thomas's shop in the Borough and doss there."

Alfred bought a bag of fish and chips on the way, and on their arrival at the shop he heated them up on a gas-ring in Uncle Thomas's bed-sitting-room. There was a note on the mantelpiece addressed to Uncle Thomas which Alfred unfolded and read. It was signed *Hector*.

. . . I've got the offer of a job in Plymouth and am going after it. As you're coming back tonight I didn't think you'd mind me going off. Hector.

"Cosy little crib, this," said Sam as he lay back in an easy chair and stretched out his legs. "You did say we could doss down here, didn't you?"

"Yes," replied Alfred abstractedly as he replaced the note. "No one'll disturb us here. The old man'll go to the Crescent when he turns up. Are you ready for the chow?"

Alfred ladled the contents of the frying-pan on to two plates, put them on the table and then put a kettle on the ring.

"I'll make a pot of tea after we've finished," he said. "It's getting cold and it'll warm us up."

When the meal was over, Alfred lit a cigarette while Sam filled a pipe. The dirty plates were pushed to one side.

"We'll wash 'em in the morning," said Alfred. "There'll be time enough then, but before we turn in I've something to explain to you. We've got to clear out of the office in Chancery Lane. You musn't go back, d'you understand?"

"What d'you mean? There's nothing—wrong, is there?"

"Oh, for God's sake don't look like that!" said Alfred. "What's the matter with you? Are you losing your nerve?"

"But why shouldn't I go back to the office? We're all ready to put through the *Karnoc* business as soon as we collect the dough from that mug Crane."

"That's all off. We'll have to get the cash somewhere else and work the whole show from some other place, too. The busies have got wind of the swindle. Someone's split the gaff. I don't know who it was, but it may have been Hunt, seeing that he didn't turn up this afternoon when he said he would."

"How did you hear about the police?" asked Sam.

"Dusty found out. I don't know how. I expect he was tipped off to it by a pal of his. I didn't ask him. What it comes to is this. You and me'll have to keep under cover for a day or two. Maybe for as long as a week, but that depends on how things turn out. Meanwhile, I'm going to see if I can't raise the cash from a bloke I know. Now, what about turning in? There's one bed and a sofa. We'll toss for who has which."

Sam won the bed with a double-headed penny, and began to pull off his coat. Alfred did the same and, as he turned to hang it on a chair, Sam uttered a shriek.

"The knife! The knife!"

"Damn your eyes, stop that blasted row!"

Alfred leapt forward and, grasping Sam by the throat, forced him backwards on to the bed.

"Will you be quiet! You'll have a flatfoot up in half a shake, you blasted little rat."

Sam suddenly ceased to struggle and Alfred released his hold and drew the knife from its sheath.

"If I have any more of that from you, you'll get the same as Hunt got."

Alfred pulled up a chair and straddled it with his elbows on the back, while Sam on the bed hitched himself up into a sitting position.

"Yes," Alfred continued, "it happened all right. You went half mad afterwards and we had to give you a shot of dope. I was going to tell you about it as soon as you had quieted down a bit."

"Why did he kill him?" Sam shot out the question between lips which trembled like a child's. "I mean, there was no sense in it."

"There's no sense in any murder if you come to that," said Alfred quietly. "And it wasn't me who did it. It was Kudorfer. Get that into your nut. It was Kudorfer who killed Hunt. He had it in for Hunt. He hated him."

"Yes, I know that," put in Sam. "Last night when we were down at the ship we met him, and Kudorfer kept saying to me he didn't like Hunt. But to kill him!"

"Hunt was a fool," exclaimed Alfred. "He realized there was something phony about the whole show and was wild that we wouldn't let him come in. Then he called Kudorfer a damned dago, and that put the lid on it."

"But why didn't you call in the police? You've landed us all in it and it's too late to do anything now."

"Oh, I thought of all that," Alfred replied. "But it would have been too risky. The knife was brought to me at the office by Hector. You brought Kudorfer to England and would have to explain exactly why you did that. The net result would have been that the *Karnoc* business would be knocked on the head and we'd have had all our trouble for nothing, besides running the risk of being charged as accessories."

"You don't mean you're going on with it?"

"Why not?" replied Alfred coolly. "I'm going to put Hunt where no one'll think of looking for him. I'll fix everything so that there won't be a fuss. Maurice Crane is our only danger. It was possible that he might start making inquiries, but I've put a stop to that."

"What are you going to do with the—with the . . ."

"What am I going to do with the body? I told you. Put it away safe and sound. In less than a week after I've finished with it no man on earth'll be able to identify it, but I'm not telling you any more. Not that I don't trust you, Sam, but if you don't know anything you can't tell anything. That's sense, ain't it? That's the line you've got to take from now on. You didn't see anything. You were blind. And all I ask is that if anyone asks you any questions you'll be deaf and dumb as well. Do you think you can do that?"

"'Course I can. I won't let you down, Alfred," Sam replied. The blind panic which had had him in its grip was ebbing, and Alfred, by the force of his personality alone, instilled into Sam a certain confidence in his powers to carry through the grisly business in hand.

"Take a pull at this." Alfred handed over a flat half-bottle of brandy. "It's fine stuff to make you forget any nasty dreams you might have had, and it'll make you sleep."

• • • • •

Uncle Thomas's last words to his wife on leaving her alone in the car outside Warbuck were: "Take the box to Town and give it to Hector at the shop. Don't go by train." So Mrs. Honeypenny hailed a passing bus and in due course reached Luton, where she changed into a Green Line coach bound for London.

Hector was putting up the shutters of the shop when Mrs. Honeypenny arrived, carrying a tin dispatch-box.

"Is your uncle back yet, Hector?" she asked.

"No, I haven't seen him. Wasn't he with you?"

She ignored the question and walked into the shop, and Hector followed a few minutes later carrying a telegram in his hand.

"Here's a bit of luck. The chance of a job in Plymouth if I can get there by tomorrow morning. Do you think it would be all right for me to go?"

"Why not? Your uncle'll be back tonight and I'll tell him. But you'd better leave a note here. He may sleep upstairs tonight. By the way, did you get the wire he sent from Royston?"

"Yes, it came all right. I gave it to Alfred, as I knew he was wanting to know when you were getting back."

Hector put on his coat and hat and picked up a small hand-bag.

"Well, I think I'll be getting along if you don't mind. Are you going to stop here the night, Aunty?"

"Not on your sweet life," Mrs. Honeypenny replied. "I'll go along to the house and wait for your uncle there. Why, it's close on six o'clock already and that's when he said he'd be home. I'll have to hurry and get the fire lit and his supper ready."

But Mrs. Honeypenny lit no fire nor cooked a meal that night, for when she was mounting the steps of the house in Graves Crescent she discovered that she had left her key in the shop. By the time she had retraced her weary steps to the High Street, Hector had gone and the iron grill in the doorway was locked. At that moment she felt like sitting down on the pavement and having a good cry, but being a woman of sense as well as of spirit she had a cup of tea instead. Then back she went to Graves Crescent, but there was still no sign of her lord and master. The windows were still shuttered and the door locked. Another cup of tea, accompanied by a plate of sausage-and-mash, filled in the time till ten o'clock.

"If he's not there this time," she muttered to herself as she turned the corner of the Crescent, "I'll give it up and he can just look after himself."

"Here, look where you're going, mother!" A man hurrying along nearly knocked her down as she walked along with bent head.

"Same to you, mister, with nobs on. Do you think you've bought the blooming— Why, it's you, Alfred! What are you doing here at this time of night?"

"I've been along to the house to see the old man, but he's not back yet."

"Maybe he's at the shop by this time," suggested Mrs. Honeypenny hopefully, but Alfred shook his head.

"No, he's not there. When did you see him last?"

Mrs. Honeypenny explained what had happened at Warbuck.

"And he shouldn't have been kept all this time," she went on. "He had the car, and even if it did break down he could always have come on by train. He knew you wanted to see him tonight particular. He told me so himself."

"He didn't give you any message, I suppose?" Alfred asked.

"No, all he said was I was to take a little box he gave me—"

"Box?" asked Alfred excitedly. "A black tin box about a foot square?"

"Yes, that's right. I saw Hector at the shop before he left and gave it to him to put away."

"Well, that's something to be thankful for, anyway," said Alfred. "But I wonder what the hell's keeping the old man? He could have walked it by this time."

"Well, I can't tell you any more than I have," said Mrs. Honeypenny. "And what I'm to do I don't know. I must have dropped my key in the shop."

"Isn't there anywhere you can go?" asked Alfred. "What about that sister of yours up at Hoxton?"

"She's no good," replied Mrs. Honeypenny. "She's 'inside' for three months for pinching a watch that wasn't worth a dollar, and some folks talk about justice. I'd like to give that beak that shopped her a piece of my mind. I'd tell him—"

"What the hell's the good of talking about that now? You come with me and I'll see if I can't fix you up with a pal of mine, Dusty Miller. He lives not very far away with his mother."

They had not gone a hundred yards before Alfred stopped.

"Strike me pink if I'm not seven kinds of a damn' fool. Your key's in the shop, you said?"

"Yes, that's right," said Mrs. Honeypenny. "That's what I said. What about it?"

"Just this," replied Alfred. "I've got the key of the shop. You'll be able to get into the house and I can do my job."

Alfred's joy at this solution of his difficulty was short-lived. When they had opened up the shop and lit the gas in the inner room there was no key to be seen.

"Well, if you were seven kinds of a fool, Alfred," Mrs. Honeypenny said, giggling weakly, "I'm sure I don't know what you'll say about me. I've just remembered that I didn't have the key with me when I got back. Your Uncle Thomas must have it himself. I'm afraid we'll have to bother your friend Mrs. Miller after all. Isn't this a fair turn-out, me bringing you back all this way for nothing, as you might say? Dearie me, what a day I've had."

"Well, if it's any consolation to you I've had a bad day too," said Alfred.

At eleven o'clock Alfred took Mrs. Honeypenny to Mrs. Miller. Then he returned to the shop and, seeking out Uncle Thomas's hiding-place in the back room, he pulled out the tin box. In it was a small collection of Sheffield plate—mustards, peppers and salts, each tied up in its own baize bag.

"Anybody who'd give a thousand quid for this lot must be a damned fool, but thank goodness there always seems to be plenty of mugs about," he said to himself. "Well, thank God Sam hasn't drunk all the brandy."

Alfred poured some out into a tin mug and sipped it. He was tired. More tired than he had ever been in his life before. The sofa was very inviting, but the thought of the body huddled in the basket would not let him sleep. Suppose some suspicious policeman lifted the lid! Alfred shuddered. He remembered the American cloth in the basket. If it was traced to the shop where he had bought it, it would be all up. He would have to run for it. If they got hold of Sam he would tell them the whole story. He recalled what Dusty had said about Sam planning to double-cross him. It would be better with Sam out of the way. . . . Alfred felt at the knife sheath and then looked over at the sleeping form in the corner. It had been so devilish easy, the way Kudorfer had done it. One thrust with all the force of his arm and Hunt had never spoken again.

Alfred walked to the window and looked out. The High Street was deserted except for a shuffling figure prying into the dustbins. A night tram groaned and swung its way along. Alfred cursed Uncle Thomas for failing him. He cursed Mrs. Honeypenny for losing her key. He cursed Kudorfer. A clock chimed one o'clock. A policeman turned the corner by the church and paced slowly along the pavement, peering into the windows of the darkened shops and trying their locks. At last he was gone.

Alfred struck a match and looked at his watch. Seven minutes past one. If Uncle Thomas didn't arrive by the half-hour he would do it. It was the only way out. If he could have put the body where it wouldn't be found it would be different, but as it was . . . Surely there was somewhere he could dump it, if he could only think? But his brain was dead. Like a catchy tune the events of the day went circling round and round in his head until he could have shouted aloud. If only—if only—he caught himself speaking his thoughts aloud and started in alarm as Sam turned in his sleep, muttering, "I saw him do it—I saw him." Like a flash Alfred was by the bed with the knife in his hand. The light of a street lamp shining through a slit in the curtains glinted on the naked blade. Sam turned again and his throat gleamed oddly white. One thrust—and Alfred's greatest source of danger would be silenced. One thrust—one . . .

It was over. Hardly had the blood begun to stream forth, soaking into the coverlet, before Alfred was at the door. He moved now like a man in a dream. Then he raised the knife and gazed at it in horror. There was a rattle of the padlock on the shop door. It was that damned policeman. He had forgotten him. Then the quiet footsteps padded on. Alfred breathed again, then crept down the stairs to the room at the back of the shop. There was a sink there and he held the knife under the tap until the water had ceased to run red. There was blood on his hands, but none on his clothes so far as he could see. That was how murderers were caught. Bloodstains. He slipped off his coat and examined it minutely. He mustn't make a mistake now, or leave anything to chance. If he was careful there would be no risk. He ran up the stairs and, with fingers that trembled in spite of himself, cut out all identifying marks from Sam's clothing.

Graves Crescent was silent and unlighted when Alfred got there. He waited for a minute or two by the pillar-box listening for footsteps, and then crept down the pavement. The road was up and there was a night-watchman at the far end. He must not hear anything. The basket was where Alfred had left it at the top of the area steps. He pulled it out on to the pavement and wheeled it round to the front doorsteps. He raised the lid, bent over and lifted the body. God! It was heavy. The basket creaked and swayed. The arms of the dead man cleared the edge and hung down dangling like those of a puppet. Alfred paused for a moment to get his breath, and then with one effort he got the body clear and dragged it across the roadway to the railings guarding the garden. If he could get it over in among the bushes there would be a good chance of it not being found for some time. And if he could raise some tool or other he might be able to bury it in some out-of-the-way corner. Under a laurustinus bush, for instance. . . .

But Alfred had over-rated his own strength. The body, as inert as only a dead body can be, defied his every effort to hoist it over the spikes. At last he gave up the attempt and leaned, panting, against the railings. That idea was no good. The blank windows of No. 96 seemed to mock his efforts. If only Uncle Thomas were back! Alfred looked up and down the Crescent. It was as deserted as a cemetery at dawn. When he had recovered his wind he dragged the body back to where he had started. The basket with the lid thrown back was standing by the steps. Alfred half bent down to lift the body into it, and then stopped. What was the good, anyway? Better to leave the body near the house, and then if Uncle Thomas came home before dawn he, Alfred, could get it inside. If not, then he would leave it to be found. There were no distinguishing marks on the clothing. He had seen to that, but the bundle of rags and the strips of American cloth were another matter altogether. The police, if they found them, might quite possibly trace them back to the office.

After a moment's thought Alfred's mind was made up. He dragged the body up the steps of No. 96 and set it in an alcove under the portico, being careful to tuck the legs well back where they would not be seen by the casual passer-by. The basket, with its tell-tale cargo of rags, he would wheel away and burn if possible, in some secluded spot. If Uncle Thomas returned he would not notice the body and all would be well. The area gate was still open. He shut it and wheeled the basket away up the Crescent.

"Spare a copper, guvnor. I've—"

Alfred stopped dead. It was the old beggar he had seen from the window of the shop rooting in the dustbins of the High Street. He was incredibly old and incredibly dirty, and his eyes, like those of an ill-used dog, peered out through a matted fringe of hair. Patient and uncomplaining. He looked at the basket and then at Alfred.

"What you got in there?" the old man croaked.

"What the hell's that got to do with you?" Alfred's nerves were all on edge.

The beggar chuckled to himself and drew his ragged coat closer around him.

"When I sees a respeckably dressed gent, same as yourself, walking the streets at this hour of the morning, ye can't blame me fer 'aving me suspicions." He edged closer to the basket and his claw-like hand began to fumble with the lid, but Alfred sent him staggering across the pavement.

"Then you is on the crooked lay? All right, don't blame me if yer pinched." The old beggar began to shuffle away, grumbling and muttering to himself. Alfred stood irresolute for a moment and then called out:

"Hi! Wait a minute!"

The old man halted and Alfred drew up with him.

"Do you know any place I can put this?" Alfred strove to speak casually. "I can make it worth your while."

The beggar thrust out his head like a tortoise.

"What 'ave yer got in it?"

Alfred ignored the question and held out half a crown. He shuddered as the nails of the beggar scratched his palm. The coin disappeared as by magic.

"Foller me an' do what I tells yer. There's a rozzer works this beat that ain't 'arf fly an' 'e's nosy, which is a bad thing fer such as us. You never know where you'll meet him next."

The old man broke into a quick shuffling trot and led the way through a maze of mean streets. Here and there at street corners a lamp shed a pool of light on the pavement, but between them it was inky dark. The sky was overcast and there was a thin rain falling.

"What's the time, guv'nor?"

Alfred stopped for a moment and struck a match.

"Close on two. Why?"

"The rozzers change over at two. We've got ten minutes clear and that'll be long enough."

The old beggar turned off down a side street. On one side was a long row of two-storied houses, on the other a high board fence.

"'Old yer 'orses a minute, guv'nor."

He stopped, and taking out a loose board thrust an arm into the cavity. Alfred could hear his fingers scrabbling about and then appeared a battered tin can. The beggar held it in both hands close to his chest and continued on at a slower pace.

"This 'ere's the swipes," he explained. "There wouldn't 'arf 'ave bin a shindy if I'd 'a' forgotten that."

They crossed a wooden bridge and Alfred could see the light of a street lamp reflected in water.

"Gettin' near the river. Not far now," grunted the old man.

At the end of the street they turned right-handed and came on the blank face of a warehouse. The beggar pointed to a door plastered with posters.

"Reach up your 'and, you'll find a bit of string."

Alfred did as he was told, and as he pulled the string a latch clicked and the beggar kicked open the door.

"Bring yer barrer in 'ere an' shut the door arter yer."

What Alfred had taken to be a warehouse was but a shell. Four walls, heaps of masonry, rubble, bricks, and twisted iron. The beggar showed him where to stow the basket, and then said:

"Come along an' meet the boys, unless you want ter be beating it?"

At that moment Alfred was content to be anywhere but on the streets, alone with his thoughts, and he followed his guide to the "Brewery". It was a side of London's life which he had never even glimpsed before, and at this hour it was alive. Round a glowing brazier the members of this queer club were ranged. Like rats they came to life when the sun went down and they scavenged the odds and ends cast away during the day. One man was picking over a pile of rags, sorting them into heaps. Another was tearing up cigarette-stubs, while yet a third was engaged in the task of sorting out odd scraps of food he had gleaned an hour before. Old Smoky, the beggar, who had brought Alfred into the midst of this queer gathering, threw a bag which he had slung round his shoulders to a man who caught it deftly and emptied its contents on the ground.

"Not so bad, old 'un. There's a bob's worth there. Got the booze?"

Old Smoky lowered the can carefully on to a bench.

"Come on, me lads, where's yer tins?"

And Alfred learnt that for a halfpenny he could purchase a cigarette-tin full of stale beer. For a penny he could buy three smokes. The man with the scraps of food plied a brisk trade when the beer was gone. No one paid the least heed to Alfred, the stranger, and he was to learn later that the one rule was that no questions were asked. "Mind your own business" was the motto of the club, and it was strictly adhered to. Alfred shuddered as he saw one old wreck guzzling his food like a dog, gnawing at a bone and searching in his tin with a filthy forefinger for scraps of food.

Then Alfred withdrew to a sheltered spot and lay down on a heap of sacking—his for the night in exchange for five cigarettes and a box of matches. He was sick with fatigue, but he could not sleep. In his mind's eye he pictured the discovery of the body at No. 96. The group of police officials and then the ambulance. The examination of the body. The tabs he had cut from the clothing of the dead man were in the laundry basket, and as long as the identity of the body was not discovered he would be safe. As for Sam —well, he was safe there too. No one had seen him go back to the shop or leave it. There was nothing to connect him with that crime. There was no motive. He conned over in his mind the points where danger might lie. Of course there was Mrs. Honeypenny, and though she was a woman and given to gossip, he knew that his warning would close her mouth as far as he was concerned. Uncle Thomas, too, he could rely upon. As for Dusty Miller, he was up to the neck in the Chancery Lane affair. There remained Kudorfer, the cause of all the trouble.

Alfred rolled over uneasily and then felt for his cigarette-case. It was no good trying to sleep now, he might as well give in and make the best of it. He would have to lay his plans with all the care he knew. Tomorrow night he would get right away somewhere. Somewhere where he could forget, and sleep. Curse Kudorfer! Why the hell had Sam ever brought him over? Well, Sam had got his—for being a damn' soft fool. Alfred shivered and drew up the rough sacking to his chin.

At last he could stand it no longer, and he rose stiffly. From near by he could hear the sound of snoring. He looked round for a minute or two to get his bearings in the half-light, and then located the place where he had left the basket. There was a brown smear on the edge of the lid and abstractedly he wiped it clean with his handkerchief. The basket could be left where it was, but the bundle of bloodstained dusters and curtains, the strips of American cloth, and the name tabs from Hunt's clothing—they must be hidden somewhere.

He made his way out of the ruined and roofless building on to a piece of waste land where nettles grew breast high and where he stumbled over empty tins and brickbats. After a few minutes' walking he came to the wharf at Spender's Draw dock. Alfred eyed the rotting planks and moss-grown bollard with approval. Somewhere round here would do to dump his stuff. He picked his way gingerly over the planks to a wooden shed and pulled open its crazy door. The flickering light of a match revealed a bench, a table and a rusty stove. Why not burn the lot? That would be the safest way out. Push the basket in the tide. It would float down-stream, and even if it were picked up no one could tell from whence it had come. The business was to get enough dry wood to burn the rags, for a soaking grey mist had risen from the river.

Alfred crept back to the "Brewery" and secured a newspaper, and then with chips of wood splintered from a plank of the floor of the hut he kindled a blaze in the stove. As soon as it was fairly going he made a second journey and cleared out the contents of the basket, which he made into a bundle and laid out on the floor of the hut. The strips of curtain he slowly fed to the flames, which charred the cloth at first and then when they took hold gave off a heavy, acrid smoke. So intent was he with his task that he did not at first hear the sound of footsteps on the wharf outside. It was a shout from a waterman in his boat alongside which caused him to start to his feet and tiptoe to the door. There was a small knot of men standing not fifty yards away, staring riverwards.

"Here she comes!" one of them cried, and Alfred saw the great black bulk of a steamship nosing her way into the dock. A tug alongside her was casting off her lines. Ropes were thrown, and in the grey half-light of the early morning the white letters of her name came into view. It was the *Karnoc*. Alfred recognized the figure of the night-watchman on board her. He was standing on the forecastle head with a coiled heaving-line in his hands.

Alfred closed the door and jammed it with a heavy baulk of timber. There was no time now to complete his task of burning the rags. With the energy of despair he wrenched at a loose board in the floor, prised it up and stuffed in the rest of the contents of the basket. Then he lowered the board back into place and looked round for some means of escape. His eye fell on a window in the side of the hut away from the wharf, and he unfastened the rusty catch, which snapped in his fingers as he did so. The broken part fell unnoticed to the floor and he raised the sash, which creaked alarmingly.

Luckily for Alfred, the men on the wharf were too intent on their work to pay any heed to the noise, even if they heard it, and he climbed over the sill and closed the sash behind him. It was not until he had made his way through the factory, past the sleeping members of the "Brewery" club, and had gained the street outside, that he paused to draw breath and decide on his destination. He examined his clothes, crumpled and creased from lying in them all night. He must have a clean up, but it was too early to find a barber open. Of course there was always the shop. It meant taking a risk, but there was the silver. That would be worth something if he could get it to Uncle Thomas.

He set out full of determination, but on arriving at the back door of the shop his courage began to fail him. For one fleeting instant he thought he saw Sam's white face pressed against the pane of the window above him, and then cursed himself for a hysterical fool. Sam was dead. Dead! Dead! He told himself a dozen times. He peered through the window into the back room. It was as he had left it. He could hear the tap dripping into the sink. The tap at which he had washed the knife. Alfred fingered the key in his pocket and half drew it out. Then he felt the coarse stubble on his chin and tried to see his reflection in the window. No, it would never do to be seen like that. Whatever the risk he must clean himself up.

The door creaked as he pushed it open, and he waited with one hand on the knob, listening. The place smelt musty and looked singularly uninviting in the cold morning light. There was some shaving gear on a shelf, and despite the coldness of the water he managed to make himself fairly presentable. Blast the tap! He screwed it down with all his strength, but still there was that maddening drip—drip—drip, only it was slower now. A church clock chimed the hour of five. People would be moving in the streets soon. Milkmen. Paper boys. If Uncle Thomas had returned to Graves Crescent during the night he would still have an opportunity of burying the body in the cellar.

Alfred withdrew the box of silver from its hiding-place, and after locking the door behind him he set off for Graves Crescent with the box under his arm. Surely the old man would be back by now? Alfred ran over in his mind what he must do first. There was the disposing of the body, and then he must look after Dusty and Johannis. The money from the silver would carry them on for a bit, and if Lena failed to bring Maurice up to the scratch they would have to think up some other way of raising the wind. At the end of the Crescent a milkman's truck was standing on the pavement and Alfred slowed up. The man was but a few yards ahead of him, carrying a cage of bottles in each hand. Alfred crossed the road to the garden side and was able to make out the windows of No. 96. They were still shuttered.

He turned and ran a few steps in the direction of the High Street and then turned off into a street of mean little houses. A navvy with a bag of tools turned into a shop, and Alfred followed him. It was one of those cheap eating-houses which abound in the poorer districts and which open at an early hour to cater for the working men. Ordinarily fastidious to a degree about the food which he ate, Alfred hardly noticed the pungent odour of cooking and cheap fat sparking and hissing in a shallow tray over a gas-jet. He took his place at a bare deal table in the farthest corner and ordered a meal of sausage-and-mash and a cup of coffee. A cheap alarm clock ticking loudly on a shelf told him that it was not yet six o'clock. He would stay there an hour and then—but at this point his tired brain refused to function.

As he was finishing his meal the street door opened and a newsboy poked in his head. Alfred bought a paper and rustled through the pages in a fever of impatience, but of course there was nothing there about the affairs of the night before. He was a fool to have thought there would be. He cursed himself for a nervy fool and called for a packet of cigarettes. He was feeling better now. The hot food was doing its work. But what to do with the box of silver—that was the question. If Uncle Thomas had been available he could have disposed of the silver at a price somewhere about its value. Alfred had never brought off such a transaction himself. If he took them to one of the regular dealers they would be almost certain to ask awkward questions, and might keep him waiting for the money. He couldn't afford to do that. Apart from some odd change, he possessed at that moment two-pounds-ten in notes, a watch worth a pound or thirty shillings, and the clothes he was wearing. It wasn't much of a look-out for a man who might have to run for it or go into hiding, in the event of the police getting on to his trail. The first thing must be to dump the dispatch-box somewhere.

Under the bench would be as good a place as any to leave it. He pushed it back with his foot until it came up against the wall. Had the woman seen him? What would happen when it was found? He could see the police questioning her. Asking who had been in the shop that morning. Later a description of the silver would be circulated. Who could tell where their inquiries would end? The box would be taken to Scotland Yard for examination. Finger-prints! God! He had never thought of that. If he was going to make such damn' fool mistakes as this, he might as well give himself up straight away and have done with it. He broke into a muck sweat at the very thought of what might happen, retrieved the box from under the bench, and polished it all over with his handkerchief. Having paid his bill, he picked up the box. For a moment he thought of asking for paper and string, but dismissed the idea as too risky. It would only call attention to himself, and that was the last thing he wished to do.

A tram, mercifully empty, brought him to the Embankment, and there he alighted. There were few pedestrians about and he looked for an opportunity to drop the box into the water, but there wasn't a chance of doing that unseen. Besides, the tide which had floated the SS. *Karnoc* into Spender's Draw dock was ebbing fast and the mud was beginning to show alongside the wall. That was no good. He walked on to Waterloo Bridge and there he found the place for which he was looking. It was under the stairs, in among the supporting beams and joists. With a sigh of relief he bent down and pushed the box well in out of sight of any passer-by. A ragged old tramp was sleeping there with his back up against the parapet. As Alfred passed on he realized with a smile that he had left what might have proved to have been a damning piece of evidence within a few yards of the Thames police-station. He halted at the board at the top of the gangway. There was a string of notices. Jewellery lost. A man found drowned. Distinguishing marks, none. Well, he'd left no distinguishing marks on Hunt's clothing. He was safe there. At Victoria Station he had a bath and felt a different man.

CHAPTER IX

IT WAS THE MILKMAN on his round who found the body. At the door of No. 96 Graves Crescent he collected the empty bottles, and when he was about to return to his barrow at the top of the Crescent he turned to give the man sitting in the alcove another look. His attitude was that of an ordinary drunk, and yet there was something odd about the way his shoulders slumped forward. The milkman set down his bottles, nudged the figure with the toe of his boot, and then leaned forward and pushed back its shoulder. The felt hat which had been balanced on the man's head fell off and rolled down the steps, and eyes that stared like those of a waxwork figure looked up at the milkman. It wasn't a drunk. It was a deader.

"Croaked, by jiminy! That's what he's done," he said, and then, remembering what he had read about not interfering with a body before the police arrived, the milkman ran up the street to the call-box at the corner.

"There's a bloke conked out 'ere. Graves Crescent. Yes, I'll wait at the corner till you come."

Three minutes later a police tender drew up at the call-box and a man thrust out his head.

"Are you the man who made that call a few minutes back?"

"Yes, that's right."

A man jumped out of the car.

"Come on, then. Show us where he is."

Sub-Divisional Inspector Lomax made a cursory examination of the body and then turned to the man with him.

"Get the Yard on the 'phone," he ordered, "and ask for the Central Branch. Tell them we want photographers and finger-print men down right away. If this isn't a murder case I'll eat my hat Oh, wait a minute, send out a call for all men off duty to report at the station."

A more detailed examination of the body and the clothing revealed that the man had died from a knife thrust. The wound was extraordinarily deep, the divisional surgeon reported, and it could only have been caused by a man of more than usual strength. "It must," he said, "have been directed from the back. That is obvious. The knife passed between the ribs, close to the spine; probably it actually penetrated the heart from the rear. Without an autopsy I can tell you little more, except that death must have been almost instantaneous."

"It's going to be a puzzle to us, Doctor. There was nothing in any of the pockets, and even the name tabs on the coat and shirt have been cut off."

The doctor put on his coat and felt for his cigarette-case.

"Well, I'll be getting along. Are you coming?"

"No, I'm afraid I must wait here." Lomax looked round the whitewashed chamber of the mortuary as he spoke. "But this place gives me the creeps. It's different for you, you're used to it."

As the door closed behind the doctor, Lomax filled and lit his pipe. It would not be long before the Scotland Yard man arrived and he must be ready with answers to the questions which would be fired at him. The body lay on a trestle table, rigid and inert like a lay figure. The milkman who had found it was waiting in the charge-room. He, Lomax, had given orders to his men to pull in every doubtful character they met. The photographers had taken photographs from every possible angle. A constable was on duty at the entrance to the house where the body had been found. The pockets of the dead man's clothes had yielded no more than dust, which had been collected in several envelopes, duly marked.

"If there's one thing I hate it is getting up before I've read the morning papers."

Chief Inspector Thompson slammed the door behind him and sat down on a bench.

"Well, it's murder, is it? I met the surgeon as I was coming along, so you can leave out the gory details. Have you pulled anyone yet?"

"No, sir."

"When was it found?"

"Six o'clock, sir, by the milkman. He's at the station now."

"He can wait. Now, Lomax, what struck you about the body when you first saw it?"

"It was in a sitting position, sir, on the top step. I knew he was dead the moment I saw his face."

Thompson rose and drew back the sheet covering the body.

"Yes. There's no mistaking a corpse, is there? What was the clothing like? Pulled about at all?"

"No, sir. The overcoat was buttoned up as you see it now," Lomax replied.

"White shirt practically uncreased. Bow tie and double-breasted waistcoat. All very posh. Now the question is, who is he? Got any ideas, Lomax?"

"No, sir. There doesn't seem to be a thing on him to give us a lead."

"Laundry marks? Name tabs? Every *good* tailor puts on a tab. Mine never does, but that doesn't signify. Maybe he's not proud of his work."

Thompson made an exhaustive survey of each article of the dead man's clothing.

"Whoever it was brought off a clean job," was his comment as he finished his survey and lit a cigarette. "By the way, Lomax, have you ever found how difficult it is to get a pair of shoes that fit? If one of 'em laces nice and tight over the instep, the other doesn't. That's nature. No two feet are the same. This chap's been lucky. He's got a perfect pair."

Thompson undid the laces and slipped a shoe off the dead man's foot.

"Made by hand, this was. I knew a man once who told me all about boots and shoes. He's making 'em in Dartmoor now. It's the sewing that gives the job away in the case of a hand-made shoe. Not quite even, the same as this one. There ought to be a name here, but there isn't. You can see where it's been scratched out. You know, Lomax, I'm beginning to think that this murder was pre—premed—well, anyway, the bloke who did it was a damned cool card. He wasn't leaving anything to chance. But I wonder if he was as clever as he thought he was? I wonder? Anyway, I'll take this pair of shoes, so you can chalk 'em off your list of exhibits. And now let's have a look at the milkman."

Joshua Ling was seated on a hard wooden chair reading a morning paper when Thompson entered the police-station. The sergeant in charge slipped off his stool and opened a door leading to an inner room. The milkman looked up expectantly.

"Do you mind coming in here?" asked Thompson, and as the man rose to follow him he continued: "Your name's Ling, isn't it? The man of the moment. Take a chair and smoke if you want to."

"Well, I don't mind if I do. I was going back to my barrer when—"

Thompson held up a restraining hand.

"Easy on. We want to start a bit farther back, and before you begin I want you to give me your word you won't say anything to the newspaper blokes. They'll be round here in half a shake. I'll tell 'em all that's good for them to know and I want you to keep your trap closed. Now tell me, when did you get up this morning?"

"'Bout five."

"Yes, and where d'you live?"

"19 Hamley Street. In the Borough."

"Where did you pick up your barrow?"

"At the shop in the High Street. There's a yard at the back and the lorries come in there. When I got round, about half past the hour, most of the chaps were gorn and my truck was standin' by the gate filled up and ready. I got the list from the foreman and checked up on it and then I started off on the round. I got to the end of Graves Crescent just as the church clock on the corner was striking quarter to six."

"Had you made any calls up to then?"

"No, sir. Graves Crescent is my kicking-off place. The road was up all the way along and I left the truck at the top end near the call-box."

"Had you seen anybody before you got to the Crescent?" Thompson asked.

"No, I don't think so. There were a few market carts about, but that was all."

"There was a night-watchman, wasn't there, at the end of the Crescent?" Lomax interrupted.

"Yes, at the far end 'e was, or that's where 'e 'ad 'is box and fire. When I found the man on the step I didn't bother about the watchman but just ran to the call-box on the corner."

"You didn't think of knocking up the people in the house?"

"That would 'a' taken a tidy time, sir. It was six o'clock."

When the milkman had gone Thompson unwrapped the shoes he had taken off the murdered man's feet. He hummed to himself as he stared at them. Just an ordinary pair of brown leather lace-up shoes. They were nearly new, but at the back of the heels on the uppers there were signs of scoring.

"Just as though the man who wore them had been lifted by the shoulders and dragged along with his feet trailing," Thompson ruminated.

"Did you notice anything about the overcoat?" he asked Lomax.

"Yes, sir. There was a tear in it on the right side and the skirts of it were covered with road dust and grit."

"How far would you say No. 96 is from the end of the Crescent?" Thompson asked.

"About a hundred and fifty, maybe two hundred yards."

"Yes. Now, Lomax, supposing that the man wasn't killed where he was found. D'you think it likely anybody would drag him all that distance from the end of the Crescent? Especially with a watchman on duty not far off. There was always the odd chance that he would be awake. You couldn't drive a taxi down the Crescent. The pavement wasn't wide enough. By the way, I suppose you've got some of your men on a house to house search?"

"Yes," Lomax replied, "that's going on now. Is there anything else you want me to do?"

"Yes. Make an examination of all the gutter-drains within a quarter-mile radius. You never know your luck, but as a matter of fact I have an idea that the actual murder wasn't done anywhere near where we found the body. I think I'll go back to the Crescent now and have a look round. And after that I shall want to see the watchman."

"I have his address," said Lomax. "16 Tacker's Rents. I was just going to send a man after him."

"No, don't do that. I'll go to his house myself," Thompson replied. "It'll be easier to get him to talk if I meet him on his home ground. A police-station has a most demoralizing effect on some people. Well, I'll be getting along. I'll leave you to organize the routine work."

There was a little crowd of morbid sightseers at the end of Graves Crescent when Thompson stepped out of his car, and for a minute he stood there spying out the land. Men were at work breaking up the roadway of the Crescent. High spiked railings flanked one side of the road, fencing in a melancholy garden of shrubs and patchy grass.

Thompson walked down the pavement.

"Not a bad place to dump a corpse," he mused, "the road being up and no traffic." He stopped opposite the door of No. 96. Though the barriers were up at each end of the Crescent the roadway at this point had not been disturbed. He walked over to the railings. They were unusually high, quite five feet. "I wonder now," mused Thompson, and then he stopped and picked up a scrap of cloth from the roadway. It was black and of a fine texture. Thompson smiled to himself. "By Jove, if I'm not being a real detective, like in one of those books. The Clue of the bit of Serge!"

The shuttered windows of No. 96 drew his attention. "That means a holiday or a death or perhaps the old man's slept in this morning." He pulled at the old-fashioned bell which clanged in response in the basement below. Then he rapped on the door with the handle of his stick. Still no answer.

"Excuse me, sir, but have you got any business round here?"

Thompson turned to his questioner and saw that he was a plain-clothes' man. "I'm Chief Inspector Thompson," he announced. "Here's my card. What job are you on?"

"I've got orders to search all the houses in this street," the detective replied. "I've been round them all, but I didn't find anything of interest."

Thompson glanced at a scrap of paper he took from his pocket and, retracing his steps, was driven to Tacker's Rents. There he found John Hancock, draining his third cup of black-and-green. After a few minutes' conversation Thompson realized that he was wasting his time. The watchman had seen nothing and heard nothing.

"You don't suffer from insomnia, I can see," said Thompson dryly at last.

"I'm a teetotaller, mister. Have been all me life."

Thompson let it go at that.

· · · · ·

There are few things more tedious than following a police investigation. Nine out of ten so-called "clues" produce no results, but the tenth one sometimes provides a link in a chain of evidence which helps to hang a man. Thompson was sick of the smell of shoe-leather before he came to the end of his quest in the workroom of a fashionable bootmaker in Chandos Street. It was a dingy, ill-lit room, littered with scraps of leather and pieces of raw material hanging from nails on the wall. The foreman, on seeing the shoe which Thompson produced, felt it and fingered it in silence, and then said:

"Yes, that was made here. Funny how one can tell, but then I was brought up to the trade ever since I left school. Leather's got a grain and every hide's different. O' course one can't keep track of every job that goes in and out of here, but that stitching! I'd know it anywhere. Ezekiah is the man you want. He made that shoe."

An old man, whose hair and scrubby beard were a silvery-white, looked up at the mention of his name.

"Wantin' me, boss?"

"Yes. There's a gent here wants to see you about one of your shoes."

The foreman, having effected the introduction, retired to his office, and Thompson produced the shoe, which Ezekiah took from him.

"And what is it you want o' me, mister?"

"I'd like to know when you made this shoe and the name of the man who gave the order."

"'E's been well looked arter," the old cobbler replied. "And no more than 'is due, for 'e's a good job, this shoe, though it's me that says it. Now, let me see." He pulled a tattered note-book off a shelf and thumbed over the pages.

"Yes, 'ere 'e be. Made for a gentleman of the name of Hunt in the month of May of this year. That be just two months ago wanting but a day."

"Did you see Mr. Hunt?"

"No, sir. I seldom sees the gents I works for. I gets the measurements from the foreman and works to them, and it's not often they sends my work back. Fifty-five year last Martinmas I handled me first tool, and that warn't yesterday."

Thompson thanked the old man and sought out the foreman. From him he gained the information that the man for whom the shoe had been made was entered in the books as Geoffrey Hunt. Thompson noted the name and address.

While Thompson was making his inquiries as to the ownership of the shoes found on the dead man's feet, Lomax had been engaged in making a thorough search of No. 96. There had been a certain delay in obtaining a search warrant, but thereafter a plumber made short work of the lock on the front door. Then a bolt and a chain were filed through. The hall was icy cold and smelt faintly of gas. Their footsteps echoed on the tessellated floor. Lomax noted that the inner hall was covered with a cheap hair carpet, threadbare in patches. The first room on the left was the dining-room, furnished conventionally with a table, half a dozen stiff-backed chairs, and a sideboard. The next room looked out on to a strip of garden and had apparently been used as a sitting-room. There were two broken-down arm-chairs and a settee through the seat of which a spring had burst. A few cheap magazines were heaped in a pile on a table in the window.

Lomax ordered his assistant to take a sample of dust from the carpets of both rooms and from the hall. He glanced into a pantry, which was the only other room on the ground floor. There was a gas-cooker in it and on the draining-board of the sink a pile of dirty dishes. A small coke boiler in one corner was stone cold and the grate full of ashes. A dish-cloth was lying on the floor.

"Looks as if they'd left in a hurry," Lomax said to himself, and made his way down to the basement. The kitchen and larder were bare and the coal-range had obviously not been used for some time. The two bedrooms also were not in use, but a wash-house at the end of the passage smelt of soap-suds. The floor had been splashed with water, roughly dried up, leaving patches of damp on the flags. Lomax found traces of soap-suds round the drain holes of two deep wash-tubs. A copper in one corner also showed signs of recent use.

The upper part of the house, with the exception of one room, was unfurnished, and the paper on the walls was dirty and torn in places. The bedroom boasted one double bed, a chest of drawers, a dressing-table, a washhand-stand and two hard chairs. Lomax estimated the value of the contents of the room at something under ten pounds. Nowhere were there signs of a struggle or of blood, but Lomax, remembering the dust on the back of the corpse, took a sample of dust from each of the rooms. When he had completed his task he locked all the doors and left a constable on guard with orders to take Thomas Honeypenny into custody should he return. A man who was digging in the gardens looked up as the door of No. 96 slammed, and when Lomax got abreast of him he leaned on the handle of his spade.

"Can I 'ave a word with you, mister? It's about suthing I found in among the bushes not 'arf an 'our back. I was waiting for one of you blokes to come along. You are in the police, aren't you?"

Lomax nodded. The gardener unlocked a gate and led him down a path till he reached a giant laurustinus bush which partly overhung the railings at one point. Then, parting the branches, he pointed to a heap of linen scattered over the ground.

"I didn't know what to make of that at all," said the gardener. "So I left it just as it was."

Lomax pulled out his note-book and made a list of the articles: sheets, shirts, socks, pillowslips.

"Someone's washing gone astray," was the detective's comment, as he noted the laundry mark and name. "I'll send a man along to pick 'em up."

The gardener was rubbing his chin thoughtfully.

"Funny things 'appen sometimes, don't they?" he said. He picked up a handkerchief. "That's the Martin's wash. Mrs. Honeypenny does for them."

Lomax offered his case of cigarettes, but the gardener pulled out a pipe and lit it. "I prefer this, but thank you all the same, guv'nor. Mrs. Honeypenny's a queer little card," he said. "But this ain't the sort of thing she'd do, nor yet 'er 'usband neither. 'Ave ye seen 'im?"

"Not yet," was the cautious reply? "But I don't expect it'll be long before I do."

"'E's a rum 'un if ever there was one. Living in a house two sizes too big for 'im an' lettin' 'is wife take in washing. 'E's got a car and they do say 'e's a warm man, but where 'e gets 'is dough I don't know, an' I don't suppose there's many as does. Not that 'e's proud. I will say that for the old codger. Many's the time I've seen 'im pushing that old laundry basket o' theirs, wearing 'is frock coat and top hat. The kids used to guy 'im once, but 'e never took no notice and they soon give it up."

"Laundry basket?" queried Lomax.

"Yes. It was a big basket affair on an old perambulator chassis. 'E keeps it at the top of the area steps. But you must 'a' seen it."

The gardener walked a few paces to the railings and peered over.

"That's funny now. It's gorn. The pair of 'em went off a day or two back in the car, an' they can't 'ave took it with them. Besides, I remember seeing it last night when I was locking up my tools."

Lomax was interested.

"What time did you leave?" he asked.

"Five o'clock. On the tick. I always go out of that gate opposite the Honeypennys' house, and I noticed it was shut up. Shutters up and all. Funny time to go orf for an 'oliday, I says to meself, and then I saw the ole basket an' wonders at 'em leaving it out. Should 'a' put it inside if they was going for long, an' then when I comes to work this morning I saw a rozzer by the door."

Lomax hurried to a telephone-box and put through a call to Scotland Yard. In less than a quarter of an hour every police-station in the Metropolitan area had received a description of Uncle Thomas's laundry basket.

CHAPTER X

THOMPSON WAS as pleased as a dog with another dog's bone when he discovered the identity of the body found in Graves Crescent. He took a taxi back to the Yard and found Lomax awaiting him in his room.

"Thank God we can make a start," he said. "That guy who was croaked ran under the name of Geoffrey Hunt. Not known here, but I've put Filson on to routing out his habitat, and if anyone can find out about him it's John Filson. I really believe that man's not happy unless he's poking his nose into someone else's business. And now let's hear what you've turned up."

"I've been over the house," Lomax began, "but I didn't find anything of interest. The samples of dust I took from the rooms were nothing like the stuff from the back of the dead man's coat."

"Call him Hunt. That was his name. So depressing to go on talking about the 'dead man'. Well, go on. What about the dust from the steps?"

"Nothing doing there, either. It's my belief that Hunt was killed somewhere else and brought to Graves Crescent and dumped there."

Thompson grunted and toyed with a paper-knife. "Yes, that's quite all right in a way, but aren't you forgetting that the road was up? It would have meant leaving the car at the end of the

Crescent and carrying the body along to No. 96, and that's a risk which no self-respecting murderer would take."

"He wasn't brought in a car," Lomax interrupted. "I've found out how it was done." And he proceeded to recount the information received from the gardener.

"In a laundry basket, eh? Well, that's a new one on me. But all the same, even if that is the way it was done, why the Halifax choose the door-way of a house to dump the body in?"

"Oh, wait a minute," Lomax interrupted. "What about that piece of Hunt's coat you found lying on the roadway near the railings? There were dragging marks on the back of his shoes too. What happened was possibly this: Hunt was brought to Graves Crescent in the laundry basket with the object of dumping him in the garden and maybe burying him there. In trying to get him over the railings the murderer tore Hunt's coat, gave it up, and hid him in the door-way of No. 96."

"Yes," Thompson agreed. "That is probably the explanation. The murderer naturally would want to put Hunt where he wouldn't be found for some time."

"It's rather an odd thing that the owner of No. 96 is missing," Lomax remarked. "His name's Honeypenny, and according to the locals they've never known him to go away for a night before, excepting when he slept at his shop."

"And where's that?" asked Thompson. "Have you been there?"

"It's in the Borough High Street. A funny-looking place crammed full of old junk as far as I could see. I knocked and rang the bell but there was no one there."

"How d'you know? You didn't go inside?"

"No. I thought of getting a warrant but I couldn't see there were any grounds for applying. You know how sticky these magistrates are about that sort of thing. The sanctity of the home and all that rot."

"Yes, it's rot as long as it isn't your own place," Thompson replied dryly. "I wonder now what we should do about it. Have you left someone there?"

"Yes. Two men. Back and front."

"That's all right. Now the man who used that laundry basket must have been either this man Honeypenny or a pal of his. We've got to run that line for all it's worth."

Lomax pursed his lips and shook his head.

"I've tried it and had no luck." He gave his chief a short resumé of Uncle Thomas's career. "You know what these old lags are like. Close as oysters."

"Or else as wide open as the deep blue sea. They're very like other folk. Some of 'em talk and some don't."

"This is a case of 'don't'," replied Lomax. "No one seems to know anything about the old boy. Nothing that matters, that is. Just that he's a queer old card who keeps himself to himself."

"I take it that you've been bullying only the more respectable members of the community. Why not try some of the bad lads of the village? They're usually much more informative."

"The local people are working them, but they don't hold out much hope. The men they wanted to get hold of seem to have cleared out."

"Yes, like rats at the first smell of fire. I was afraid of that," said Thompson. "Well, we'll just have to smoke a pipe of shag and solve the mystery that way. Oh, by the way. This Honeypenny gink. Is he married? And if so, where is the lady?"

"Yes, he's got a wife. She runs a sort of home laundry in the basement of No. 96. She's gone off too."

"Leaving a consignment of clean laundry behind, which somebody dumped in the gardens," commented Thompson. "That's not like a woman. What made her clear out, d'you think? She must have had pressing business somewhere or else her old man had. Who was boss in that household?"

"Oh, the man," replied Lomax. "He's a real strong character by all accounts."

"And he left the district two days before the murder. If he had an inkling of it coming off, that would explain his clearing out, but he couldn't have known."

"It might have been planned beforehand," suggested Lomax.

"It might have been and I might be Commissioner one day. One's as likely as the other. Murders don't happen that way, except poisonings. They happen differently in books; but can you think of a murder by violence that wasn't committed on the spur of the moment? I can't. That's why we catch 'em as a rule. Now this man Hunt was stabbed in some building or other. The dust on the back of his coat is made up of very fine fluff, hairs, coal ash, dried earth, and a few particles of plaster, according to this report."

Thompson compared the samples taken from the rooms at No. 96 with that from the dead man's coat. When he had completed his scrutiny he re-read the laboratory report on the subject.

"Yes, there doesn't seem to me much doubt that Hunt wasn't done in at No. 96. We'll have to look farther afield."

•••••

It was Detective-Sergeant Woods who provided the first useful information about Geoffrey Hunt. His photograph had been circulated to every police-station shortly after the discovery of the body, and Woods, when he reported at Vine Street on coming off duty at 6 p.m. that same evening, recognized Hunt at once, and a report was sent to Scotland Yard. Thompson had left by that time to visit Uncle Thomas's shop in the Borough. On his return he found Woods waiting for him.

"Well, what is it?" Thompson snapped.

"I've come about the man who was found murdered, sir."

"Which one? There's two of 'em now."

"The man whose photograph was sent out to-day."

"Yes? Well, go on."

"His name was Geoffrey Hunt, and he lived in Clark Street."

"I know that. What else?"

"I've had him under observation for the last six months on and off. I suspected him of working the 'con' game and about a week ago I warned him. He was going about with a young fellow of the name of Crane. Maurice Crane."

"Where did Crane hang out?"

Woods consulted his diary. "At No. 25 Hilberry Mansions, W.I. I saw Hunt with Crane. They dined together and went to a theatre. It was after they parted I warned Hunt, and I followed

Crane up to try to get a word with him and put him wise to the sort of man Hunt was. I wasn't quite quick enough to catch him before he went into his flat, but I made a few inquiries about him, and left it at that. I kept an eye lifting for Hunt for the next few days, but he seemed to have taken the hint and cleared off, so I let the matter drop. I had no real evidence against Hunt, you understand."

"Lomax, make a note of that address. It doesn't sound as if Crane could help us, but you never know, and we can't afford to take a chance." He turned back to Woods. "Did you ever see anyone else with Hunt? A short, fat man, for instance. Age about thirty-five. Sandy hair. Wearing a suit of blue serge reach-me-downs. He's been murdered too. Stabbed."

Woods denied any knowledge of Sam Hartford.

"All right. Wait downstairs. One of my men—Filson's his name—is looking up Hunt. When he reports in an hour's time tell him all you know."

When Woods had gone Thompson poked the dying fire into a blaze and lit his pipe.

"I wish to hell we could get hold of this man Honeypenny. One murdered man outside his house and another in his shop. . . . If he doesn't know something about 'em I'll resign from the Force and keep chickens. I always did like a fresh egg for my tea."

Lomax sighed wearily. When his chief started on this particular idea there was no knowing when he would stop. He had explained to his subordinate once that day dreaming was the best thing out for clearing the brain and enabling one to get a fresh outlook. Lomax only wished that he didn't have to listen. Ten o'clock struck before Thompson gave up the planning of the ideal poultry-farm.

"That was as good as a sleep to me," he announced.

Lomax yawned. "Yes, to you," he thought to himself, and gathered up a pile of papers on which he had been typing a report of the day's work. Thompson glanced through it and made a pencilled correction here and there.

"Maurice Crane," he said. "As soon as Filson gets on to him we'll have him up here. Then there's this old lag Wheeler, whom

Truscott saw in the shop. It shouldn't be long before we get our hands on him. Hector Brown. He's vamoosed. Truscott said he was O.K., but we can't accept that. Lastly there's 'Uncle Thomas' Honeypenny and spouse. A total of five for us to work on, not counting anyone the locals may find for us. You know, Lo, it's an odd thing that both these men were stabbed, and in each case the murderer had the nerve to remove the name tabs and laundry marks from their clothing. It was devilish lucky for us that he overlooked the shoes which Hunt was wearing, and luckier still that we found the maker so soon. I had quite expected it would take a week to find him, and if it hadn't been a London-made shoe we should have been properly stuck."

·····

Mrs. Honeypenny, after her encounter with Alfred on the night of Sam's murder, slept in the house of Dusty Miller's widowed mother. One night was enough for her, however. The bed was nothing but a flock mattress laid on bare boards, and she was in such a bad temper next morning that it was all she could do to thank Mrs. Miller for her hospitality. She completely forgot Alfred's advice to keep out of the way until she heard from him again, and decided if she couldn't get into No. 96 she would sleep over the shop.

The plume on her old black bonnet nodded furiously as she stumped along. She'd have something to say to Thomas when he turned up, that she would. Leaving her to tramp the streets like this without a proper place to lay her head. Even if she had mislaid the key of the house, that was no reason why Thomas shouldn't arrive when he said he would. "I may be a bit late, but I'll be in London tonight," he had said when she had left him, and here it was tomorrow morning. Seven o'clock and cold enough for a Polar bear.

The shop was locked and shuttered when she reached it. She gave a loud rat-tat on the knocker. She rang the bell and knocked again. There was no response. A passing tramwayman on his way to work stopped to give her a hand. His onslaught on the door, however, had no effect, and at the end of a few minutes he continued on his way.

Mrs. Honeypenny felt in her bag and unearthed two pennies and a farthing. If she couldn't get into the shop the only thing to do was to get some breakfast and return later, but what was the use of twopence-farthing to a hungry and very cold old woman? Then she remembered the consignment of clean laundry she had left behind at No. 96 when Uncle Thomas had made her go away with him to the country. All she had to do now was to deliver it and collect the sum due to her for her work. Then she'd have a breakfast! Mrs. Honeypenny had sketched out the menu in her mind down to the last piece of toast and pat of butter before she had traversed the length of Graves Street, which led to the Crescent. An ambulance with its clanging bell swept past her, followed by a crowd of small boys. It turned into the Crescent and suddenly, for no reason at all, Mrs. Honeypenny's heart began to thump and she hastened her pace. One of the boys lagged behind his friends and she caught him by the arm.

"What's the trouble?" she asked. "'As there bin an accident or what?"

The boy struggled to free himself but she held him tight.

"It's a murder, that's wot it is," he said. "Now leggo, can't yer?"

"Murder?" said Mrs. Honeypenny, in a voice little above a whisper. "Where?"

"In the Crescent. At No. 96. The postman told us. The cops is there nah."

Mrs. Honeypenny loosened her grip and the boy sped off. Murder! No. 96! Was that what Alfred had in his mind when he told her to keep out of the way last night? He had seemed a bit funny, she remembered now. Sort of excited. Not calm and collected as he usually was. Murder! She held on to a railing for support. Yes, perhaps it would be better if she did keep away. Alfred must have gone or else he would have answered her when she was at the shop.

Since the day she was married at the age of thirty-two, Martha Honeypenny had never known what it was to act on her own initiative. Occasionally she had flared up in a petty revolt against the rules Uncle Thomas had made. Then he had retired to his own chair in a corner of the living-room and maddeningly ignored her tantrums. She would leave him. She had said that a dozen times, but even as she had uttered the words she knew it could never be. On her own she would have been as helpless as a chip in the swirl of a millstream.

Murder! Supposing it was him! She must know. She must! Nervously she crept down the street, her bag brushing the railings as she went. The ambulance had stopped at the end of the Crescent by the pillar-box. A policeman was keeping back a crowd of boys and loafers. She altered her position until she could see down the Crescent. Yes, that was right. They were at her house. Three or four men in dark overcoats and bowler hats were talking together while the two men from the ambulance stood at a little distance with the stretcher they had brought leaning against the area railings. Mrs. Honeypenny cornered a butcher's boy who was standing near her.

"Who is it?" she asked in a voice which she did not recognize as her own.

"I dunno," was the reply. "They say it's a young feller. I was going down to 'ave a look but I was sent off."

"Did you see his hat?" Mrs. Honeypenny quavered.

The boy eyed her curiously. "Yes, I saw it; a green felt, I think it was. But what's that got to do wiv you?"

"Oh, nothing, nothing."

Mrs. Honeypenny turned and almost ran down Graves Street, through Tanner Place into the High Street. It wasn't him. It wouldn't be. Thomas was over sixty and he never went anywhere in London without his top hat. She hailed a tram which took her northwards and westwards to Blackfriars Bridge. She gave the conductor her last twopence and sat there on a front seat clutching her little black bag and staring ahead with unseeing eyes. It was only when the conductor came along jingling his coins and calling out "Any more fares, please?" that she realized that she had travelled as far as she could for her twopence, and clambered down.

Where she walked that day Mrs. Honeypenny could not have told anyone had she been asked. She had lived nearly all her life in the Borough, and except for an occasional pilgrimage to visit an aunt in Camden Town she seldom crossed the river. When night fell she made her way back from the Edgware Road, whither she had wandered, to Westminster Bridge, and from thence via the back streets to the shop in the High Street. The shutters were still up and the grill was closed. A man was standing near by smoking a cigarette. Something about him made her hesitate and draw back into the shadow of an adjoining doorway. If that wasn't a copper in plain clothes, then she'd never seen one. Maybe she could get in at the back. If there wasn't food somewhere in the place, there would be something she could pawn even if it were only for a few shillings. It would be enough for a meal and a bed at least, and she felt she'd die if she couldn't get a bite to eat and a lay down. The street at the back was almost deserted, and as she opened the door of the backyard of the shop Mrs. Honeypenny thought she was in luck. The door leading to the back shop was ajar and there was no sign of anyone about.

"Hullo, hullo! Where are you off to, Missis?" The man who had stepped out of the shadow of the water-butt laid a hand on her shoulder and shone a light in her face.

"Here, lemme go! What's the idea, jumping out like that and frightening people?"

"Do you live here?"

"Yes. No. What's it to you where I live?"

"Quite a lot," replied the detective quietly. "You're Mrs. Honeypenny, aren't you? I've been looking out for you."

•　•　•　•　•

"All right. Have her sent along here right away. No, don't give her anything to eat. I'll look after that."

Thompson slammed the receiver back on its hook and grinned across at Lomax.

"They've got Mrs. Honeypenny. Walked right into their arms. She's about done in they say and hungry, which is all the better for us. Order up some coffee and a hot pie or something and keep it next door."

Ten minutes later Mrs. Honeypenny arrived in the care of a matron, who whispered a few words to the Chief Inspector and sat down in a corner of the room.

"Come and sit down by the fire, Mrs. Honeypenny," urged Lomax and pushed forward a chair. "I expect you're cold."

The woman looked nervously at the two men and then edged up to the fire and spread her thin, worn hands to the blaze.

"I'm hungry, too," she said simply.

"Yes, I know that," Thompson replied. "I've ordered you a meal. While it's being prepared I want you to tell me where you've been the last few days."

"Oh, just knockin' round."

"With your husband?"

"Part of the time, yes."

"Where have you been?"

"I can't tell you that, and you can't make me." Mrs. Honeypenny shut her mouth like a trap. She had not forgotten Uncle Thomas's last words to her that she was to keep quiet about his movements.

Thompson changed his tactics.

"Why did you go to the shop this evening?"

"To get something to eat and to sleep there."

"I see, but why not go to your house in Graves Crescent?"

"I'd lost the key. When I got back last night I found I'd dropped it somewhere. I saw . . ." Mrs. Honeypenny bit off the word which rose to her lips. Alfred must be kept out of this. She thought for a moment and then continued: "I saw there was no good me hanging around so I went to a friend for the night. I went back to the shop this morning, but the old man wasn't there, so I spent the day walking about and tried again not half an hour ago."

"You were expecting your husband to come back today, were you?"

"Yes. I thought he might come, but he's not very regular in his habits. I weren't surprised he didn't turn up."

"Where d'you think he'll go when he does turn up?" asked Thompson casually.

"Well, I don't rightly know," replied Mrs. Honeypenny doubtfully.

"I suppose he might go to the house?"

"Yes. Maybe."

"And yet you didn't go there to look for him? You tried the shop and then just walked around?"

"I didn't say I didn't go to the house."

"Did you?" Thompson shot out.

"No."

"Why not? Wait a minute. I'll tell you. You didn't go there because you knew that Geoffrey Hunt had been murdered and that his body—"

"No—no—I didn't know that. I swear I didn't! If I'd known that I'd never have come . . ." Mrs. Honeypenny stopped short. What was she saying? She mustn't talk too much.

Thompson reassured her with a smile. "I'm quite sure you knew nothing about what happened at No. 96 until—let me see—say early this morning. By the way, who was it you met last night?"

"Nobody."

"Where did you sleep?"

"With a Mrs. Miller."

"Where does she live?"

"I don't rightly know. It's a little street off Surrey Street, about the third or fourth on the right."

"Had you known her before you went there last night?"

Mrs. Honeypenny burst into tears and the matron, at a sign from Thompson, advanced to comfort her. When the sobs had eased to an intermittent snuffle the matron whispered to Thompson that she thought Mrs. Honeypenny had had about all she could stand and that the supper was ready. She had heard it being brought into the adjoining room a few minutes before. At the word supper Mrs. Honeypenny raised a bleary face.

"Supper, did you say? God! Why can't you give it to me? I'm starving—you know that."

"You'll get it all right," said Thompson easily. "But there's two things I want to know first. First, how long have you known this Mrs. Miller?"

"Only since last night," sobbed Mrs. Honeypenny. "And I never want to see her again."

"The other question is: Who took you to her? Was it your husband?"

"No, I told you I haven't seen him since I came back. That's why I went to the shop."

"You said you went there to sleep and get a meal."

Mrs. Honeypenny again sought refuge in tears, and Thompson waited until she had quietened down a little before he asked: "If it wasn't your husband, who took you to Mrs. Miller's—who was it?"

As Thompson was putting the question Lomax slipped out of the room and returned with the supper tray. The coffee was steaming and the meat-pie was piping hot. Mrs. Honeypenny looked up and smiled through her tear-filled eyes.

"Here, gimme that."

"Just a minute," said Thompson. "Who was the man who took you to Mrs. Miller's?"

"It was her son. They call him Dusty Now will you let me eat?"

CHAPTER XI

After he left Victoria, Alfred boarded a No. II bus bound for the City. For the moment he had forgotten completely all that had happened during the last twenty-four hours. It was a faculty he had possessed all his life—that of dismissing from his mind all unpleasant thoughts, and it had turned him into a man with a soul like a shrivelled pea. If he thought of Sam Hartford at all he did so much as a golfer might recall the worm-cast he had removed from the green. He had had to do it. The action assisted him in the game he was playing and that was all there was to it. Hunt had threatened to become a nuisance and perhaps it was as well he was gone too. Of course it was awkward that Kudorfer should have selected the office in Chancery Lane as the place for losing his temper. Alfred had tried to stop him, and it was just a bit of bad luck that the knife sent by Nick Wheeler should have arrived when it did. But that was the way things happened, and it was no good worrying. It had been a good idea of his to use Uncle Thomas's laundry basket. It had been devilish risky, but now that it was well hidden he wouldn't have anything to worry about in that direction.

The bus was passing the Law Courts, and a few yards farther on it was held up at the foot of Chancery Lane. Had he cleared everything out of the office? Would it be safe to go in now and have a final look round? The carpet was gone and the boards scraped. Dusty had put a coat of brown distemper over the lower panels of the wall where the string of bloodstains had been. No, there was nothing more to do there. The bus lumbered on down Fleet Street. There was another wait at Ludgate Circus, and Alfred conned over in his mind the advisability of going to the office where he was employed, and finally decided to give it a miss, for that day at any rate. It would be safer to keep out of the way until he saw how things were shaping. He could always say he'd been ill.

Habit, however, drew him to the sandwich dive in Lombard Street, which it had been his habit to patronize daily, and it was not until he was perched on a high stool before the long counter that he asked himself if he wasn't a fool. He'd be sure to meet someone he knew, perhaps even one of his confrères from the office, though that was unlikely. The employees of Hare & Johnson, for the most part, patronized a café in the building itself. The man behind the bar, who served him with his customary glass of bitter and ham sandwich, was a stranger, and as he paid his bill and was about to slip down from his stool Alfred felt he was a great deal luckier than he deserved to be. It was then that he met Blacker, the man who had put him on to the idea of buying the *Karnoc*.

"Hullo, Alfred, old scout. I've been looking for you. You weren't at your office this morning and they didn't know where you were."

"No, I've had a job to do outside," Alfred replied. "And now I'll have to be toddling."

"But wait a minute. What about the *Karnoc* deal? I thought you were going to put that through yesterday and let me have the papers today. The sale'll have to be registered."

"The *Karnoc*? Oh yes, of course. As a matter of fact that'll have to hang over for a day or two. I had a bit of trouble with my partner and I haven't got the dough yet."

"Well, it doesn't much matter to me one way or the other," Blacker replied. "But if you want her you'd better get a move on. The boss is talking about selling her for breaking up. He's shifted her up to Spender's Draw dock."

"Thanks for the information. I'll let you know within the next few days if I can go on with it. Bye-bye."

Alfred bought an evening paper and boarded a bus without bothering about its destination. He had made no plans and wanted time to think out the next move. As he had half expected, the paper had a short account of the discovery of the body of Geoffrey Hunt, and he read it eagerly. "The body of a well-dressed man was found early this morning . . . stabbed . . . identity unknown." He hurried through the other sheets to the Stop Press, but even there there was no mention of Sam Hartford. He had done his work well in cutting out the names and marks on the dead man's clothing.

Alfred spent the afternoon at the Zoo. It was his first visit, and with his faculty for living in the present he was able to forget for a time the difficulties and dangers which lay ahead. At six o'clock he thought of Kudorfer, and he made his way to the Warham Hotel, where he found Johannis sitting solemnly in the lounge smoking a very black cigar. There was a glass of wine on the glass-topped table before him and a litter of cigar-butts in an ash-tray. As Alfred advanced he looked up and something like a smile crossed his face, then he resumed his usual stolidity.

"So you have come at last. I have been waiting. I do not know what to do or where to go."

"That's all right," replied Alfred. "You leave everything to me. I'll see you through as long as you keep your mouth shut.

You understand that? If anyone questions you, make out you can't speak English."

"I understand. I am not a fool. Now tell me where can I buy cigars the same as this one I smoke now?"

"Gosh, you're a cool hand," said Alfred, with the admiration of one artist for another. "You've—well, you've had a bit of trouble. You're in a strange country with precious little cash, and you ask me where you can buy a cigar. I think you and I'll get on all right."

"I am sure of it. I said to myself when first I saw you, 'That is a man I can trust'. Mr. Hartford is no good, he is a weakling, and I wasted my drug on him. Still I have a little left. Tell me, is this Hartford recovered?"

"He's O.K." replied Alfred coolly. "He won't give us any more trouble."

"He thought it was all a dream. That was funny. A good joke. I shall tell it to my brother when I return to Posnik."

"Yes, and I expect you'll have a lot more to tell him by the time you get there."

Johannis lit another cigar.

"My knife. You have him safe? Yes?"

"Your knife at the present moment is on its way to be dumped in the Thames estuary, and that's the best place for it. It was broken, anyway."

"Broken? I do not understand."

"The tip of it was snapped off about half an inch from the end. I didn't notice it until late last night when I was cleaning it. The broken piece must be in the body of the man you killed. In one of his ribs, most likely. If the knife was found on you now, you'd swing. It wasn't safe to keep it a moment longer than I had to, so I threw it into a dust-cart that was waiting to shoot its load into a barge. The barge will be towed out and its cargo dropped into the sea."

"Yes, that was well done. I am sorry to lose my knife, but yes, it had to be. I will get another."

During this conversation Alfred had been thinking hard. The *Karnoc* was still for sale. If he could raise the money to buy her she would provide an excellent hiding-place and a means of getting Kudorfer and himself out of the country. It might even be possible to carry out the original plan of scuttling her and collecting the insurance money, but there would be time enough to go into that later. Spender's Draw dock in the meantime would be as quiet a berth as could be wished for. There were men close at hand in the "Brewery" who could be used as messengers and who could be relied upon not to talk. The only flaw in the scheme was the almost total absence of money. It was maddening to think of the silver dumped on the Embankment which, if properly handled, would have realized somewhere about the desired sum. If only Uncle Thomas had got back in time!

"Well, what is to be done? I cannot stay here for ever."

"You have got some money, haven't you?"

"A little, yes. Not much. But you—you promised that you would pay me. Is that not so? If you do not, I will—"

"Yes, go on, what will you do?" Alfred dropped his good-humoured pose and for the first time Johannis saw him as he was. Hard as agate and as selfish as the devil.

"I will go home."

"You will stay here till I give you the word. From now on you will obey me. If you do not—the rope, the nine o'clock walk. One word from me—"

"So that is the way of it? I see. The pleasant Mr. Alfred Brown changes his tune. He would give me away, he would—"

"I would do anything to any man who stands in my way, but if he is useful and will do what I want, of course, that would be different. I've got an idea in my mind. A way in which you and I can get out of England which will mean freedom to you and money to me. Your wage shall be paid the day we land on Posnik."

"You mean you are going on with this plan? You have the ship, the *Karnoc*?"

"Practically. In two days, three at most, we will start our work. There will be a lot to be done. Engaging the crew, overhauling the engines, and buying stores and bunkers."

"Mr. Brown, I salute you. You have the nerve of a—of an Englishman. I can say no more."

"Then you are with me?"

"Of course. I am your servant. You will take me to my home and pay me the one thousand pounds."

"Five hundred," said Alfred sharply, then cursed himself for a fool, but comforted himself with the thought that promises could be broken as easily as they were made.

"All right," replied Johannis with unexpected meekness. "Five hundred pounds the day I land on Posnik."

"Provided the *Karnoc* is sunk."

"Yes, yes, of course. There will be no difficulty about that. The compass will go wrong, most unfortunately. I will arrange everything."

• • • • •

At about the same time as Alfred left Victoria for the City a telegram was delivered to Lena. She had been out for a walk with Maurice along the cliffs and was unwinding her scarf in the hall when the porter appeared with a buff envelope on a salver.

"For you, miss."

Lena tore open the flimsy envelope. The words seemed to dance before her eyes and a full minute passed before she took in their full meaning.

They have discovered it. When can you come.

She crushed the paper into a ball and turned to meet Maurice's alarmed and questioning gaze.

"Bad news?" he queried. "Is it anything about that swine?"

"No, no. What do you mean?"

"Tonio, of course."

"Please do not mention his name again."

"I say, I'm awfully sorry. Come out on the verandah and have a cocktail."

"No, Maureece. I thank you, but I must go to my room for a little while to lie down. I am tired after our walk."

At the sound of the luncheon-gong Maurice left his chair on the lawn and waited for Lena in the lounge. Five minutes passed. Then ten. When the clock struck the half hour he rang the bell for a waiter and told him to find out if Lena was coming down.

"The young lady? Your sister, sir?"

"Yes, of course."

"But, sir, she has gone. An hour ago she ordered a car and I understood she was to take the 1.35 train to London."

"But her luggage?"

"She took one small bag, sir."

Maurice strode over to the office.

"Did Miss Crane leave any message?"

The clerk scanned the rack behind him.

"Oh yes, sir. She asked me to give you this note when you came in to lunch."

I am sorry, Maurice [he read], *But I must leave you. Some day I may be able to explain, but meanwhile you must stay in this hotel. A life depends upon it. If I can, I will write.*

A scrawled "L" ran across the page. The ink was smudged as though in her hurry she had omitted to blot the words she had written. Stay in the hotel! Like hell he would . . .

"Here waiter, have my bill made out. I'm leaving in three minutes' time."

The train which Lena had intended to catch had left the local station by the time Maurice climbed into the Lagonda and let in the clutch, but there was still a chance of catching her at Willowby Junction, fifteen miles away, where she would have to change into the London train. The car ate up the miles of white moorland road, leaving behind it a cloud of dust. It was an exhilarating run, swooping down into the dips and breasting the slopes at a speed which at times caused all four wheels to leave the road. When the little town of Willowby hove in sight Maurice heaved a sigh of relief. Far below in the valley he made out a plume of smoke from the panting engine of the local train as it toiled upwards. He had five minutes in hand, and it was at a very modest thirty-five that he dropped downwards to the station.

He was waiting for her on the platform as she stepped out of her carriage.

For a moment she looked utterly amazed, then glad. Was it pleasure? Maurice could never be sure, for immediately a look of fury supplanted all other expression.

Her black eyes flashed fire at him.

"Maureece! I thought I told you to stay! That you must not follow me. Did you not receive my letter?"

"Of course. That's why I'm here."

"But why? Oh, you fool, you will ruin everything."

Maurice picked up her bag and led the way to the exit, while she followed protesting. He threw her bag on to the back seat, picked the girl up and deposited her in the front seat.

"Maurice! You kissed me!"

"You're telling me, baby. About a quarter of an hour ago I discovered that I love you."

"You—love—me?"

"Yes, as soon as I found you'd vamoosed, my heart started to go tinketty-tonk, and it was yo-ho for the open road and a gallon of petrol."

"Will you please be serious. My hair! Look at it."

"It's AI."

"Where are we going?"

"Where would you like to go? Say the word."

"I think you are horrible."

"And I think you're adorable. You must always do your hair like that and promise you'll always wear that dress."

"I shall do no such thing, and at the very next town you must set me down. I will take a train to London, while you will return to the Linden Hotel and stay there."

Maurice merely laughed in reply and pointed to the speedometer. "Seventy-five," he said. "Are you scared?"

Lena shot out the tip of her little red tongue.

"You devil," was all she replied, and sank back in her seat.

As they neared Town Maurice dropped to a decorous thirty and Lena, who had been so silent that he had thought her to be asleep, sat up with a jerk.

"Are we here already?"

"Not far off it. Another ten miles or so. Had a good snooze?"

"I have been thinking what to do. What time is it?"

"Half past five. Why?"

"I'm meeting Alfred Brown at six at Paddington."

"Look here, Lena, there's something going on that I know nothing about and I don't believe there's any such person as Tonio."

"Well, and if you are correct, what then?"

"I'm not going to let you out of my sight."

Lena sighed. "Maureece, please do not be difficult, and ask me no questions, I implore you. If there is a chance of buying the *Karnoc* I promise that you will have your share, and if you wish you can sail in her. I would like you to see my home. There is a beach there were no one goes but I. Where the sand is coral, white, the cliffs black as night and the sea is bluer than any sky you have ever seen."

"I'd like to go to Posnik," said Maurice. "But isn't Hammersmith the devil with all these trams and buses?"

"I love it. It is all so new and strange. I wish I was not meeting this Alfred man."

"Then why meet him? Come away with me. We can get married in next to no time if I get a special licence."

"No, Maureece. You do not understand, and I cannot explain. You must trust me. Promise that you will?"

"Of course, Lena; but is there nothing I can do?"

"I do not know. Later, perhaps, I may have need of you, but now I must go to my father. He needs me."

When Maurice set Lena down at Paddington Station he parked the car in a side street and followed her at a discreet distance into the booking-hall. Ten minutes later Alfred appeared and the pair of them got into a taxi. Maurice was able to hear the words "Warham Hotel", and arrived there a few minutes after the taxi.

"Can you give me Miss Kudorfer's room number, please?"

The clerk at the reception-bureau looked at Maurice coldly, and then glanced at the register.

"There is no lady of that name in the hotel, sir."

"Are you sure?"

"Quite sure, sir."

"But she came in a few minutes ago. I saw her."

The clerk proceeded to manicure his nails.

"I'll wait."

"If you wish, sir, but I'm afraid you'll be disappointed."

Maurice took up a strategic position in one corner of the lounge where he could keep an eye both on the lift and on the staircase. Half an hour later Alfred appeared. He looked worried, and was coming down the stairs two at a time.

"I say, wait a minute!"

It was with something like panic that Alfred recognized Maurice's voice, and his first impulse was to brush past him and make his escape. The body of Geoffrey Hunt had been discovered, and if its identity was revealed by some unlucky chance the papers would make a front page splash of the story. Maurice would see it sooner or later and go to the police and give his, Alfred's, name as one of Hunt's late associates. Lena had been right and all would have been well if she had kept him down in Dorset.

"Sit down for a minute," Maurice urged. "I want to ask you about Hunt. I suppose you've been seeing him lately?"

Alfred passed his tongue over his dry lips and shook his head dumbly. Curse the fellow. What the devil did he mean by saying that?

"I'm in rather a hurry," Alfred mumbled. "Got to meet a man."

Maurice forced him into a chair.

"You look a bit queer. You'd better take a rest for a minute. Your pal can wait."

Alfred grasped the side of the chair to stop the trembling of his hands. God! He was losing his nerve! And with Maurice loose in Town!

Maurice pulled out a pouch and slowly filled his pipe.

"There's that fellow Hartford, too. I had a note from him when I got back from Norfolk. It was waiting for me at my flat. Apparently he wanted me to come along to the office and produce the dibs for the *Karnoc*. As a matter of fact I'd really decided to give the show a miss if it didn't mean letting Hunt down, but I went along on the chance of seeing him there."

"And did you—see—Mr. Hartford?" asked Alfred slowly, forcing his voice to a dull monotone.

"No, nor Hunt. I only met Miss Kudorfer there. As a matter of fact, I'm waiting for her now."

Alfred made an excuse and hurried out of the hotel. A half-crown tip to a porter gained him a re-entry through the staff door, and ten minutes after leaving Maurice he was back with Johannis. Lena was lying on the bed puffing at a cigarette. Alfred let out a curse and sat down on a hard chair.

"What is the matter?" Johannis asked. He was standing at the window looking down on the traffic in the street far below. The inevitable black cigar was between his teeth.

"Everything's the matter," snapped Alfred. "Maurice Crane is here in the hotel, and what the hell I'm going to do now God knows." He turned to Lena. "You were a fool to let him come here." He jumped to his feet and began to pace up and down the room with short, nervous steps.

"Oh, please sit down," Lena entreated him. "I am tired after my drive, and if I cannot rest I will have a headache. I did not bring him here, he must have followed me."

"I think it would be better if you would go away Mr. Brown," Johannis added. "There is nothing more to say. We have already had our talk, have we not?"

"If that man stays in London and the police find out that Geoffrey Hunt is the name of the man you killed—"

"Not so loud, my friend." Kudorfer was across the room in one bound. He clapped a horny hand over Alfred's mouth. "Killed," he whispered. "That is not a pretty word. Be careful, my friend."

Alfred wrenched himself free from Johannis' restraining grasp and addressed himself to Lena.

"It is all your fault his being here. I thought you were going to be clever and keep him out of the way."

Lena brushed some ash from her dress before answering.

"Yesterday I got him to take me to Dorset and I would be there now had not I received this."

She searched through her bag and then tossed a crumpled scrap of paper over to Alfred.

"Who sent this?" he demanded angrily.

"My father."

Johannis glanced at the telegram and nodded agreement.

"When I heard that you had been unable to hide the body and that the police had found it," he explained, "I was naturally a little alarmed. Lena is clever and will be able to help."

"I had to come," said Lena. "There was no choice, but I left a note in the hotel in Dorset addressed to Maureece, telling him to wait there until I returned. He followed me."

"And now we're in the hell of a jam. Maurice is sitting in the lounge. We've got to do something about him and do it quick."

· · · · ·

Alfred left Kudorfer in his room puffing away at his cigar. Lena acknowledged his departure with a wave of her hand and then sank back in her chair. Alfred sped down the service stairway and gained the street, where he stood for a minute thinking. What the blazes was he to do now? Everything depended on him, that was obvious, and with Maurice in London he would have to act quickly, or . . . Alfred hurried on. Maurice! He was just the sort of fool who might queer the whole show, and then there was the question of raising the wind. His thoughts went back to Uncle Thomas. If he knew anything of the old fox he'd lie doggo as soon as he got word of the murder of Geoffrey Hunt. If there was one thing Uncle Thomas hated worse than the police it was a murder. Well, if the old boy didn't choose to come along he, Alfred, would just have to bide his time, that was all about it.

He recalled his last meeting with the old man when he had spotted that queer key on his ring. It was one of the barrel type usually associated with deed boxes or a simple type of wall safe. There had been a tradition in the family that Uncle Thomas kept his wealth in a sock under a loose board, and Alfred, as soon as he had developed a use for plenty of cash, had shed his last scruple and had carried out a systematic search of the shop and of the house. He had even bought a steel tape and had measured every room, tapped every foot of floor and wainscoting, and picked at every board with a chisel, but with no success.

The search had taken months to complete, but even when he had finished Alfred would not own that he was beaten. He had only been able to make a most cursory examination of the basement before Uncle Thomas had fitted a complicated lock to the door leading down there. It looked almost as though Uncle Thomas suspected his nephew, and Alfred, realizing that the old man was a good friend, did nothing further to risk rousing his enmity.

That had been the state of affairs a year or two ago, but now things were different, and besides, as Alfred assured himself, it was only like taking a temporary loan to rifle the old man's savings. Not, of course, that Alfred would have hesitated to rob a child of its Saturday penny, but he still wanted to keep in with Uncle Thomas.

Alfred sauntered along, turning over in his mind the possibility and also the propriety of breaking into No. 96. There would be no difficulty about making an entrance into the house itself. When he was a boy he had, times without number, scaled the back garden wall and crept through the stunted, sooty laurels. The windows in the basement were barred, and though he had long tried to loosen a bar with a broken file, in the manner of Dick Sheppard, he had failed. But it was child's play, he had discovered, to shin up to the flat roof over the wash-house and lever up the window into the room on the ground floor which Mrs. Honeypenny had converted into a kitchen. There was a catch on this window designed to foil the most skilful burglar, and every night Mrs. Honeypenny slipped it into position. Fortunately for her own peace of mind she had never noticed that the effective part of the device had been snapped off half an inch from the end. That had been Alfred's doing, and now he began to appreciate the misdeeds of his youth at their true value.

The first question to decide, once he had made up his mind to break into No. 96, was the method of approach, and for the purpose he bought a map of London and studied it over a cup of tea and a crumpet in a tea-shop in the Strand. First of all he located Graves Crescent, the High Street, and the approximate position of the shop. Then he ran his finger northward from the Crescent and to his astonishment he found it was quite close to the river. There was a maze of small streets with here and there the uncompromising bulk of a factory barring the way to a street which had essayed to run from the High Street to the river. Of course, yes, it was at that corner he had met the old beggar who had showed him the way to the "Brewery". If he could land at Spender's Dock it wouldn't be difficult to make his way to the street which ran parallel to, and on the north side of, the Crescent.

For some reason, which he could not have explained even to himself, he was distrustful of treading the populous streets of the Borough. In the City it was different, but once in Southwark he felt he would have to be wary. Some of the police there might know him by sight and possibly connect him with Uncle Thomas and No. 96. But before he went farther there was Maurice to be dealt with. It was essential that he be kept out of the way at least until the *Karnoc* sailed. Alfred paid his bill and rang up the Warham Hotel and asked for the reception-office. Then he gave a brief description of Maurice, who he said was in the lounge, and asked the clerk to give Maurice a message.

"Hold the line a minute, sir." There was a pause and then: "Yes, sir, the gentleman is in the hotel. Perhaps you'd like to speak to him yourself."

"No, no. I want you to tell him this."

The clerk wrote a message down at Alfred's dictation, repeated it and then rang off.

So far so good. Alfred, after another glance at the map, slipped it into his pocket and took a bus to Ludgate Circus. From there he proceeded by way of Water Street, past the Apothecaries Hall, across Queen Victoria Street to Thames Street. He was searching for an outlet on to the river, but warehouses had wiped out the many steps and taverns which in bygone days had fringed the water front. Puddle Dock had gone, and Trig Stairs, and Queenhithe Little Stairs with it. It was not until he had passed Tower Bridge that he came on Whitefriars Stairs wedged in between two towering warehouses, so high that they made the little public-house look like a shanty even though it did boast of two storeys, a red-tiled roof, and a bow window looking out across the river. The steamboat pier, where the *Karnoc* had laid on the night when Sam and Kudorfer had boarded her, was vacant. Alfred walked into the "Seven Seas". The barman looked up from his paper.

"Well, mister. What are you 'aving?"

"I don't want a drink. I was looking for a waterman. I want to be put across the river."

The potman raised his eyebrows.

"Ain't the bridge good enough for you?" he asked. "By the time Fred finds 'is sculls you'd be 'arf way across. It ain't five minutes' walk from 'ere."

"Where is Fred?"

"Round the back, most likely."

Alfred slipped a shilling into the man's ready palm.

"Get hold of him for me. I'm in a hurry."

But hurry or no hurry Fred had one speed, which he didn't think fit to alter.

"Where was it you wanted to go, mister?"

"I'll tell you when we get afloat," replied Alfred, and clinked the coins in his pocket.

"I twig, guv'nor. Mum's the word."

The young flood was making and tugs with barges astern were starting up river when Alfred took his seat in the stern of the wherry and Fred pulled out from the Stairs.

"I want you to land me somewhere near Spender's Dock," he said, and Fred lay on his oars and spat on his hands.

"Spender's? Why, what d'you want there, mister? It's all gone to pieces, that dock 'as. Nothin' ever lays there these days. Oh, lor lumme, of course, I forgot! The *Karnoc* went up there on the tide this very morning early. It's her you want to go to, I expect."

"Land me at the wharf," Alfred replied shortly. "I don't know anything about the *Karnoc*."

"It'll be 'arf a dollar."

"Oh, all right, but let's get a move on for God's sake."

A quarter of an hour later Fred edged his boat in alongside the rotting piles of Spender's wharf and Alfred clambered up a rickety ladder. It was almost dark and the wharf was deserted.

On the *Karnoc* there was a faint light and Alfred could make out a figure moving about in the galley. It would be the night-watchman, he decided, and he walked across to the shack where he had hidden the contents of the laundry basket. Twice he stumbled over piles of rope and a bollard before he reached the door of the shed and pulled at the handle. Damn the thing! It was jammed! He tried again but without success, and then walked round to the window at the back. He had left it half open, he remembered, but now it was closed and as immovable as the door had been.

It would not be wise to break into No. 96 yet awhile, and he had thought that the time of waiting would be well spent in destroying the bloodstained rags and curtains he had left in the hut, but his luck was definitely out. The door of the window could be forced no doubt, but the danger of rousing the watchman on the *Karnoc* was too great a risk to take, besides, his only available tool was a pocket-knife. He took the path he had trodden before, through the waste ground to the "Brewery", which was deserted save for one figure seated on a box by a coke brazier. By the light of the glowing fire Alfred recognized the face of Nick Wheeler and heaved a sigh of relief.

"Nick!"

The man slipped from his box into the shadows.

"It's all right. It's me, Alfred. What the hell's the panic?"

"Panic! Who the blazes wouldn't 'ave the wind up with every flatfoot in the Borough camping on 'is trail? You know Truscott?"

"Yes, what about him?"

"'E's after me. God knows what for, but 'e is. Thinks I knows about this killing, but strike me pink I don't know no more than you do."

"You mean in the Crescent—at ninety-six?"

"Ninety-six be damned. Didn't you know old Sam Hartford was croaked larst night in Uncle Thomas's shop? Stabbed he was, right through the 'eart. Blood all over the place so they tell me, and all because I was round at the place yesterday the rozzers thinks it was me. Me, I tells yer! A self-respecting burglar what wouldn't hurt a fly, let alone a soft old geezer like Sam.

Every time I've been took I've gone quiet and yet they 'as to pick on me to be the goat."

Nick lit a cigarette and looked moodily into the hot coals.

"Did ye get that little souvenir I sent you? Hector picked it up and he said he'd see you got it."

"Yes, I got it all right," said Alfred curtly.

"Why, what's the matter? Didn't you like it? I thought you was nuts on curios. That's why I lifted it. Lovely 'andle it 'ad and it warn't 'arf sharp neither."

"Yes, it was sharp enough."

"'Ere, what do you mean, talking like that? I sends you a little present. A bonus, as you might say. Something extra, and you speak as if I'd socked you one."

"Oh, for the love of Mike don't gas about that knife! It was all right and I'm obliged to you, Nick, for getting it for me, but I don't want to talk about that now. I'm in a hell of a hole."

"How's that? I turned over the box to Uncle Thomas. That was all right, wasn't it?"

"Yes, I got it, but the old boy hasn't turned up. I don't know what's happened to him."

"Oh, he'll be along when it suits 'is 'ighness, you see if he don't. It's meself I'm thinking abart. Truscott's bin down 'ere twice since the murder, but I dodged 'im each time, an' now I 'as to pay that old blighter Smoky a bob a night to keep a look out an' give me the office if there's anything moving. I tell yer it's no blooming joke. 'Ere I am down to me last bob and what's the odds on me doin' a job? Not an 'undred ter one chance. The Borough's like a blinking wasps' nest when you've chucked a stone in it, and every one of the cops are ready to sting at sight. God! I'd just as soon be back in clink. There's nothing to put yer out there and you gets your meals reg'lar. But 'ere! Lor' love a duck, 'ave you ever tasted that stew old Barmy dishes out?"

"I had something out of a tin the other night." Alfred shuddered at the memory of bits of fat floating in a tepid grey liquid.

"Well then, you know what it's like. But Alf, you're not stoppin' 'ere, are you?"

"For a bit, at any rate. I've got a job on later." He thought for a minute and then went on: "Do you feel like making a quid? I thought about doing it on my own but there might be a snag. I'm not too strong on locks. Have you got your tools?"

"I don't need no tools, except these." Nick pulled out a piece of wire from one pocket and a couple of screw wedges from the other. "That's all I need. I can open most anything with this 'ere little bit of wire and the wedges—why, I can jam a door that tight with them that anyone that comes arter you 'as to file the 'inges orf before they can foller."

"All right. We'll start about midnight."

"What sort o' crib is it? An 'ouse or a shop?"

"A house."

"Then we'd better wait till later. You hear people talk about the best sleep being afore twelve o'clock, but that's all my eye. The time a bloke sleeps soundest is round about four or five. He gets inter his stride abart then as you might say. Now where abarts is this place?"

"Not a quarter of a mile from here." Alfred was naturally of a secretive nature, and for the time being he thought it unnecessary to mention that it was Uncle Thomas's house they were to break into. It was clear to him that Nick Wheeler was, to put it vulgarly, "in a flat spin" about the murder of Sam at the shop and would naturally fight shy of entering the house in Graves Crescent.

At two o'clock they made a move, and on their way dismissed Old Smoky from his vigil at the street entrance. The old man blinked at the sight of Alfred.

"Back again, guv'nor?" he said wheezily. "I thought ye'd gorn fer good and all. I was just saying—" But Alfred cut him short.

"I'm coming back later on," he said. "And I'll want a doss."

"That'll be all right, guv'nor. I'll fix suthing up fer you nice and snug and 'ave some chow ready too."

It was anxious work threading their way through the narrow streets to the mews in the rear of Graves Crescent. The street lamps had been extinguished and there was not a light showing anywhere when they halted by the door in the wall leading to the back garden of No. 96. Alfred shone his torch on the wall and located the niches in the mortar he had made use of as a boy to climb into the garden, and a minute later he was following the path through the bushes to the back door, with Nick at his heels. There was no difficulty in forcing the window into the kitchen on the ground floor and, as Nick closed it behind them, they stood listening. Save for the ticking of a cheap clock the house was silent and apparently untenanted. Nick felt his way along the passage into the hall and eased back the bolts of the front door and removed the chain.

"It's always best to have an extra getaway," he explained when he rejoined Alfred at the top of the stairs leading to the basement. "Somebody might have seen us come in, but I don't think so. Still, I always like to be on the safe side."

He produced his bit of wire and Alfred switched on his torch and illuminated the door leading to the basement. After an exploratory feel round the lock Nick straightened up.

"I'll manage it all right." He inserted the neck of an oil-can into the key-hole and then set to work. In less than a quarter of an hour the door was open and Alfred led the way down the stone steps. Despite the most painstaking search of every room, which was not completed until half past four, the two men found no trace of what they sought, and Alfred had almost made up his mind to give it up, when Nick stumbled over a pile of clay in a corner of the wash-house. It was obvious at first sight that it had been lying there for a considerable time, for it was covered with a thick coating of dust.

"Where the devil did that come from?" said Alfred, and Nick replied with the directness of a simple mind. "Looks as if some bloke had dug a hole somewhere."

"Yes, that's it." Alfred flashed his light over the flags of the wash-house. He did not dare to put into words the thought that had come to his mind. "Yes, dug a hole, but where?"

"Maybe in the garden?" suggested Nick.

"Don't be a fool. He wouldn't have carried the clay in here if that had been the case. No, it must be in the house. In one of these rooms. Perhaps in here. It's the only place where there are flagstones."

"There's a crowbar here behind the door," Nick reported. "And it's bin used not so very long ago. See! There's marks on the toe of it."

But Alfred was down on his knees examining every joint of the flags.

"I say, bring the what-d'you-call-it here. This looks a likely one. There's a piece chipped off the corner."

Together they pressed down on the bar and with a sucking sound the flag came away from a bed of yellow clay. The clay had been disturbed, that was obvious, and when the flag had been laid on its back Alfred probed gently with the crowbar. Almost at once he unearthed an oiled-silk bundle.

"That's what I was after," he muttered. "Put back the stone, Nick, and square up. We don't want to leave any traces."

With fingers which trembled in spite of himself, Alfred untied the securing tape and unrolled the covering. A touch told him that the contents were a thick wad of banknotes, and he hurriedly refastened the package and slipped it into his pocket. There was no point in letting Nick know what it was. A fiver would do for his share.

"Come on, let's get out of it." With a last quick look round he led the way up the steps. As they reached the ground floor and Nick was about to close the door Alfred caught him by the arm.

"Quiet!" he whispered. "Listen!"

A man was coming down the staircase above them. They could hear the creak of the boards and the bump-bump of a bag against the banisters. Nick motioned towards the kitchen, but Alfred still held him tight in his grasp. Whatever happened an alarm must not be raised or . . . The man had reached the foot of the staircase. Alfred waited tense to see which way he would go. The bag was dropped on the floor and footsteps advanced in the direction of the basement door behind which Alfred and Nick were waiting. A hand felt along the wall. Nick sank back on his heels and then sprang forward. His fingers met round the man's gullet and strangled the scream which rose in his throat.

"Get his legs! And hold on!"

It was a fierce struggle but a short one, and a minute or two later Uncle Thomas found himself bound hand and foot. A strip of plaster sealed his lips.

"Come on, Nick, let's stow him away quick. You take his feet. There's a cupboard in the sitting-room. Open that door behind you."

Nick was breathing heavily before they had finished their job and he straightened himself with a sigh of relief.

"That was a bit of luck. Copping 'im quick like that. He didn't see who we were, did he?"

Alfred shook his head and took out his cigarette-case.

"Well, let's beat it."

"We haven't finished yet," Alfred replied. "Light up."

Nick, with the caution of his kind, closed the shutters and drew the curtains before he struck a match.

"Haven't we done enough for one night?" he asked.

"Not quite," Alfred replied as he sank back into an easy-chair. Then he drew a stocking from his pocket. It was partly filled with sand and tied with string.

"I'm expecting a man any minute now, and we've got to put him to sleep for a spell along with the old man. They'll be company to each other."

Nick grinned.

"I thought this was goin' to be an easy job," he said.

"Well, it has been, hasn't it, up to the present, and we won't need to take any chances with the next one. He'll be a bit livelier than . . ."

"Quiet!" Nick whispered, and Alfred held his breath for a moment.

"That wasn't anything. You're losing your nerve, Nick."

"Listen, you damned fool. There's someone at the front door."

Then Alfred heard a faint rat-tat and he reached for his sandbag.

"Come on, Nick. You keep to the right and open the door quick. I'll do the rest."

For one fleeting instant Maurice looked into the face of Nick Wheeler and then he fell, an inert, unconscious form, on the tiles of the hall. Alfred dropped his weapon, pulled him clear of the door and pushed it to with his foot.

"We'll tie him up and leave him here," he said.

CHAPTER XII

UNCLE THOMAS was arrested by a police-constable about thirty seconds after he had broken out of his own house. Uncle Thomas's feet had apparently lost their cunning, for one of them shattered a pane as he was clambering over the lowered sash.

"Why, bless me soul if I haven't been looking for you," said the constable as he took a firm grip of Uncle Thomas by the elbow and propelled him up the area steps. "This is a bit o' luck."

"You're making a mistake, officer," said Uncle Thomas, trying to keep his temper under control. The policeman halted under a street lamp and twisted his prisoner round until he got a good view of his face.

"Yes, I knows who you are all right. I thought I couldn't 'a' made a mistake even if you have left off wearing that mouldy old top hat of yours."

"I repeat, officer, you have made a very grievous error. I shall make it my business to see that the papers hear of this and I shall bring an action against you for wrongful arrest. That'll cost you something."

"It'll give me a hearty laugh. Meanwhile, you'd better keep your trap closed, and I'm saying that for your own good."

At the police-station the sergeant on duty took one look at Uncle Thomas and then stretched out his hand for the telephone. Within ten minutes of putting through the call Thompson arrived and, after hearing the report of the constable, he had Uncle Thomas shown into the Inspector's office where he was sitting.

"So you've come back, eh? Where have you been these last two or three days?"

"I've been touring in my motor-car," said Uncle Thomas loftily. "I thought a little country air would do me and my wife a bit of good."

"Went away in a hurry, didn't you?" snapped Thompson.

"I go when the spirit moves me. I'd been working very hard, and on Monday after dinner I says to my wife, 'What about a turn in the country?' and as she was agreeable, we went."

"Do you often go away like that? All of a sudden?" Thompson asked.

"If I want to go, I go," replied the old man.

"Have you ever been out of Town for more than a day before this trip of yours?"

"That, I am afraid, I cannot remember."

"You left on Monday? What time?"

"About two o'clock. It may have been later. I don't know."

"Where did you go to?"

"Norfolk. The air is very fine on the East Coast."

"I've no doubt it is, but whereabouts in Norfolk did you stay?"

"We travelled round. A day here, a day there. We had no settled plans."

"Where did you sleep on Monday night?"

"On Monday night? Now let me see. We followed the Great North Road as far as Stevenage and then we went on through Baldock and Royston to Newmarket."

"Yes, and from there?"

"Well, really, I didn't notice the places we passed through, but that night we slept at a village called Starring."

"That was Monday night," commented Thompson. "What did you do next?"

Uncle Thomas passed his hand across his forehead and wrinkled up his eyes.

"To tell you the truth I have very little recollection of where we went next. It's my memory. It's not so good as it was and it often plays me tricks. Now where was it we slept on Tuesday night?"

"Yes, that's what I want to know," prompted Thompson. "You memory's done very well up to date."

"It's no good," replied Uncle Thomas after a pause during which he was apparently thinking deeply.

"It's a very curious coincidence, if I may say so," said Thompson. "But your wife's memory is even worse than yours. She doesn't seem to know what happened to her after she left London on Monday." Uncle Thomas's features relaxed and an expression of something very like relief passed over his face.

"That is the effect of age, my dear sir," he explained. "Neither of us are as young as we were."

"Your wife takes in washing, I believe?"

"Yes. She does do a little in that way. Just to oblige some old friends."

"And she left a clean lot of laundry behind her on Monday. Now why was that? One would have thought that she would have delivered it before she left."

"You surprise me," the old man replied. "If I had known, of course I would have delayed our departure. It must have slipped her memory. Such a thing has happened before."

"I suppose you came back to London by car?"

"No, I took a train, but where from I cannot remember. I know it sounds odd, but one must put it down to an attack of asphasia."

"Can you tell me at what point this memory of yours started work again? From Tuesday up to today it has been a blank?"

"That unfortunately is the case," Uncle Thomas agreed urbanely. "It must have been some time between two and three o'clock this morning that I found myself crossing Southwark Bridge in a taxi. It was a very curious sensation, I assure you, travelling I knew not where. The driver evidently had had his orders, for he drove straight to my house in Graves Crescent. Of course I had my keys, but somebody had apparently bolted the front door from the inside and I had to make my entrance through a window in the basement. You mentioned my wife and her washing just now, well, when I opened the area gate I found that the basket she was in the habit of using in her work had disappeared."

"That struck you as odd, then—that it wasn't in its usual place? Might someone not have borrowed it?"

"That of course is a possibility, but one I must confess I did not envisage at the time. Who would have a use for such an article?"

"Search me, unless someone wanted it to carry some article or other in it—such as a body, for instance."

"A body?" Uncle Thomas's usual resonant voice sank almost to a whisper. "What do you mean? A body—a dead body?"

"Yes, something like that."

"But—but . . ." the old man quavered, dropping abruptly his affected pedantry of speech.

"For God's sake let's quit beating about the bush. You know as well as I do that a man was found murdered on your doorstep yesterday morning. It's been in all the papers. Splashed all over the front page."

"No. No, I know nothing about it. Nothing, I tell you, and I can prove it if you'll let me!"

"There's no need to shout," Thompson assured him. "Have a 'bine and take a pull on yourself. I've got another bit of news for you. There was a man murdered in your shop on Thursday night or maybe early on Friday morning. Do you know anything about that?"

"In the shop?"

"Well, in the room over it."

"I swear here and now that I know nothing of no murder nowhere, so help me. On Thursday night I was in the police-station at a place called Warbuck near Baldock. I was coming along steady in my car in the direction of London when a young toff in one of them sports cars passed me and stopped in front of me, so that I had to pull up. What does this young feller do then but give me in charge for failing to stop after an accident. According to him I'd forced him off the road some way back on the Tuesday afternoon, which was clean ridiculous. I'd never set eyes on him before. There was a lot of talk at the station and they was going to let me go when, bless me, if the Inspector didn't think I'd been mixed up in some business or other—a burglary, I think it was, in Norfolk."

"Your memory's improving," said Thompson dryly. "Whereabouts in Norfolk was this burglary?"

"In a little place called Starring," replied Uncle Thomas. "Where I stopped on the Monday night. As I was a stranger they picked on me and sent my description all over the country. Two fellows came down from Starring yesterday and said I was the man who'd been in their district, but that didn't prove anything, and after a lot more palaver they said I could go. That was at four o'clock on Friday afternoon, and here I am."

Thompson consulted his notes.

"You left London on Monday. Slept at Starring that night. You were at the police-station at Warbuck on Thursday night and were released on Friday afternoon. Now what about Tuesday and Wednesday? Don't tell me you can't remember where you were, because I won't believe you and you stay here till you split."

"All right, then, you can tell someone to get a bed ready. I've told you all that's necessary. You said the bloke that was murdered was found yesterday morning—that was Friday. My alibi is that I was at Warbuck from Thursday noon up to Friday tea-time. That covers it. And I knows the law. You've got to bring me up afore a beak within twenty-four hours and make a charge, or else you've got to let me go, so there's no good you trying to come it over a bloke like me."

Thompson grinned. "I'll take the risk of keeping you locked up for a bit," he said. "Alibis have been busted before now. Well, that'll be all for the time being. I'll see you in the morning. Have him taken away, Inspector."

As Uncle Thomas went out Lomax entered the room.

"I'd heard you'd come here, Chief. What's doing?"

"The old gentleman from No. 96 has thought fit to return. A local bobby snaffled him as he was leaving his own house and the explanation was this: he—that is this old Wreck of the Hesperus, Uncle Thomas—found that he couldn't get into his house because the front door was bolted from the inside. I was responsible for that, you remember. I left by the door in the area. The old man was locked out so he climbed in through a window. I haven't asked him what he did inside. I thought we'd have a look round there first. We'll go along there now."

When they reached the area of No. 96 Lomax trod on a piece of broken glass and a torch revealed the gaping hole made in the window by Uncle Thomas's foot. Thompson tried to raise the lower sash, but it had jammed tight.

"Hence the climbing act," said Lomax. "The top part is free enough."

Thompson produced a key for the area door and they walked into the narrow passage within and opened the door of the wash-house.

As he crossed the floor, Thompson's foot struck against a *loose* flagstone. "Someone's been playing about here," he said. "Ah! The very thing." His eyes had lit on the crowbar standing in a corner of the room. He fitted the sharp edge into the crack and, as he heaved, the stone came up until Lomax could get his fingers under it and lift it clear. By the light of a torch Thompson discovered that a hole had been dug in the place where the flagstone had lain, but whatever may have been hidden in it was gone, leaving no trace.

A brief examination of the other basement rooms revealed nothing of interest, and Thompson led the way up the stone stairs to the ground floor. As he made his way along the passage to the front door he stumbled over a gladstone bag. Thompson carried it into the dining-room and lifted it on to the table. It was strapped up but not locked, and, as the lid was opened, there was revealed a collection of clothes. Suits, underwear, handkerchiefs and socks.

"The old boy must have left this behind," said Thompson.

They found the front door unbolted.

"That old scoundrel Honeypenny must have been lying when he said he found it fastened from the inside," said Thompson.

Lomas turned the handle and pulled.

"There's something holding it!" he exclaimed. "Yes, by Jove! There's a screw wedge here. I wonder who put it there—and why?"

"It's a funny business," Thompson went on. "One body was found outside Honeypenny's house and the other in his shop, but he swears he knew nothing about either. That may or may not be true. We'll find out that tomorrow when we test his alibi."

Uncle Thomas was awake when the gaoler came to call him. He was an old man who had slept soft for many years, and the so-called bed in his cell had found out the knobbly parts of his old bones. Besides, there had been some talk of murder. A body had been found outside his house and another in his shop. . . . Though he knew that his alibi was sound yet he was frightened. He had known of a man who had got "life" for being an accessory before the fact. A man who had been a hundred miles away from the scene of the crime at the time it was committed. Like most of his class, he had in his mind the fixed idea that the police, if they could, would fix a crime on a man no matter if he were innocent or no.

The gaoler piloted Uncle Thomas into the brightly lit room where Thompson and Lomax were waiting and pointed out where he should sit.

"I've been to your house," Thompson began. "And have had a good look round. What did you have hidden under the wash-house floor?"

The colour drained from Uncle Thomas's face.

"In the wash-house? Under a stone?"

"Yes, in about the middle of the room."

"How the hell did you find it? And what's the idea of asking me? If you lifted that stone you must have found it and it's mine! You've no right to take it! It's mine and rightly come by."

"You'd try the patience of a plaster saint," said Thompson. "I've had the stone up and there's nothing there but a hole in the clay. What I'm asking you is what did you keep there?"

"My savings," replied Uncle Thomas in a weak voice. "Every penny I've managed to scrape together was hidden there and you're lying. It was there when you looked. It's just like you ruddy policemen to pinch it."

"If we'd taken it why should we ask you what was there? That's sense, isn't it?"

"Yes, I suppose so," said Uncle Thomas grudgingly.

"Now, who knew your money was there?"

"Nobody. Not a soul. I never even told my wife in case she talked."

"Did anyone ever come to your house except tradesmen?"

"No. We live very quietly, just the two of us. Sometimes Alfred would come in for a bite of supper but that was all." Then a light broke. "Alfred, that's who it must have been, the mangy little cur, and not more than I would have expected of him. Now I come to think of it, I caught him once up in my bedroom. He was down on his hands and knees tapping on the skirting-board. After that I fitted a lock to the basement door and kept the only key myself."

"Alfred?" Thompson interjected. "Who was he?"

"Alfred's my brother's boy. I kind of brought him up when his pa died. Not that he needed much looking after. That's the sort Alfred is."

"What does he look like?"

"Well, he's not much to look at. He's short and has got sandy hair."

Thompson signed to the station-sergeant to make a note of the description, then he turned back to Uncle Thomas.

"He knew you kept a pile of cash in the house, then?"

"He suspected it. And to think all I've done for him. Jobs a-plenty and hardly a word of thanks. Was there nothing left?"

"Not a cent," replied Thompson. "I'm afraid he's cleaned you right out. He left a bag of clothes behind."

"A bag?"

"Yes, it was at the foot of the stairs on the ground floor."

"You mean an old portmanteau with 'T. H.' on it?"

"Yes, that was the one," Thompson agreed.

"I packed that bag," said Uncle Thomas. "I'll tell you what happened. I got in through the basement window, went up the stairs and locked the door at the top behind me. Then I went up to my bedroom and took out the bag from under the bed and put some duds in it. It took me a tidy time to find all the things I wanted, and I suppose I must have been in the room nearly an hour. Then I came down again and when I was on the last step I heard a noise. I couldn't make it out, so I dropped the bag and walked along the passage to the basement door. When I was within two or three feet of it a man sprang at me. I couldn't see his face. It was too dark. I tried to keep him off, but it turned out there was two of them and atween them they tied me up and shoved me in a cupboard in the sitting-room."

"How did you get loose?" asked Thompson eagerly.

"All right, all right. I'm coming to that bit. I'll tell me story me own way. There I was trussed up and stiff and sore from the way they'd handled me. I heard them whispering together for a bit, and after a while there was a knock at the front door. I didn't hear anything after that except a kind of thud and I could hear footsteps scrabbling on the tiles in the hall. After that it wasn't long before I heard footsteps coming back. They went into the kitchen, and that was the last of them. I began to get the wind up then, for the door of the cupboard I was in was locked and it began to get mighty stuffy. My legs was aching something cruel, not to mention me arms, and there was a tickle on the back of me neck that was near driving me mad."

"Oh, never mind your neck. Get on with the story," Thompson urged.

"You won't believe what I'm agoing to tell you," said Uncle Thomas.

"I'll try," said Thompson dryly.

"A girl came into the room. I didn't hear her steps, but when she called out not a couple of feet away I was sure I was dreaming. 'Maurice, Maurice!' she was saying, kind of agitated like, and I twisted meself round till I could get me foot agin the door and tapped away with it as hard as I knew how. Then I heard her hands feeling over the door and I could have cried when she found the key. 'Maurice!' she said again as I rolled out, and down she went on her knees, picking away at the string me hands were tied with. It was dark as a tomb, but she didn't do so bad, and all the time she was talking away nineteen to the dozen."

"What did she say?"

"I didn't pay much heed really, but she did say someone was a swine and it wasn't her fault and a lot else besides. She was crying too. As soon as I got me hands free I struck a match and then she gave a sort of a screech. I thought she was going to pass out, but she was a game one all right. She took one more look at me dial and then lit out of the room like as if the devil was after her. I heard her striking matches in the hall and then I smelt something which made me jump. It was gas. Not strong, but I wasn't taking no chances. 'Put out that light!' I shouted at her, and I think she must have sniffed it at the same time because she called back: 'Yes, all right, I understand. But come and help me to find him.' She had a funny way of talking. Like some kind of a foreigner. 'Find who?' I asks. 'They've gone, whoever they was.' 'No, no,' she answers back quick like, 'Maurice is here.'

"The smell of gas was getting stronger, and I knew it could only be coming from one place, and that was the cooker in the kitchen. I felt me way down the passage and opened the door. The curtains weren't drawn and it was light enough for me to see something lying near the cooker. I ran across the room holding me breath all the time and damned nigh came a cropper on a bloke lying stretched out on the floor. I could hear the sound of gas whistling out of one of the burners and I turned it off sharp and then threw up the window. Gawd, it wasn't half good to get a breath of clean fresh air! He was as near a deader as any I've seen, but he came round after a bit. The girl, she fussed round with wet cloths and suchlike wiping his face, but after all said and done, it was the fresh air that did the trick."

"What was she like? This girl?" queried Thompson.

Uncle Thomas sucked at his cigarette for a minute or two in silence. His brow was wrinkled and two or three times when about to speak he checked himself.

"I didn't know quite what to make of her at first," the old man said at last. "But there's one thing I can say and that is she's a good looker. We didn't have no more than a couple of candles, but you can tell a high-stepper by the way she moves. I hardly saw her face, but I could sort of feel her eyes, and her voice was low and husky. More like a man's than a woman's."

"She was calling for Maurice when you first heard her?" asked Thompson.

"Yes, that's right, but you know the way she said it was funny. I wouldn't be suprised if she wasn't some kind of a foreigner."

"Now tell me about the man you found in the kitchen. Was that Maurice?"

"Yes, but what his other name was I can't tell you."

Uncle Thomas gave a brief description of Maurice, and Thompson looked over to Lomax.

"That sounds like young Crane all right," he whispered. "I wonder what the devil he was up to in that house?" Then he turned back to Uncle Thomas. "Well, tell us what happened to this man and the girl."

"They didn't stop long. As soon as the young chap got his breath back he and the girl had a palaver out in the passage and I sat smoking in the sitting-room. I needed a rest, I don't mind telling you. I was proper shook up. I sat there thinking and wondering to myself what it was all about, when the next thing was I didn't hear anything from the couple outside the door. I could hear a clock ticking in the kitchen as clear as anything. I called out and got no answer, so I opened the door and called again. They was gone. I soon found that out, and as far as I could see they'd used the window into the back garden. The front door was fastened with a screw wedge."

"Why didn't you tell me all this before?" asked Thompson, exasperated.

"I didn't tell 'cause I thought it might be Alfred and I didn't want to get him into trouble. He thought I was out of Town and took me for a burglar most likely as I came down the passage."

"And you don't mind telling me now that you thought it was him. What's made you change your mind all of a sudden?"

"If you can get back the dough he's taken off me I'll tell you anything you like," replied Uncle Thomas vindictively.

"If you want me to do that you'll have to spill the beans first," said Thompson. "Let's start at the beginning. What was Alfred's last name?"

"Brown. He was my sister's boy. He has a job in the City, as a sort of commission agent I think it is. He'd never tell me what he did."

"Where did he live?"

"I don't know that either, but there is a bloke who might be able to help you there. His name's Dusty Miller. If you give me a pencil I'll write down his address for you. It's not far from here."

Thompson handed the paper to the station-sergeant with the order that Miller be brought along for examination right away. Then he read out the description of Alfred which he had obtained from the old man.

"Does that sound all right?" he asked.

"Yes," said Uncle Thomas. "And he's got a gold tooth on the left upper side."

Thompson made a pencilled note.

"You said a few minutes ago that you did jobs for Alfred. What were they?"

"Selling stuff, mostly," replied Uncle Thomas a little vaguely. "You see, I had the shop."

"I know. When were you last in it?"

"Monday dinner-time I left."

"Did you lock it up?"

"No, I left Hector in charge. I expect he's there now. He was going to sleep in the room above."

"Why didn't you sleep at No. 96 last night when you got there, and where were you going with the bag?"

"Well, I suppose I might as well tell you," said Uncle Thomas. "It wasn't true what I said about driving in a taxi. I've never been in one in my life. I walked across Southwark Bridge, and on the south side there's a boarded-up shop. When Alfred wants to send a message to me he often writes it on the boards in chalk. I go past that place most days and it saves him a long walk."

"What was the message?" asked Thompson.

"You wouldn't understand it as it was written. We have a code. A circle with a dot means I'm coming to the house tonight. A cross means . . ."

"Never mind about that. What sort of sign was there on the hoarding?"

"A cross with a dot in every quarter, and that was a warning to keep away."

"And you didn't?"

"I hadn't any spare clothes or boots or anything and I was down to my last half dollar. I had to go to the house to get supplies."

In response to a call from Thompson, finger-print men got to work at No. 96 and inquiries were sent out to Starring and Warbuck.

"Amend that description of Alfred. Add the gold tooth and the name is Brown. Get through to the City police. I fancy they may be able to help us." Thompson gave his orders and returned to the questioning of Uncle Thomas.

"I've got your story straight now," he said. "Except for that time on Tuesday and Wednesday. It's no earthly use keeping anything back now, and you might as well finish it."

But the old man was dumb.

"You went up to Norfolk to pull off a job at a house called the Grange at Starring," Thompson suggested. "Alfred put you on to it and you brought away a box of valuable Sheffield plate. What happened to it?"

"I don't know what you're gassing about," said Uncle Thomas. "I went for a little pleasure trip in the car. That was all."

"Alfred knew of the silver at the Grange, didn't he?"

"He might have done and then again he mightn't. I dunno. I haven't seen Alfred since Saturday, or it may have been Sunday."

"Where did you meet him?" asked Thompson.

"He came to the house and had supper, but he didn't stay long. He said he was going to meet somebody but he didn't say who and I didn't ask him. Alfred's not one to answer questions."

"That seems to be a family failing," commented Thompson dryly. "And you're not going to do yourself any good by following his example. Now, look here, if you help us we'll help you and if we can lay our hands on the cash Alfred pinched from you we won't ask you where it came from."

Uncle Thomas looked up with a crafty gleam in his eye.

"I've heard of promises like that before," he said. "And they never came to anything. It may be all right and as you say, but if it wasn't—where would I be?"

"All right, if you won't take my word for it I can't make you. You'd better think it over and let me know in the morning if you change your mind. Have you ever met a man called Hartford?"

Uncle Thomas shook his head.

"Or Hunt?"

"No. I ain't either seen or heard of any blokes by those names. What are they like?"

Thompson gave a brief description of the two men, but it apparently conveyed nothing to Uncle Thomas.

"Anyway, you know Dusty Miller. Did he go about with Alfred?"

"I've heard Alfred speak of him once or twice," Uncle Thomas replied.

"Your wife met him, she said, when she got back to Town. That was Thursday night."

"She got back all right then?"

"Yes, I was wondering when you were going to ask that. Have you seen her since you arrived in Town?"

"No, and I wasn't worrying. Mrs. Honeypenny can look after herself."

"She brought something with her," said Thompson quietly. It was a shot in the dark, for he had no more than a suspicion in his mind that Mrs. Honeypenny had conveyed the proceeds of the burglary from Warbuck to London. But Uncle Thomas was too old a hand at the game to rise to such a bait.

"I don't know what you mean," he said, and Thompson left it at that.

· · · · ·

"Well, my Maureece, and how are you now? Better?"

"Not so bad, but I still feel a bit dizzy. Someone landed me a beauty just as I was coming in at the front door."

They were standing before the open window in the Honeypennys' kitchen. Uncle Thomas had retired to the sitting-room, "to have a sit me down and pull myself together", as he had expressed it. Lena was leaning against a dresser smoking her inevitable yellow cigarette.

"Yes, you are looking more bright," she said. "Shall we go?"

"Yes, rather. I'm on. We want to get hold of a bobby as soon as we can."

"A bobby?"

"Yes; you know, a policeman."

Lena's face clouded with anxiety.

"Before you do that I must tell you something. When I have finished you will decide what will be the best thing for all of us."

Maurice took Lena in his arms and kissed her on the mouth.

"That's one of the best things," he laughed.

"And someone told me that Englishmen could not make love! He was a liar. But now please be serious just for five minutes. My father came to England some days ago. A ship was to be bought and he was to sail in her. Before everything was arranged there was a quarrel between the men who were to buy the ship. One of the men was killed."

"Heavens alive! When was that?" Maurice ejaculated.

Lena hurriedly continued her story.

"This man died two days ago. My father was present at the time, but of course he had nothing to do with what happened."

"Where is your father now?"

"At the hotel to which you followed me this evening. Soon, if all goes well, we will sail for Posnik in the *Karnoc*, and . . ."

"But, dammit, he must go to the police first and tell them all he knows! A man was killed, you said? It may have been murder . . ."

Lena pressed against the dresser to still the trembling of her legs.

"If he is innocent, as you say," Maurice went on, "your father will have nothing to fear."

"It is not so easy as that, my Maureece, or I would have made him do as you say as soon as it occurred. My father is an alien and landed in this country without a permit. He could be sent to prison for doing that."

"Yes, I dare say, but in the meantime the man who did the killing will get clear away."

"I do not think so, Maureece, if you will do as I ask. You know Alfred, do you not?"

"Yes, rather. I met him once at the office in Chancery Lane and then he came to see me at my flat one night. What has he got to do with this affair?"

"He was present when Captain Hunt was stabbed. He—"

"Hunt? You mean Geoffrey Hunt?"

"That is the man."

"Good God! Hunt killed? And it was me that brought him into this business. How on earth did it happen—and why?"

"He quarrelled with Alfred. They did not like each other."

"Do you mean that Alfred murdered him?" Maurice whispered, with a white face, but Lena ignored the question as she fitted another cigarette into her long holder and went on:

"Alfred hopes to arrange for the purchase of the *Karnoc*, and when he does so my troubles will be at an end. When she sails I will send you word and *then* you can go to the police and satisfy your conscience, once my father is out of the way."

"And what about you?"

"Does it matter what happens to me?"

"My poor innocent child! That's one of the few things which does matter—to me. I don't want to do anything that may worry you or have your father embarrassed with awkward questions, but you don't seem to realize how serious this business is. If Hunt was really murdered you can't expect me to stand by and do nothing. It would be criminal."

"No, no, Maureece. I do not want to upset your English idea of justice. I did not mean to tell you all this, but I thought—I *knew* I could trust you and depend on your help. All I ask is that you will let it go a day—two or three days perhaps—until my poor father is safely away, and then you must do all you can to help the police and revenge your friend Hunt. Just a few days. . . . Can you not do that for me?" She laid a hand on his arm.

"Oh, I suppose so," said Maurice. "God knows, we seem to be in enough of a mess already. Anyhow, let's get out of this place now."

"Very well. But there is much more that I must say to you. We can talk on the way back to my hotel."

"Hotel be damned! We're going somewhere where I can get a good strong drink and a couple of bites of chow."

Maurice found both the front door and the area door locked.

"Nothing for it but to drop out of this window. Are you any good at dropping?"

Lena gathered up her skirts and vaulted lightly on to the sill.

"With you beside me, my Maureece, I can do anything."

A prowling night-hawk of a taxi picked them up and took them across the river, and after a few minutes' drive stopped outside a door in a mews. Maurice paid off the driver and Lena looked doubtfully at blank windows and a closed door.

"Are you sure this is the right place, Maureece?"

"Sure thing. You wait half a mo'."

He knocked on the door and a shutter in a grill slid back to reveal a face which looked at them in silence for a minute and was then withdrawn. A key was turned in the lock and Maurice and Lena were ushered in through a tiny lobby to a long low room, blue with tobacco smoke, where a dance band was droning out the latest fox-trot. Maurice chose a table in an alcove and ordered bacon and eggs and a bottle of Mumm. When the waiter had taken the order Maurice turned to Lena.

"I don't want to talk about this business. The less I know about it the better, perhaps. But tell me, why did you come to that house in Graves Crescent?"

"Because you were there and I was frightened. I did not know what Alfred would do."

"Alfred again! How does he come into it?"

"He sent you a telephone message, did he not?"

"Well, I got a message, certainly, but the clerk told me it was from you."

"I did not send it. Listen. After Alfred left our room in the hotel I stayed there for a time resting. Then I went down to the lounge to see if you were still there, but you were gone. I asked at the desk if you had left any message and the clerk looked at me a little queerly and said, 'No, madam, but I gave him your message.' Of course, I realized then there was something wrong. He said he told the gentleman that he was to go to No. 96 Graves Crescent at 3 a.m. Was that not right?' 'That was quite correct,' I said, 'I wished to make sure that Mr. Crane had been told.' I left the hotel at once and drove in a taxi to the house in Graves Crescent, but I could not get in. There was but one person who could have sent such a message. It was Alfred. I feared that he would do something violent, and at half past two this morning I slipped out of the hotel. I had to walk and walk until I could find a taxi. That was why I was late. I had to climb in through the area window, which was open."

"I'd have been a gonner if you hadn't turned up."

"Please do not speak like that. It is too horrible . . ."

"Righto, old lady. Ah! Here's the food. Stoke up."

When the champagne had been lowered and the bacon and eggs despatched Maurice ordered liqueur brandies.

"I don't know about you, Lena," he said, "but I'm about ready for bed. What's the programme for today?"

"Maureece, you must keep out of sight until I send for you. Will you promise me that?"

"But why?"

"Because if you are seen by the police you may be in a very difficult position. That unfortunate affair of Captain Hunt took place at the office in Chancery Lane very shortly before you arrived there on Thursday evening. If Alfred was cornered he might say that you were there at the time, that you were the one who . . . Oh, can't you understand?"

"Oh yes, I see what you're getting at all right. This is going to take some thinking over,"

"Please do as I say. Where can you stay?"

Maurice scribbled an address on the back of a menu.

"I'll remain there till six o'clock tonight. I shall probably sleep till then, anyway."

"And if you want me before then I shall be at the Hotel Warham. Do not ring me up unless it is absolutely necessary."

"I shall want to see you long before six o'clock," Maurice replied. "But I'll try and be good and not bother you. Give me a kiss before you go."

CHAPTER XIII

ON SATURDAY MORNING at nine o'clock Thompson had Filson's report. Hunt's flat in Clark Street had been searched but with singularly little result. There was not a scrap of writing to indicate how Hunt spent his time nor whom were his associates. The porter of the block of flats had been questioned, but again the police had drawn a blank.

"And now where do we go from here? It's not often one comes up against such a dead end as this."

"No. It's devilish odd," Lomax replied. "Of course, there's this fellow Maurice Crane. According to Woods he'd been out with Hunt."

"Yes, that's right. They'd been in the Navy together, but Crane was only a pigeon, if Woods is right."

Lomax picked out a paper from the pile on the desk.

"This is Filson's report on Crane," he said. "He hasn't been able to locate Maurice, but Henry Crane, his brother, is in Town and can be found during the day at Plum Court, Temple."

"Hasn't been able to locate him, eh?" Thompson filled his pipe thoughtfully. "It's not often Filson slips up on a job. I wonder why he couldn't trace young Crane. He must have left some tracks unless, of course, he didn't want to be followed. The best thing we can do is to trot along and interview the brother."

A quarter of an hour later Thompson knocked on the door of Henry Crane's Chambers and was admitted by a clerk.

"Mr. Crane, sir? Yes, he came in not ten minutes ago. He's got an appointment at 10.30, and I don't know whether he will be able to see you. Have you an appointment, may I ask?"

Thompson handed his card.

"No, but my business is urgent, and if he can spare me a few minutes I would be much obliged."

"I'll see what I can do, sir."

A moment later the clerk reappeared.

"Will you please step this way, sir? Mr. Crane will see you now."

He held open the door. "Mr. Thompson."

Henry Crane looked from the card before him to Thompson. There was a puzzled frown on his face as he rose to shake hands.

"You are a police officer, I see," he said.

"Yes," Thompson replied. "I'm sorry to bother you, as I know you're busy, but I think you may be able to help us. It's about your brother, Maurice Crane."

"Maurice? Why, I haven't seen him for the last couple of days. It was Wednesday he went away."

"Where?"

"To Norfolk. You see, what happened was this. Our house at Starring was burgled on Tuesday night and the police wanted someone to go there and tell them what was missing. My brother left on Wednesday morning in my car. He said he would try to get back that night if possible, but I've heard nothing from him since he went. I suppose it is in connection with that affair that you wished to see him?"

Thompson coughed.

"Well—er—not exactly. It's about a man named Hunt."

"Hunt? I've never heard of the man."

"Your brother knew him. Are you sure he never mentioned the name to you in conversation?"

"Of course he may have, but I've no recollection of his having done so."

Thompson thought for a moment and then asked:

"It is rather curious, isn't it, Mr. Crane—your brother not communicating with you?"

"Yes, I suppose it is in a way, but he's like most young men of his age, rather irresponsible. If he ever makes a plan he never sticks to it."

"But he'd know that you'd be anxious to hear of the result of his visit to Norfolk."

"Yes, of course. As a matter of fact, I've been very busy during the last two or three days."

"Yes, I understand that, Mr. Crane, and I don't think I need bother you any more this morning." Thompson rose and turned towards the door. "Oh, there is one favour I want to ask of you and that is that I may have a look round your flat? I'm very anxious to get into touch with your brother, and it is possible I may find some indication as to where he has gone."

Henry Crane hesitated.

"It is rather unusual," he said after a short pause. "But if you wish I could arrange to be at the flat at six o'clock this evening. Will that suit you?"

"I am afraid I can't wait until then, Mr. Crane. This matter is urgent."

"Do you mind telling me what it's all about, Inspector? You mentioned a man Hunt a few minutes ago. Is it him you're after?"

"No, Mr. Crane. He's safe enough in the Southwark mortuary. He was murdered on Thursday evening."

"You should have told me of this before you questioned me."

"I'm sorry, but I do not see why," Thompson replied quietly.

"My brother knew this man Hunt, you say?"

"That is my information. It is only natural that we should want to trace anybody who had seen Hunt lately."

"Yes, I understand that, but . . . Oh well, I suppose it's no good objecting. I'll ring up my butler and let him know you'll be round some time this morning."

Thompson picked up his hat. "Thanks very much, Mr. Crane. I'm glad you're being so reasonable. Good-bye."

"Reasonable be damned," thought Henry Crane to himself. "If I had refused he would have got a search warrant."

· · · · ·

From Plum Court Thompson took a taxi to Scotland Yard, where he picked up Lomax and then ordered the driver to take them to the Crane's flat in Hilberry Mansions. Lomax glanced at his Chief as he entered the cab and grinned.

"I can see you're on to something. What is it?"

"We're going to the Crane's flat now to see what we will see."

In answer to Thompson's knock a manservant opened the door of the flat in Hilberry Mansions.

"Mr. Thompson?" he asked.

"Yes, that's right. How d'you know?"

"Mr. Crane rang me up a few minutes ago to inform me that you might call."

Thompson laughed. "'Might' is good," he said. "He knew damn' well I'd be right along. Well, let's get on with it. You needn't wait about. I'll ring when I want you."

The servant bowed and withdrew. Thompson turned the handle of the door opposite him and walked into the sitting-room. It was a very ordinary room, furnished with deep comfortable chairs and a thick pile carpet. There was an array of invitation-cards on the mantelpiece and Thompson examined each one in turn.

"Now let's turn out that bureau."

Swiftly and methodically the two detectives examined the contents of every drawer and pigeon-hole. Stuffed away at the back of a pile of envelopes Lomax came on a sheet of crumpled paper stuffed into an envelope. There was a printed heading which read: *International Developments, Ltd., Chancery Lane,* and below a few lines of typewriting.

"*Dear Crane* [Lomax read out]. *We are having a final meeting here on Thursday afternoon at 4 p.m. when I hope to complete the preliminary matters in connection with our venture. I am counting on your support.*"

It was signed *Samuel Hartford.*

Thompson took the sheet from Lomax and carried it to the window.

"No sign of dust on it as far as I can see," he said at last. "I wouldn't mind betting it was written quite recently. The ink of the signature appears to be fresh enough." He pushed the bell, and when the servant appeared he handed him the envelope.

"Have you seen this before?"

"Yes, sir. A man brought it on Wednesday evening. He asked me to make it clear to Mr. Maurice that it was essential that he should attend the meeting on Thursday at 4 p.m."

"What was the man like?"

"About the average height, sir. Rather fat and red-faced. He wouldn't give me his name. I laid the note on the top of the bureau so that it would catch Mr. Maurice's eye if he came in when I happened to be out."

"Did you notice anything particular about this man? What sort of hat was he wearing?"

"I didn't see, sir, I'm afraid." The man scratched his head. "But he was wearing one of them old-fashioned watch-chains, Alberts I think they're called, with a bunch of seals and keys on it."

"I found this note tucked away at the back of one of the pigeon-holes. Do you know how it got there?" Thompson queried.

"I'm afraid I can't say, sir. I hadn't noticed that it was gone from where I had laid it. I remember seeing it on Thursday morning because it was then a gentleman called to see Mr. Maurice. He was rather upset to learn that he was out of Town. I suggested he might like to write a message. He said he would, sir, and I left him in here alone. About five minutes later he rang for me and gave me a note to give Mr. Maurice, and now I come to think of it I didn't see the other letter after that."

"Have you got the note he left?"

"Yes. I'll get it. It's in my pantry."

A moment later the servant returned with an envelope addressed to Mr. Maurice Crane, which Thompson took and opened.

"Gosh! This is a queer go," he muttered and handed it to Lomax. "It's handwritten and word for word the same as this other letter except for the fact that 'Friday' has been substituted for 'Thursday', the signature of 'Samuel Hartford' is in quite a different handwriting to that in the typewritten letter. The man who wrote it obviously did so for the purpose of keeping Maurice Crane away from the meeting on the appointed day."

"Perhaps the date of the meeting had been altered," Lomax suggested, but Thompson shook his head.

"No, that won't work. You see, the signatures are entirely different." He turned to the butler, "What exactly happened when this man called? After he had asked for Mr. Maurice Crane you left him in here to write a note?"

"Yes, sir, and then he rang the bell and handed me the letter I gave you."

"Did he leave a card or anything?"

"No, sir, he just told me to tell Mr. Maurice that Captain Hunt had called."

"Hunt? Are you sure that was the name?"

"Oh yes, sir. Quite sure."

Thompson and Lomax exchanged a look.

"What were Mr. Maurice Crane's movements during the week-end?" Thompson asked.

"He went down to the country with his brother, sir, and came back on the Monday morning. He slept here Monday and Tuesday nights, and on Wednesday he took the car to Norfolk on account of the burglary at the Grange."

"And when did he return?"

"Thursday evening, sir. But he rang me up first. It would be about five o'clock, I think, but it may have been later. I told him there were two letters for him and I gave him the verbal message about the meeting taking place that afternoon at four o'clock. He said he knew about that, and that he would go round to the office."

"Where was this office?"

"Mr. Maurice didn't say, sir. He came to the flat about half an hour later. He ran into his bedroom and picked up a few things. 'I shall be away for a few days,' he said. 'Tell my brother when he gets back.' "

"Oh, Mr. Henry was out of Town, then?"

"Yes, sir, he was on circuit and he was to arrive back in Town this morning. I haven't seen him yet, as he drove straight to his Chambers."

"I see. Thank you."

Thompson and Lomax left the flat and hailed a taxi.

"This is a damn' funny show, Lomax," said Thompson, after he had given the driver instructions to go to Chancery Lane. "The fat red-faced man who left the first note was apparently Hartford, and the description that butler fellow gave us of him fits the man who was murdered in Honeypenny's shop in the Borough. You'll remember there was just such a watch-chain as he described on the body. If that is correct we have both the murdered men calling on Maurice Crane within approximately twenty-four hours of their being knocked out. Hunt's body was found outside Honeypenny's house, and the other man, who may be Hartford, was murdered in his shop. On the face of it it looks as though Maurice Crane may have been mixed up with one or both of the killings. At least he knew both the victims."

The taxi drew up outside an office block in Chancery Lane. Lomax paid off the driver and followed his chief up the staircase to the offices of International Developments Ltd. The half-glazed door with its fresh black lettering was locked. The name "Samuel Hartford, Managing Director," caught Thompson's eye. He pointed to it and said:

"You see! Hartford's name again, and the paint has not long been dry. Go and hunt up the janitor. I'll wait here."

A few minutes later Lomax returned with the custodian of the building in tow.

"I hears you wants to 'ave a look at this 'ere office, guv'nor? Well, I 'ardly knows if I can let you in. Not without a written order, that is, from the boss."

A half-crown, however, settled his scruples and he unlocked the door.

"You're not agoin' to take anything away, are ye?"

Thompson reassured him.

"No, no, we just want to have a look round. You'd better stay. I'll want to ask you a few questions later on." He looked round the room. "Carpet gone," he muttered, and dropped on his knees on to the bare boards. "Bring your torch here a minute, Lomax. Someone seems to have been scraping the boards and a pretty rough job they've made of it. Look out you don't get a splinter in your hand."

Thompson rose to his feet and resumed his scrutiny. A book-case filled with ledgers and account-books caught his eye and he pulled one out at random. The date of the last entry was for the month of October three years before. Lomax looked at the page over Thompson's shoulder.

"It seems to have had something to do with a corn chandler," he said, and picked out a fat ledger. "I say, look here, this is quite different." He turned back to the first page and read out, "John Silver, Haberdasher, in account with Carnew, Atkins & Co."

Thompson made a brief examination of the other books.

"This is a proper job lot and no mistake," he said. "It looks to me as though International Developments Limited was a very queer concern and all this lot was mere window-dressing, bought to make the room look like an office."

He walked over to a typewriter in one corner of the room and slipped a sheet of paper under the roller. Then he tapped out a line of characters and compared it with the typewritten note which had been left at Crane's flat. Then he handed the two sheets to Lomax.

"What d'you make of that?" he asked.

Lomax examined them in silence for a minute or two and then handed them back.

"I'm not an expert on this sort of game," he said. "But it certainly looks as if this note signed Samuel Hartford had been typed on this machine. There are several characteristics which seem to tally. That 'e', for instance, and the tail of the 'f' is cut off in each case."

"Yes, that's what I thought," Thompson agreed. "And now let's get on with it."

He opened the door which led into the inner office.

"You do that while I finish off here."

The janitor lit a cigarette and watched Thompson stolidly as he turned out every drawer and pried into every corner. Now and again the detective would gather up a pinch of dust and place it in a seed envelope.

"Lucky you come today, mister. If it had been tomorrer you'd 'a' bin out of luck."

"How's that?"

"New crowd's comin' in next week, and I've got me orders to clean the place out. I would have had it done already if I 'adn't bin that busy. This lot's bin behind with the rent and the guv'nor is givin' 'em the push."

Thompson lit a cigarette and perched on the edge of the table.

"I see there's a name on the door. 'Hartford, Managing Director.' What was he like?"

"Oh, 'e was quite an ordinary kind of bloke. Quite a jolly sort. Fattish."

"Anything else about him you noticed?"

The janitor scratched his head.

"No, I don't think so, guv'nor."

Lomax reappeared from the inner room with the report that he had found nothing of interest. Thompson nodded and turned to the janitor.

"When did you last see this man Hartford?" he asked.

"I can't say when it was. Maybe a week ago, but there was some pals of 'is come to the back of the building round about nine o'clock on Thursday night. They had a basket with them. It was a laundry basket, I think, on pram wheels. They took it off the chassis and hoisted it up to this floor on the outside lift we use for taking away the rubbish."

"A laundry basket?" Lomax repeated, then asked: "How many men were there?"

"Two. One was a sandy-haired little chap and the other was taller. I didn't pay much attention to 'em as I was in a 'urry to get away to the pickshers."

"Did you go the pictures?"

"Yes, as soon as I saw they could work the lift. I told 'em to lock the door when they'd finished and leave the key under the mat."

"So you didn't see what they did with the laundry basket?"

"No, guv'nor, I didn't, but the little feller, the sandy-haired one, said as 'ow they'd come to take some books away from this 'ere office."

"It was a bit risky, wasn't it, to leave them here alone?" Thompson suggested. "They might have been burglars."

The janitor laughed.

"No, not them. They wasn't burglars. I'd seen 'em in and out of 'ere two or three times."

"What time did you get back from the pictures?"

"It was after eleven, guv'nor. The door was locked and the key was where I told 'em to put it, under the mat."

Thompson gave a description of Maurice Crane and asked: "Did you ever see that man about the place?"

"No, sir. Not to my knowledge."

"You're sure he wasn't one of the two men who came with the basket?"

"I'm certain sure he wasn't," replied the janitor. He thought for a minute. "I say, hold on, mister. Now I come to think of it I did see that young chap. I was up on this floor on Thursday afternoon mending a sash-cord on the passage window."

"What time was that?" Thompson asked.

"Some time after five it would be. I was busy on my job when I heard someone rattling this 'ere door handle. I turned round and I saw the door open and a girl come out. They talked together for a bit and then went off down the stairs."

"What was the girl like?"

"I didn't see much of her, to tell the truth, and I couldn't make out what they was saying all except one word. 'Maureece' it sounded like to me, and I wouldn't be surprised if she didn't turn out to be some kind of furriner."

"Did this man go into the office?"

"No, guv'nor. Didn't I tell you? They had a bit of a chat and then the two of them went off down the stairs arm in arm."

Two hours later Thompson sent for Lomax to come up to his room.

"I've been thinking over what that janitor fellow told us," he said. "And as far as I can see it appears to let Maurice Crane out. What do you think?"

"Yes, it certainly looks like that," Lomax replied. "But we'll have to trace him all the same and find out what his story may be."

"Yes, of course," Thompson agreed. "But meanwhile have a look at this little lot." He pointed to a pile of typewritten sheets on his desk "It's a report from the lab. I'll read it to you. 'A careful comparison has been made between samples of dust labelled G.C. 96 and C.L., and though it is impossible to come to any definite conclusion there are certain factors present in both samples which would appear to indicate that they were obtained from the same source'. There's a lot more of it, but it boils down to this: that the dust on the back of Hunt's coat was very similar to that found in the Chancery Lane office, which means—"

"That Hunt was murdered in the office of International Developments Ltd.!"

Thompson nodded agreement.

"And his body was taken to Graves Crescent in the laundry basket belonging to Thomas Honeypenny," Lomax continued. "The men concerned with the disposal of the body were Alfred Brown and another we haven't fixed."

"Yes," said Thompson. "By the way, I've looked up old Honeypenny's alibi, and it seems to be sound enough, and in doing so, I unearthed another interesting fact. The police at Warbuck say that the man who made the original complaint against old Honeypenny was Maurice Crane. Crane left Warbuck at about four o'clock, which would mean he would arrive in London just about the time mentioned by the Cranes' butler. After telephoning Hilberry Mansions he went to the office in Chancery Lane. What happened there, of course, we don't know, but it's odd that he should have returned to the flat apparently in a hurry and then disappeared without leaving a trace behind him."

"You think he had a hand in the killing of Hunt?" Lomax queried.

"Well, what else would have made him light out like that?"

"But he's not the type of man you'd expect to be a murderer," Lomax objected.

"Murderers aren't a type. You know that as well as I do. It's impossible to classify them. I don't know whether I was right," Thompson continued, "but I've got the evening papers to publish Alfred's and Maurice's descriptions."

"I think it was the only thing you could do," replied Lomax. "But it's going to mean the hell of a lot of work. Every damn' fool in the country'll be writing in that they've seen 'em."

"Yes, it'll be hard work right enough," Thompson replied. "But what does that matter if we catch the man we want?"

There was a knock at the door and Filson entered carrying a parcel.

"This has just been brought in by one of my men, sir. I thought you'd better see it straight away." He cut the string and disclosed a dagger in a blackwood sheath ornamented with inlaid silver. "It was found on a hawker's barrow in Sole Street," he explained, and withdrew the blade. The point had been snapped off about an inch from the end. Thompson held out his hand.

"I say, give it to me a minute." He took a piece of steel from an envelope. "By Christopher, it fits! D'you see that, Lomax? This was the knife with which Hunt was stabbed. What an astounding bit of luck! We'd better have it tested for finger-prints, but I don't expect we'll get any results."

"Do you think it would be any good showing it to Henry Crane?" Lomax asked.

"What d'you mean?"

"Well, if Maurice is our man his brother has probably seen this knife before. We could spring it on him and see how he reacts."

"Yes, I'll do that. Take a taxi to the Temple and bring Henry Crane here. Don't tell him what we want him for."

Half an hour later Lomax showed Crane into Thompson's room, and the latter rose and indicated a chair facing the window.

"I'm sorry to bother you again," he said. "But there are a few points I would like to clear up. First of all, I believe your brother was in Town on Thursday afternoon?"

"He may have been. Inspector, but I've been in the country for the last few days and I haven't been back to the flat yet."

"He didn't communicate with you in any way?"

"No. But I told you that when you came to see me this morning, and I don't see why I should have to go through all this again," Henry protested.

Thompson picked out the dagger from under a pile of papers and drew the blade with a flourish.

"Ever seen this before?"

"Good God, it's . . . No, of course not." But his eyes were fixed on the gleaming steel.

Thompson looked over at Lomax.

"I don't think we need bother Mr. Crane any more," he said.

CHAPTER XIV

ALFRED WAS NOT the man to sit back and take it easy if there was a job to be done, and as soon as the offices were open in the City he sought out Blacker.

"I've got the dough," he said simply. "I want you to put through this *Karnoc* deal as quickly as you damn' well can."

Blacker looked at his friend curiously.

"You didn't seem too keen on it yesterday, Alfred."

"To tell you the truth, old man, I wasn't too sure I could raise the wind, but I had a bit of luck and managed to raise the ready from an uncle of mine, and I want you to put the deal through in his name."

"He'll have to sign the contract and the application to the Register," said Blacker.

"There won't be any trouble about that," Alfred replied. "You let me have the papers and I'll do the rest."

From the City, Alfred journeyed westward to Kudorfer's hotel. There he found Johannis sitting at the same table in the lounge drinking wine and smoking a foul cigar.

"Ah, here you are. Sit down, my friend. I have something to tell you. I have heard from my son in Posnik. He is ready to do what we wish, but he says we must hurry. The fogs now are good and thick, but next month it may be clear. It need not be very bad, you understand, but a fog we must have or else the under-writers may how you say?—smell a mouse."

"There needn't be any delay," said Alfred. "I've got the cash— the money."

"From this Mr. Crane?"

"No, he's out of it."

"I'm glad of that. He was altogether too big a fool. He was also an honest man and that's what we do not want. Mr. Hartford is also a fool."

"He's out of it too," said Alfred shortly.

"So? Then it is just we two. That is better and better. When do we start?"

"Today's Saturday. I ought to be able to complete the sale on Monday. There's the crew to get, but that shouldn't take long. Let's say Tuesday."

"Must I stay here till then? This hotel, I tire of him. All day I sit and think of my home. I have nothing to do."

Alfred took out his wallet and produced a five-pound note.

"Go and settle your bill now," he commanded. "Pack your gear and warn your daughter. I'll wait for you both in the lounge downstairs."

"That is good news. Thank you, my friend. In ten little minutes we shall be ready."

As Alfred was descending the staircase a man approached the lounge from the outer hall. There was something about him which Alfred didn't like. He couldn't have analysed his impressions if he had tried. Perhaps it was the man's clothes, though in themselves they were undistinguished. A blue serge suit with a pin-stripe pattern. Double collar and polka dotted blue tie. He was carrying his felt hat in his hand and a raincoat over one arm. Alfred sensed that he was a policeman and stood stock still in the shadows where he could watch, although he couldn't hear the visitor. Detective-Sergeant Woods strolled up to the reception-desk and produced his card.

"Do you mind if I look through your register?" he asked, and the clerk on duty swung it round on its swivelled stand.

"There's not many in the house," he said. "Were you looking for anybody in particular? Perhaps I can help you?"

Woods ran his eye down the entries.

"The man I'm after is a short, sandy-haired chap, five feet six or thereabouts. Clean-shaven."

The clerk laughed.

"You've got a job on all right. What d'you want him for?"

"Nothing special. Just like to have a talk with him. Have you got anyone here that would answer that description?"

"No. I'm afraid not."

A name in the register caught the detective's eye. "Kudorfer. I've never run across that name before. What's he like?"

"Short and fat. Thick, frizzy sort of hair and a black moustache. He's usually in the lounge about this time, but he must have gone out."

Woods turned over the pages of his diary and read over an entry.

"He's no use to me," he replied. "I'll have to be beating it. I've got two days' work to do before I knock off tonight. Fifteen hotels to visit and I expect it will be the same tomorrow. So long."

Alfred waited on a bend of the stairs until Woods had gone and then ran up to Kudorfer's room. The "ten little minutes" were nearly up, but there was still a pile of clothing on the bed waiting to be packed.

"I am not sorry to leave, no," said Johannis as Alfred entered. "But where do we go now?"

Alfred looked at his watch. It was nearly twelve o'clock. He had no doubts as to their destination, but to get there in safety was the difficulty. If by mischance the police had traced a connection between himself and Geoffrey Hunt or Sam Hartford, every man on duty would be on the look out for him. His description would have been broadcast in the form of a Printed Information. He had seen one once and he had never forgotten the black headline—"Wanted for Murder". An hour ago he had felt safe, but the visit of the detective to the hotel bureau gave rise to doubts and fears. What had that "busy" been after? Was it only a formal examination of the register? Kudorfer felt that there was something wrong and looked up from his job of closing the lid of his over-packed suit-case. Alfred had ignored his question as to where they were bound for and was standing at the window beating a tattoo on the pane.

"I am ready now," said Kudorfer, and lifted his heavy case off the bed.

"Hell! We can't lump that thing round with us."

"You mean—"

"That bag of yours. It's too big. And I s'pose your daughter's got one too?"

"Yes. But I do not understand. We can go by cab," Kudorfer replied.

"Yes, I know, but it'll be better if we go separately." Alfred handed Johannis a handful of silver. "You and Lena go downstairs. Carry the bags yourself and when you get into the street turn left and walk for ten minutes. Then take a taxi and give the driver this address." Alfred printed in pencil a few words on a scrap of paper and under it drew a small plan. He indicated the route which Kudorfer was to follow in order to reach Spender's Dock and finished with, "You'll find the *Karnoc* lying there. Go on board and wait till I come. If anybody questions you say you're the night-watchman. Do you understand?"

Kudorfer nodded and folded the paper.

"When you get on board burn that," Alfred continued. "And keep under cover, both of you. You'll find the charthouse unlocked."

Alfred waited for a quarter of an hour after Kudorfer had gone and then walked down the stairs to the hotel lobby. The clerk whom he had seen talking with the detective was busy with a visitor. He waited until he was free, then he strolled up to the desk and inquired if Sergeant Sims had called.

"You mean a soldier, sir?"

"No, no, a detective." He gave a short description of Woods.

"Yes, sir, there was a police officer here not more than half an hour ago. We get him in here fairly often, but I'm glad to say he's never found anyone he's after in our hotel. That sort of thing would do us quite a lot of harm. Why, I knew one case where an old gentleman was murdered in a small hotel not far from here and the manager told me afterwards that it took him a year to pick up the trade he'd lost through that. That's the sort of publicity which does nobody any good."

"Then he didn't have any luck?" queried Alfred.

"No, sir, and I don't envy him his job. There must be hundreds of men with sandy hair knocking about when you come to think of it, but all the same I wouldn't mind betting the police'll get their man in the end. They don't give up in a hurry."

"Oh, I don't know about that," replied Alfred, and sauntered out into the street. Was it a mere coincidence that the police were looking for a man with sandy hair, or had they got his description? Alfred dithered between hope and fear, and pulled his hat farther down over his eyes. He was beginning to experience for the first time since that fatal meeting in the office the cold fear of a hunted man.

A policeman was approaching from the end of the street a hundred yards distant and Alfred, in spite of himself, turned into a bookshop. His hand was shaking as he took a book at random from the shelves. God! What wouldn't he give for a pinch of 'snow'! He'd had some once and it had brought sleep in exchange for a ten-shilling note. The sleep of forgetfulness. His eyes focused on the picture on a book wrapper. It was of a masked man with a revolver in his hand, and he was about to thrust it back into its place when he hesitated. A mask? That, of course, was impossible, but the idea was good. He glanced out through the door and saw the constable pacing slowly by.

As soon as he was past the entrance Alfred left the shop and inquired the way to the nearest chemist. There he bought a roll of bandages, some lint, and a packet of cotton wool. In a draper's he bought a large, black silk handkerchief, and finally in a tobacconist's he purchased a heavy ash walking-stick. Then he walked to Oxford Street and in an underground lavatory near Tottenham Court Road he unpacked his parcels. The bandage he would round his head in such a way that there remained only slits for his eyes and one for his mouth. The handkerchief did duty as a sling for his left arm. He had some difficulty in adjusting his head bandages so that his hat would remain on, but he managed it in the end and hobbled up the stairway to the street.

There are few things quite so annoying to an active man as to walk slower than his usual pace, and Alfred, unaccustomed to playing a part, had to force himself to maintain the unsteady gait of a sick man. At Charing Cross he took the Underground to the Monument, and after crossing London Bridge turned left down Tooley Street, and so through Marshall Alley to the "Brewery". Once inside the walls of the ruined factory he removed his bandages and made them up into a bundle in the black handkerchief. There was not a sign of a living soul between the "Brewery" and the wharf, but to be on the safe side he hid behind a pile of debris and whistled softly. The door of the chartroom on the *Karnoc* slid back and he saw Kudorfer poke out his head.

"Is it all clear?"

"Yes, come on board. There is no one here."

Alfred found the keys of the ship hanging on a nail in the chartroom and opened up the captain's cabin.

"I'll sleep here," he said. "Your daughter can have the wireless operator's room, and you must look out for yourself, until the crew come on board, then we'll have to find somewhere else."

"How long will it be before they arrive?" asked Lena.

"They'll be here on Monday and we can shove off the day after."

Kudorfer gave a short laugh and went up on the bridge to return a few minutes later with a book, which he threw down on the bunk.

"It was spring tides two days ago," he said. "Next Thursday it will be neaps."

"Well, what about that?" asked Alfred, puzzled.

"When I come on board at one o'clock," replied Kudorfer slowly, "it was high water. There was no tide running in the river and this ship she was still aground. Every day until Thursday the tide it will not rise so high as the day before. After that day the height will increase again, so that twelve days from now at about this time the ship will float once more."

For a moment or two Alfred failed to grasp Kudorfer's meaning, and then, "Damn the tide! Do you mean to say we're stuck here for a fortnight?"

"I mean just that," Kudorfer replied, and opened the book he had brought down. "These are tide tables and you see what

I say is quite correct. The ship was berthed here on the spring tide, and it will take such another tide to float her out. Come with me."

He took Alfred by the arm and led him out on deck.

"You see the mud now is almost bare and it is not yet low water. Now do you understand?"

Alfred swore. He understood only too well. That the getaway on which he had been depending might not prove available after all was a possibility that he had not contemplated for one moment, and now, after the strain of the last few hours, he felt suddenly very weak and helpless. Kudorfer, with the bunch of keys, was walking forward.

"I go to the store to get some bedding. We must have that. Lena cannot sleep on a bare mattress."

Sleep! Ye gods! And here they were cooped up in a ship with only one line of escape. The police were on his track and Alfred knew in his inmost heart that if he remained in England he would be caught sooner or later. He had given himself two days in order to get the ship ready. That was risky enough. But a fortnight! A great deal could be discovered in that time by those whose business it was to find out things. There was nothing for it but to remain on board with Kudorfer and Lena. Smoky could buy food for the two of them and act as watchdog. Alfred returned to the captain's cabin and sat down in the swivel chair before the desk. So far he had been able to act on his own, but now he must depend on others while he waited. Kudorfer and Lena passed the cabin with their arms full of blankets and pillows. Lena went up to the boat deck to make up her own bed in the wireless operator's cabin. She was silent and thoughtful, but appeared to be content to leave all the arrangements to the two men.

"We are in luck," said Kudorfer. "The stores are all on board. We shall not starve. We can stay here for months."

Alfred swung round in his chair.

"You talk as if this was a blasted picnic. Now get this into your head. The police are wise to the killing and we've got to keep under cover."

"That is not difficult. As I have said, we have everything we need on board here. In time the police, they will forget."

"They will never forget. Never."

Kudorfer spread out his hands in surprise.

"What a lot of fuss about such a little thing. In my country it is different. If the police will not forget we give them money and they wink the eye. We can do the same here, can we not? Of course we can."

He went on with his task of making up the captain's bunk.

"These blankets, they are not thick. How many do you like?"

"Look here, Kudorfer, try not to be a damned fool. The police can't be bought. Nothing on this earth will stop them. The papers have printed your description," Alfred lied, "and if you don't want to hang you must do exactly what I tell you."

"So? They know? Why did you not tell me this before? You allowed me to go through the streets alone. I should have stayed at the hotel or taken a ship abroad and yet you make me come here. Like a rat I will be trapped. Like a rat I will die. Who brought me to this country? In Posnik I was happy. In Posnik I was king."

"Yes, and in Posnik you were bored. Tired of life. The chance of making money made you leave your happy home. Besides, it was Mr. Hartford who asked you to come, was it not?"

"I was forgetting. Yes, it was him. Oh, if I meet him again let him watch out."

"You won't meet him again," said Alfred quietly, and blew out a cloud of smoke. The excitement and the anger of Kudorfer had the effect of quieting his own nerves and calling up his reserves of power.

"Sit down," Alfred commanded. "Smoke."

Kudorfer felt for his case of cigars, lit one, and smiled.

"Sometimes I get like that. I am a fool. I am sorry."

"You blamed me for bringing you here," said Alfred, leaning forward in his chair and looking into Kudorfer's eyes. "You think I brought you into danger? Think. I am here too. I was in the office when you had that little quarrel with Captain Hunt.

How do you suppose I would stand if the police came here and found us two together?"

"I had not thought of that. Yes. Truly I am a fool. It is as you say."

Alfred dropped his eyes and Kudorfer rose.

"I will finish making your bed and then I will help Lena get something for supper. It is early yet."

It had taken more out of Alfred than he had reckoned to quell this crazy dago. He again experienced the feeling of a man who is about to lose control over his senses. He wished he could lie down now and, relaxing, perhaps sleep. He was very tired, but round and round in his brain there began to revolve the scenes of the last two days. Hartford hysterically accusing. The nightmare passage through the streets with Hunt's body in the basket. That meeting with Mrs. Honeypenny when he had had to force himself to appear ordinary and unexcited. Sam's discovery of the knife. The moment when he found that the door of No. 96 was locked and Uncle Thomas was not at home. While he was awake he could in a sense control the wild inconsequence of these memories. If he slept he would be at their mercy. He leaned forward until his head was between his knees, and as in the case of a fainting man, the action brought temporary relief. Hell! If his head would only stop throbbing. His pulses were working like trip-hammers.

"Kudorfer. What was that dope you gave Hartford?"

"Just a little mixture of my own."

"It makes one sleep, I know that, but does it make one feel foul afterwards?"

"Foul?"

"Yes. Ill?"

"No, no. It is good stuff. It will make you sleep like a man with no conscience, and when you wake it will be like a baby. In my country men would sell their wives for ten drops. Sometimes that is a small price to pay in order to forget, even if it be for but one night. That depends on your wife."

"How much have you got?"

"Sufficient to defeat an army if it was put in their soup or their coffee. Seven times distilled from the root of the Yamuki bush. From a ton of wood and months of labour one gets a bottle such as this half full. It is called in our tongue, 'Nico Laki', the passport to oblivion."

"Give me enough to last twelve hours. Last night I couldn't sleep and now I dare not."

"Very well. Lena will make some coffee first. It will not be long. Wait."

Alfred heard the door of the galley clang open and the noise of a stove being raked out. Damn those tide tables. He threw the book into a corner. Well, if they were going to stay here for a fortnight precautions must be taken. Alfred peeled off a pound note from the remainder of the haul from Uncle Thomas's house, and after a cautious look around stepped out on deck and thence on to the wharf. He found the inhabitants of the "Brewery" asleep, and it was with some difficulty that he was able to rouse Old Smoky from his bed of filthy rags and straw.

"See here, Smoky. I'm stopping in that ship over there and I want you to hang around and keep a good look out for you know who."

Smoky winked one bloodshot eye and laid an incredibly dirty finger to his nose.

"I twig, but I 'as to 'ave me lay down some time."

"You can get one of the others to give you a hand. The pay'll be two bob a day and here's a thick 'un in advance."

The note disappeared as though by sleight of hand.

"You can trust me, guv'nor. I tell yer I won't be sorry to give a miss to picking over the cans. I'm gettin' old. That's the trouble with me."

Alfred returned to the *Karnoc* to find Kudorfer coaxing the galley fire to burn. There were patches of soot on his face.

"Lena has a headache and has gone to bed," he explained. "Tomorrow I will sweep the flues. Your coffee will not be ready for some time. Such a mess that I find here. It is terrible. Dirt! Look at this pan."

Alfred beat a retreat to the captain's cabin and filled and lit his pipe, and as the blue smoke filled the room he ran over in his mind his plans for the future. He must see Dusty at all costs. Uncle Thomas? Alfred wasn't so sure about him. Of course, he needn't know who had burgled his house. He had had a perfectly easy job to carry out and he had bungled it, If he had come back as arranged on that Thursday night there would have been nothing to worry about. Hunt at that very moment would be resting in a bed of quicklime under a flagstone in No. 96 Graves Crescent with Sam Hartford alongside him to keep him company. Sam! It was strange how that man still haunted him. He had been a good chap enough in his way. Cheery, and always ready with a joke. It had been like killing a trusting dog, and yet what else could he have done? If the police had got their hands on Sam he would have squeaked.

"Anybody about?"

The voice outside caused Alfred to leap from his bunk to the door. It was Smoky bringing an evening paper. Alfred cursed him for calling out.

"Haven't you any more blinking sense than that?" he snarled. "Next time you've anything to say come aboard quiet and whistle like this. Two long and a short."

Smoky handed over the paper.

"Thought you'd like to see this," he explained apologetically. "Sorry if I did wrong, guv'nor."

"That's all right, Smoky, but keep quiet the next time. I was nearly asleep and you gave me a start."

"Yes, I knows what it's like to be on the run, guv'nor. But you'll find suthing in that there paper that'll give yer something to think about. It's about that murder up in Graves Crescent, and it seems they've got on to the bloke what done it, but ye can read it for yourself. I'll be getting along. So long."

The sun had set and it was too dark to read in the cabin. Alfred closed the door, drew the curtains over the ports, and lit the oil-lamp slung in its gimballed holder overhead. Then he spread out the newspaper on the desk.

The Police desire to interview two men in connection with the death of Geoffrey Hunt, whose body was found early yesterday morning on the steps of a house in Southwark. Description of one of the wanted men: about five feet six or seven. Fresh complexion, sandy hair worn rather long and brushed back. Last seen wearing a blue serge suit with a herring-bone pattern and yellow tie. Gold tooth in left upper jaw.

Alfred walked over to a glass and took off the yellow tie he was wearing and stuffed it into the narrow space between a chest of drawers and the bulkhead. What fools the police were to publish such a description. He could dye his hair and change his suit for another. Smoky would buy it for him. There was a knock at the door and Kudorfer entered with a steaming jug of coffee, a cup, and a plate of baked beans. He set down the plate on a table in the corner and poured out the coffee.

"You will eat first and then drink this."

He produced a phial from his pocket and measured out ten drops of the liquid it contained into the cup.

"Stir it well first, and when you have finished undress and go to bed."

"When will it act?" Alfred asked.

"That is difficult to say. With some people the effect comes soon. Sometimes within ten minutes or so. With others it is different. With you who are excited it may take as long as half an hour before you sleep. It is not possible to tell. But it will make you sleep. You will have no dreams and will wake refreshed."

When Kudorfer had gone Alfred ate his simple meal and then stirred the cup of coffee and drank it off. One last pipe and he would turn in and forget. Forget! If only he could. He could see Sam's face now as, convulsed with fear, he had stared at the knife like a man who had seen a ghost. Alfred was seeing ghosts now, but thank God he was tired. He would sleep. A delicious feeling of lassitude was creeping through his veins. He staggered as he felt for the bunk. The light was getting dim.

"I suppose the oil's run out in that blasted lamp," he muttered, as he crawled on to the bunk and groped for the coverlet.

But the lamp was burning as brightly as ever when Kudorfer came to clear away the dishes.

CHAPTER XV

THE PLYMOUTH POLICE arrested Hector Brown at 4 p.m. on the Saturday afternoon, and he was met at Paddington by Detective-Sergeant Truscott and escorted to Scotland Yard. Thompson did not take long in making up his mind that Hector was in no way implicated in the murder of Hunt nor in that of Sam Hartford. The wire which had been sent to Hector offering him the job in Plymouth was proved to have been genuine by the police in that town, and a ticket-inspector definitely identified him as having left Paddington by the 5.45 p.m. on the Thursday afternoon.

"Well, you're cleared, young fellow," said Thompson, when he had received the evidence of the railway official. "And now I'm free to ask you some questions. I expect you've read in the papers that a man was found murdered in the shop in the High Street on Friday?"

Hector nodded. "Yes, and I don't mind telling you it put the wind up me. You see, I realized at once that it must have taken place not long after I left. I laid low so that I wouldn't be mixed up in it."

"You would have saved yourself a lot of unpleasantness if you'd come forward right away," said Thompson. "But we won't say any more about that. What I want to know is what happened on Thursday. What time did you get up that day?"

"Seven o'clock, sir. I took down the shutters as usual and swept out the shop and then had my breakfast. One or two customers came in later in the morning, but they were strangers to me."

Truscott leaned forward and whispered to Thompson, who asked, "You know a man called Nick Wheeler. Who was he?"

"Yes, I knew him," Hector replied. "But I didn't cotton on to him much. He used to come round to the shop at odd times to see Uncle Thomas, but what his business was I never know. They used to shut themselves into the back room."

"When did you last see Nick Wheeler?"

"On the Thursday morning about one o'clock. He wanted to see the old man, and when I said that he was still away he was rather put out. Then he asked me if I'd oblige him by collecting a parcel from an address in Kennington that afternoon and take it to Alfred. I said I would, but I told him I didn't know where Alfred would be, and he gave me an address in Chancery Lane."

"Do you remember what it was?" asked Thompson.

"No, I'm afraid I don't. I jotted it down at the time but I don't know what I did with the paper."

"That was about one o'clock, was it?"

"Yes, round about then. There's never much doing in the afternoon, so after I had my dinner I locked up the shop. The address Nick Wheeler had given me I found was a greengrocer's shop, and when I mentioned Alfred's name the man handed me a parcel."

"What shape was it?" Thompson asked.

"As long as that." Hector indicated with his hands a length of about a foot. "And about three or four inches across. It was addressed to Alfred, so of course I didn't open it, but took it back to the shop as it was. Nick had told me that Alfred wouldn't be at the office much before four o'clock, and I didn't leave the shop till five-and-twenty to four. A telegram had arrived for Alfred and, of course, I took that with me too. I went by bus to Ludgate Circus and walked up Fleet Street to Chancery Lane. The office was in a big block at the lower end."

"What was the number?"

"I'm afraid I can't remember that," Hector replied. "But I could take you there. The name of the firm was something Developments, and it was on the third floor."

"International Developments?" Thompson suggested.

"Yes, that was it. Well, I knocked on the door of the office and Alfred let me in. He seemed surprised. I fancied he was expecting somebody else."

"Wait a minute, I want to get this quite clear," Thompson interrupted. "What did you first see when you entered?"

"Alfred took the parcel and the wire and then took a pace or two to a side table. In front of me, running pretty near the length of the room, was a long, polished table, with three or four men sitting round it."

"What were these men like?"

"There was a fat, red-faced man at the far end facing me. Alfred had been sitting at the end nearest the door. On the left side of the table I saw Dusty Miller."

"You knew him before, then?"

"Yes, in a way. I don't suppose I've spoken to him more than twice in my life, but I've seen him about with Alfred now and again."

"He was on the left, you say? Which end was he nearest?"

"He was on the chair farthest from me and the one on his right was empty."

"And what about the other side?"

"There was one man there but he was a complete stranger to me, and I didn't take much notice of him."

Thompson read out the description of Hunt and of Maurice, but Hector shook his head.

"Neither of them were there I'm quite sure. The man nearest where I was standing I might be able to recognize again, but I couldn't be certain. I couldn't see how tall he was, but I did notice he was very broad across the shoulders, and had a black moustache, rather long. I thought at the time that he was a foreigner, but I didn't have much chance of examining his features because, as Alfred was unwrapping the parcel at the side table, he twisted round in his chair and I could only see his back view."

"Then the side table was to your right as you were standing?"

Hector agreed.

"Did you see what was in the parcel?"

"I only sort of caught a glimpse of it. It was a dagger in a black sheath with a white design on it. I'm sorry not to give you a better description, but it was hardly out of its wrapping before

Alfred turned and told me I needn't wait, and there was nothing for me to do but go."

"What did you do when you left the office?" Thompson asked.

"I walked down to Fleet Street and at the corner I saw by the clock on the Law Courts that it was well after four o'clock, so I thought I'd have a cup of tea before I started back to the shop."

"What do you mean by 'well after four'? Do you remember the exact time?"

"Yes, I do," answered Hector. "It was between the quarter and twenty past. I worked it out that if I took ten minutes for tea I could get back to the shop by five with something to spare."

"At what time did you reach the shop?"

"Before five. I can't say exactly. I had a job in hand, mending a chair, and I got on with that right away, and while I was working on it a boy came in with a telegram from a friend of mine down at Plymouth. It was about a job that was going there, and ended up with the words, 'Cannot keep it open after noon tomorrow'. When Alfred had read the telegram I took to him he said that Uncle Thomas was on his way home, and I thought there wouldn't be any harm in my going off to Plymouth."

"We know all the rest," said Thompson. "I won't bother you to go through all that again. Now I think it would be to your interest if you didn't go to your home. It's possible Alfred may hear that you've been here and that might cause trouble if you fell in with him. I'll fix up somewhere for you to stay in the meantime, and I'd like you to remain there in case I want to see you again. Understand?"

Thompson turned to Lomax as Hector left the room.

"Do you see what it means if that lad's speaking the truth? At a quarter past four on Thursday afternoon Hunt was alive. Maurice Crane was expected. For you remember the note and the message from Sam Hartford which his valet gave him? And then there's the vacant chair at the table in the office."

Thompson took up a pencil and made a rough sketch plan of the office at the time of Hector's arrival.

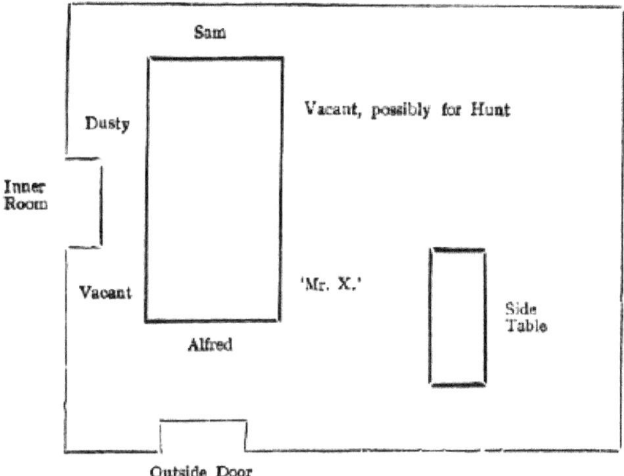

"You see, I've put Sam Hartford at the end of the table farthest from the door with Dusty Miller by his right hand. I'm assuming that Hartford was the red-faced man Hector described. Opposite Miller I've put an empty space. Alfred is at end nearest the door. It is pretty clear that when Hector arrived someone else was expected. It may have been Hunt, or Maurice Crane, or perhaps both of them."

"You haven't forgotten Hunt tried to put Maurice off," Lomax interrupted.

"No, but the butler said he gave Maurice Hartford's message over the 'phone and that made it clear that Thursday was the day. No, we can't rule Maurice out of it. Now there's one thing I'm clear about and that is that Hunt was murdered in the office between 4 p.m. and 9 p.m. on Thursday. There are four men who could have killed him. First, there's Hartford. He's dead, so we'll leave him out of it. That leaves Dusty Miller, Alfred Brown, Maurice Crane, and Mr. X. Crane is very unlikely, that's obvious, and from what I've heard from Truscott about Miller he's not a probable. I have an idea that it lies between Alfred and Mr. X."

"Yes, but it's all a matter of guess-work really," said Lomax. "I wish to blazes we knew who 'X.' was, what part he was to play in the swindle, and what exactly it was. Oh, you know you said just now that the murder of Hunt could not have been planned?" Lomax went on. "Well, what about the knife having been delivered at the office shortly before he was killed?"

"Coincidence," replied Thompson. "It must have been. Now, let's work back. Originally it belonged to Maurice Crane. It came to London by post. Nick Wheeler knew about that. Nick burgled the Grange, the Crane's house in Norfolk. Did he steal the knife at that time? And if so, how did the knife get up to Norfolk?"

"Damned if I know," Lomax replied. "What was stolen?"

"Some rather valuable Sheffield plate."

"When Woods met Wheeler on his return to Town he hadn't anything on him which would connect him with the burglary," said Lomax.

"That proves nothing. As like as not there was a carrier ready to pick up the goods and bring them to Town by some roundabout route. Uncle Thomas would fill that bill. He's an old lag and has been acting as a fence since he left Dartmoor. He went to Starring on Monday. What he did on Tuesday and Wednesday we don't know, until he was arrested on Thursday. As far as the murders are concerned he's clear enough. The police at Warbuck have more or less corroborated his story and it's certain that he wasn't released until six o'clock on Friday evening."

"If he had the stuff from the Starring job he must have cached it somewhere before the Thursday afternoon when he was arrested," said Lomax.

"Aren't you forgetting his wife?" said Thompson. "I fancy she played a part in this game. As a liar she wasn't up to her husband's standard, but she did fairly well, considering she was dead beat. When the Warbuck police brought in Uncle Thomas's car the woman wasn't there, and it doesn't need much of a brain to guess what happened. Her husband sent her on to Town with the loot."

"Yes, that hangs together all right," Lomax agreed. "But what connection had this burglary with the killing of Hunt and Hartford?"

"None that I can see," Thompson replied. "Except for the knife."

"You don't think the Grange was burgled in order to get a knife to kill Hunt with, do you?" queried Lomax.

"No, of course not, but you can't get away from it that the knife used may have come from the Grange, and it was definitely taken by Hector Brown to Alfred at the office. Alfred was connected with Uncle Thomas, who had something to do with the burglary. If the knife was taken from the Grange at the time of the burglary it may mean that Alfred was the man who arranged for it to be carried out."

· · · · ·

The inquiries into the history of the knife with which Hunt was killed began immediately after the interview between Thompson and Henry Crane on the Saturday morning. Having ascertained that the knife originally belonged to Maurice, it only remained for Thompson to discover how it had got to the hawker's barrow in Sole Street where the detective had seen and purchased it, suspecting it to be stolen property. The detective, accompanied by another, had no difficulty in identifying the barrow. The owner was one Simon Darling, and his story was a simple one. As well as a stand in Sole Street he ran a junk shop in Lambeth, and shortly after he had opened his shop on the Friday morning a dustman came in and asked him if he, Simon, would like to buy a curio. The knife—which he identified as the one bought later by the detective—was produced and, after a bit of a haggle, changed hands. As it was his day for Sole Street he loaded up his barrow and added the knife to the load, telling his boy not to sell it for less than a couple of shillings. And that was all he knew about it except when his boy reported on his return in the evening at half past six that the knife had been sold for half a crown.

In their search for the dustman the detectives in charge of the investigation inquired of the local police for the nearest dump for dust carts, and were directed to a wharf west of London Bridge on the south side of the river. By the time they had found the wharf it was nearly dark and the wharf was deserted save for a night watchman. Anyone other than a police officer would probably have called it a day and gone home, but members of the C.I.D. know no limits to their working hours when they are on a job.

A call to the Yard produced half a dozen detectives swiftly delivered in a plain van, and the search for the dustman who had sold the knife continued until he was finally run to earth in the early hours of Sunday morning in the wilds of Bromley. A certain amount of time was wasted in making it clear that he was not being arrested and that anything he said would most certainly not be used in evidence against him.

This point having been made clear, and his wife having been prevailed upon to stop screaming, a patient detective learned that on the Thursday night the dustman had arrived at the wharf with a full load. As it happened there wasn't a lighter under the tip, so he backed in his cart, unharnessed his horse and went off duty. Next morning he came down early, about half past six, because he knew that the tide would be flooding then, and a barge would probably have been brought in. The wharf where his cart was standing was open to the street, and as he came along he saw a man walking in front of him about a hundred yards ahead. At that hour in the morning it was unusual enough to meet anyone, but what drew his attention was that the man appeared to be well dressed and not a workman like himself. "He looked like a toff," were the dustman's own words.

"And I thought it was funny like. All of a sudden he left the pavement and darted across the roadway, and I saw then he'd got a parcel or suthink in his hand. After he'd passed my cart his hand was empty. O' course, people do shove things into the carts now and again. I've seen 'em do it meself, but the way he did it made me think, and when he'd gone I rummaged round and brought out a parcel tied up in newspaper. It was a knife, or, rather, a dagger, just the spittin' image of the one you've showed me, that I'll take me Bible oath on. Would I know the bloke again if I saw 'im? Well, that's 'ard to say. He weren't young exackly nor yet old. Not more than forty year I'd say, with one o' them sharp, ferrety faces. He was wearing a light overcoat, but as to what 'at 'e 'ad on I couldn't say. I never noticed that."

Thompson, when he received the report next morning, tossed it over to Lomax.

"There's just a chance he might be able to recognize the man again. You never know. These sort of chaps are never any good at giving a description, but that doesn't mean to say they can't identify a man."

"It sounds like Alfred," said Lomax. "As far as it goes."

Thompson nodded agreement.

"If we lay our hands on him we've got enough evidence to make a charge." He ticked off the items on his fingers. "Hector Brown can say he saw him at the office at 4.15 p.m. on Thursday. The knife was delivered to him. He was probably the man who dumped it in the dust cart. He stole old Honeypenny's savings, I suppose in order to help him to make a getaway, and now he's disappeared. By the way, Truscott is out after Nick Wheeler with half a dozen men. I'm told he'll speak, and I have a hunch that if he does we'll be able to tie up a few loose ends. The other man we want is Dusty Miller. I got the Sunday papers to run his photo. Something may come of that. By nine o'clock tomorrow morning he'll have been seen in a hundred different places. It's odd how many people get a kick out of writing to the Yard. It makes 'em feel important, I suppose."

· · · · ·

At eleven o'clock on Sunday morning a constable on his beat passed an old beggar squatting in the doorway of a shop. As the policeman approached he made an attempt to hide something behind a sack. The constable stopped and asked what he'd got there, whereupon the beggar reluctantly brought forth a shiny, black tin dispatch-box stamped with the letters O.R.C. A brief examination showed that the box was filled with a collection of green-baize bags, each one of which contained a piece of silver. The beggar and the dispatch-box were duly taken to the nearest police-station and a search was made through the lists of articles lost or stolen. The sergeant on duty was able to identify the box as one stolen from the Grange, Starring, on Tuesday of the same week.

At first the old beggar, who gave his name as Daniel Chadwell, refused to disclose where he had found the box, but at the end of half an hour's questioning by the station-sergeant, assisted by a constable, he broke down and in return for a cigarette he told how he had been sitting on the Embankment under the stairs leading up to the temporary Waterloo Bridge when he had seen a man thrust the box under a timber and walk quickly away. No, he hadn't seen more than the man's back, and he wouldn't know him again. That he was certain sure of. Apparently he had stayed where he was for a couple of hours and then he had put the box into his rag bag and made off.

Thompson, when he saw the box, recognized it at once by the published description as the one which had been stolen from the Grange at Starring. He piled its contents up on a table and checked them by a list which Lomax produced.

"Yes, they are all here. All present and correct. That's the lot, isn't it?"

"Yes, but look at this!" Lomax exclaimed.

Thompson adjusted the shade of his reading-lamp so that the light shone on the piece of silver Lomax was holding, which was half out of its green-baize cover.

"A thumb-print!" Thompson exclaimed. "Good. Of course it may belong to the old tramp who had found the box, or it may not. Have it sent up to the Finger-print Department, will you? Let's see, who was the last person to handle the box, according to our theory? Mrs. Uncle Thomas. Maybe it's her thumb-mark, but that we'll soon find out. By the way, where is the old dame?"

"Lodging with a policeman's wife in Balham."

"How very respectable," commented Thompson "And I expect she's hating it. Policeman's wives have to be so very proper. At least some of them have to. Others show a pretty leg at night clubs in search of evidence. Have you ever been to a night club, Lomax?"

"No, but I'd give a week's pay to get on to that line. You have the time of your life and all exes paid without a murmur, so I'm told."

Thompson shook his head slowly.

"You'd loathe it. Bad air, no beer, and a hell of a din. Bring Mrs. Honeypenny along. She may be at church. You'll have to yank her out if she is."

When Lomax had gone Thompson smiled to himself. Things were really beginning to get a move on at last. He picked up the telephone and was put on to the Finger-print Department, who sent up a man to remove the piece of silver for examination. Twelve minutes later a messenger brought the report. So the man who had handled the silver was the same man who had been at the office of International Developments and had broken into No. 96 Graves Crescent. And it wasn't Dusty Miller. The Records Office, in conjunction with the Finger-print Department, had established that fact. Thompson took out his sketch of the office which he had made on Hector's information and studied it afresh, though to tell the truth every detail of it was fixed in his mind. Alfred was his man, or was it this Mr. X? It must be one or other of them Maybe Mrs. Honeypenny would help. At that moment the telephone-bell rang. It was Truscott calling from Rotherhithe to report that he had arrested Nick Wheeler, and asking for instructions.

"Come right along," Thompson ordered. "And you'd better ask the people down there to lend you a man to give you a hand. I don't want you to take any risks."

$$\bullet \ \bullet \ \bullet \ \bullet \ \bullet$$

Mrs. Honeypenny strutted into Thompson's room and flumped down in a chair before him.

"Well, how long is this going on, mister? That's what I'd like ter know."

"If I knew that I'd leave the Force and become a ruddy fortune-teller. What's biting you? You've nothing to worry about."

"That's what you think, mister, but let me tell you one thing. I've had all the religion I want to last me my life, and I'm not having any more."

"The woman she's living with has family prayers every night," Lomax explained.

Thompson grinned.

"It hasn't done you any harm," he said. "You look twice the woman you were the last time I saw you."

Mrs. Honeypenny sniffed.

"I've been making some inquiries about you," Thompson continued. "And it appears that when you arrived in London on Thursday evening you brought with you"—he stooped down and lifted the tin box on to the table—"this."

"Well, what about it?"

"It wasn't your property."

"I know nothing about that," Mrs. Honeypenny answered quickly. "I don't know where it come from or what happened to it."

"Don't be stupid," Thompson snapped. "This isn't the time to fool around. Did you leave it at the house at Graves Crescent?"

"I told you, didn't I, that I'd lost me key? How could I have left it there?"

"Then you took it to the shop. What time was that?"

"I dunno exactly. Young Hector was putting up the shutters."

"What had he got to say for himself?"

"Nothing much. He asked where my old man was and said he was going away somewhere. I don't rightly remember what he said."

"Did he say he was going to Plymouth?"

"He might have said that, but I wasn't paying much attention to him."

"Was that because you were wanting to get rid of the box?" Thompson suggested.

"I wasn't bothering about that. I was looking for some place to sleep."

"But you left the box at the shop?"

"I might have done."

"Where?"

"Just lying about."

"Well, we won't bother about that now," said Thompson. "There's something else I would like you to tell me. You told us before that, as you found yourself locked out of the shop and your house, you slept at Mrs. Miller's."

"Yes, and that were the truth. You can ask her if you like."

"I have," was Thompson's reply. "She said Alfred brought you."

"Well, what about it? He can take me where he likes for all it's got to do with you."

"Oh yes, but you remember when I asked you about this on Friday night you said it was Dusty Miller you met the night before."

"I may have said that. I was in such a state then, the way you kept on at me that I wasn't really responsible, if you know what I mean."

"You were a bit upset," Thompson agreed. "But now let's get it straight. It was Alfred, wasn't it?"

Mrs. Honeypenny nodded.

"Why didn't you want to tell me it was him?"

Mrs. Honeypenny smoothed out her skirt and adjusted the fur round her neck before replying.

"Alfred's a bit funny at times, and he doesn't like people talking about him. I'm sure I don't know why, but that's the way of it."

"You were afraid of him?"

"In a way, yes, I was. So was my old man. Though for the life of me I couldn't say why. If you did anything to cross Alfred he just gave you one look. That was all. He didn't say anything—much."

"What time did you meet him on the Thursday night?"

"Oh, it was some time after I left Hector. I'd been walking to and fro between the shop and the house, looking for my old man and expecting him to turn up at any minute. It was dark, of course, and I hadn't the price of Guinness. I can tell you I was feeling proper low when all of a sudden I runs into him. 'Where d'you think you're agoing to?' I said."

"Where was this?" Thompson interrupted.

Mrs. Honeypenny pursed her lips in thought.

"Now let me think. I was going towards the shop. No, I wasn't. I was coming away from it. It must have been just past that little fish shop at the corner of Minnan Street."

"He was going the opposite way?"

"Yes, and I wouldn't have noticed him but I ran right into him."

"Yes, go on. What did he say?"

"He wanted to know what had come over the old man, but o' course I couldn't tell him."

"Did he seem worried, or upset?"

"Well, now you come to mention it he was a bit that way. I can't describe it quite, but he wasn't hisself, and when I told him I hadn't the key of the house he gave me one of his looks."

"What happened after that?"

"We went back to the shop."

"Why?"

"'Cause I thought I'd left the key there when I dumped the box, but it wasn't there. I must have dropped it somewhere."

"Was there anybody in the shop when you got there?"

"Not that I saw. I had an idea of sleeping there, but Alfred said he'd made up the bed for hisself and that I'd have to go to Mrs. Miller's. I wish now I hadn't. The bed was as hard as a board, but there's no gainsaying Alfred when he makes up his mind."

"Did you see Dusty that night?"

"No, I can't say as I did. Old Mrs. Miller wasn't 'arf worried about him though."

"She's not the only one who'd like a word with him," said Thompson. "All right, Lomax, have her taken back. Good-bye, Mrs. Honeypenny. Sorry about the hymns, but you'll have to stick them for a day or two longer. There's worse places than Mrs. Howlett's. You haven't been to Aylesbury, have you?"

Mrs. Honeypenny rose uncertainly to her feet.

"For God's sake, mister, say it's not going to be that. You've treated me fair up to now, and surely you wouldn't—"

"Where you are this time next week depends largely on yourself," Thompson cut in. "If you tell me everything—well, I promise nothing, but it might help. In the meantime do what you're told. It'll be safer for you that way."

"She stinks a bit, doesn't she?" said Lomax, as he threw open the window and filled his lungs with the fresh morning air. "That's the worst of this job I always think."

"She's talking at last, anyway," said Thompson. "And that's all I care about. Have you ever thought what would happen if everybody we questioned stayed dumb?"

"There'd be three thousand warders out of a job."

"Exactly," Thompson agreed. "It's a wonderful thing, the human speech."

· · · · ·

Nick Wheeler was a graduate of many prisons and convict establishments, but despite that fact he was never at ease when in the company of police officers. His attitude to them was like that of a small boy when hailed before his house master for some peccadillo. Usually he was suspicious of all that was said and as communicative as a dead oyster, but as a master may sometimes obtain the confidence of a difficult boy so Detective-Sergeant Truscott had succeeded in getting Nick to talk. How it was done Truscott could not for the life of him have explained, and he didn't bother to try. On his arrival at the Yard Truscott left Nick in charge of the detective who was accompanying him and went up to make his report to Thompson.

"It's no good my bringing him up here," he said. "He won't talk, but if you'll let me have a go on my own I may be able to do something."

"You know, Truscott, you're not being too tactful."

The sergeant flushed and Thompson laughed.

"It's all right. I know what you mean, but get a move on and remember that this bloke Alfred is the one we want to hear about. There's another man whose name I don't know. Lomax will give you his description. I'm calling him Mr. X. Find out if Wheeler knows him."

Nick gave a deep sigh of satisfaction as Truscott piloted him out of Scotland Yard and into a car.

"That's a place I don't care about," he said. "Why the hell do they want to make it like the way it is? It fair puts me in mind of Brixton, I dunno why."

"Have a 'bine and think of something else," Truscott urged.

Nick drew deeply and blew out a cloud of smoke.

"Where are we bound?" he asked.

"Southwark."

"How did you get on to me?" Nick went on. "I thought I was clear."

Truscott smiled.

"As long as you stick around the big Smoke you're never clear," he said. "And you know it. Why don't you let up for a spell and see what it's like going straight?"

"Why? 'Cause I don't know how and I've been too long at the game to make a change. Say, what's happened to the rest of the crowd?"

"Inside, mostly."

"Bet you a quid his blooming highness ain't."

"You mean the old geezer they call Uncle Thomas?" questioned Truscott.

"Like hell I do." Nick looked out across the river as they sped down the Embankment. "No," he continued slowly. "I was thinking of a little bloke round about my size, with kind of gingery hair."

"Oh, you mean Alfred?"

"I might."

Nick relapsed into silence until the car drew up at the police-station, but at the sight of the station-sergeant he broke into speech.

"Home again," he said. "Got me bed ready?"

Truscott opened a door leading into a bare, white-washed room with bars across the window.

"Sit down. I want to have a talk with you first. You might be able to do yourself a bit of good." He locked the door and sat down with his back to the light. "See here, Nick, you know me, don't you?"

"In a manner of speaking, yes."

"Well, listen here. We haven't got any witnesses. I won't take down anything you may say, but if you'll help me I may be able to do something for you." He pushed a packet of cigarettes across the table. "Help yourself."

Nick squashed the butt of his cigarette on the table and lit a fresh one.

"You want a squeak, I s'pose?" he said. "Well, that's not the way I'm made. I've got me living to make, and if you shop my pals where the hell am I going to be?"

"Alfred's not a pal of yours. He's not your sort," replied Truscott. "He'd let you down as soon as look at you."

"You're not far out there," Nick agreed. "He's a kind of an amateur. Thinks he knows everything an' knows nothing. Not but what's he's fly enough. You'll have a job catching him."

"He got you to do that job at Starring. Has he paid you yet?"

"No, he hasn't". . . . Nick checked himself, but too late. "What d'you mean, job at Starring? I knows nothing about any job there."

Truscott ignored the denial.

"He owes you some money, doesn't he?"

"I'm not saying he doesn't."

"You're broke, aren't you?"

"Just about it, or else you'd never have caught me the way you did."

Truscott took a folded poster from his pocket and spread it on the table.

"See that? 'Wanted for murder. £50 reward'."

"Fifty quid! Blimey, that's a new one on me. Getting a bit desperate, ain't you? Who's the bloke you're after?"

Truscott read the description.

"Recognize him?"

"Blimey, I'd never've thought it of him. Are you certain sure?"

Truscott re-folded the bill and placed it carefully away in his pocket-book. "As certain as I've ever been of anything," he said. "And anyone who's helped in this murder'll be as badly off as the man who did it. The man who provided the knife, for instance."

Nick shrunk back in his chair.

"The knife," he said. "Was that what it was done with?"

"You've read the papers, haven't you?"

"Papers?"

"Yes, the newspaper. There was a picture of it on the front page of the *Globe* this morning."

"I never read the *Globe*."

"It was a dagger, really," Truscott continued. "About a foot long in a black wood sheath inlaid with silver. Have you ever seen one like that?"

Nick shivered and drew back still farther.

"A knife of that description was delivered by post at a shop in Kennington on Thursday morning addressed to Mr. Alfred Brown. The postmark was Mercham, a town up in Norfolk, about twenty miles from Starring. A similar knife was stolen from a house in Starring. As a matter of fact this knife was the same as the one sent by post to Kennington. It was used to murder a man named Geoffrey Hunt in a Chancery Lane office at approximately 4.15 p.m. on Thursday afternoon."

"I know nothing about that, Mr. Truscott. I swear I don't. I don't know why I sent it. I wasn't told to. I picked it up and as it looked a kind of a curio, and remembering Alfred was a bit of a collector, I just . . ."

He broke off and, rising, pushed back his chair which fell with a crash on the bare wooden floor.

"You're a devil!" he shouted. "That's what you are! You'd make the dead speak. I had nothing to do with it, I tell 'you. Nothing! Nothing! . . ."

"Sit down, and don't be a fool."

The quiet, insistent voice of the detective had its effect, and the outburst ceased as suddenly as it had begun.

Truscott picked up the fallen chair.

"Sit down, man, and take a pull at yourself. I haven't made a charge—yet."

"What do you want of me?" Nick asked, his voice strangely flat and without expression. Cold fear had given away to despair.

"I want to know all about Alfred Brown," said Truscott quietly, and Nick Wheeler told him all he knew.

CHAPTER XVI

After Kudorfer and Lena had boarded the *Karnoc* the latter
had retired to her bunk, pleading a headache. But when the sun
had set she slipped out of her tiny cabin and took up a position
from whence she could keep a watch on the landward end of
the wharf. There she waited, smoking cigarette after cigarette,
until a low whistle caused her to start to her feet. Again came the
signal. The first few bars of a popular song. She looked forward
along the deserted decks. The windows of the cabin where Alfred was sleeping were dark. She crept to the rail and completed
the refrain.

"Lena!"

"Be quiet. Someone may hear."

Maurice ran lightly along the planking of the wharf and
climbed up over the rail of the *Karnoc*.

"I say, what's going on here?"

She laid a hand on his arm and whispered:

"It is not safe to talk here. Follow me."

The flame of the oil-lamp flared up smokily as she opened
the door of her cabin.

"Come in. We shall be all right here." Then as he closed the
door she turned and held out her arms. "And how are you, my
Maureece? We seem to have been parted a week. That is what it
has seemed like to me."

"Then let's make up for lost time."

A moment later Lena pushed him away, laughing.

"What will happen if we do not see each other for a month?"

"I shall take darned good care that that doesn't happen. You
seem to forget that we're going to be married just as soon as I
can fix up about a licence."

Lena became suddenly grave.

"I wish I could be sure about that, Maureece. Sometimes I
wonder if it can ever be. My father is in danger and it is of him
that I must think."

"Yes, I know there's heaps to be done. The man I want to get my hands on is the one who killed Captain Hunt."

"He is on board this ship now."

"Does he mean to sail with her?"

"Of course. He wants to leave the country, and who would not, if he were a murderer?"

"Hell's bells! What the Hades are we going to do? Once your father was safely out of it I was going to put the police on to Alfred's trail. Once they have his name and description he wouldn't stand a dog's chance of getting away, but as he's on board it's going to complicate matters considerably."

"Maureece, I have a plan. You shall sail in the ship with us."

"But—"

"No, please do not interrupt. It will be quite simple. You will hide in one of the boats."

"But I can't stay in a boat all the time."

"Oh, please do not be difficult! At night you can come out when the others are asleep. I will bring you food and water. The moment my father lands on Posnik you will make yourself known to the Captain and this will be your proof that Alfred is wanted by the English police." Lena took a newspaper from the bunk. Maurice read the account of the murder of Hunt, the description of Alfred, and then turned over a page.

"But, good heavens alive! Did you see this? The police want me too! Here's my name and description, as well as Alfred's."

She snatched the paper from his grasp. "That is not true! I did not see that."

"Well, it's there plain enough on this other sheet." He smiled grimly. "It seems I'm in this mess too, and I don't know the first thing about it. Tell me, when did it happen?"

"On Thursday afternoon about half past four."

"How do you know, Lena?"

"I will tell you. I was in the office in Chancery Lane, in the inner room. There was a meeting in the big room and it was then that Hunt was killed. I did not see it and I was not told who dealt the blow."

"Who was with Hunt at the time?"

"There was Alfred, a man named Miller, Mr. Hartford, and—and my father."

"You told me before that Alfred was the man, but now you say you were never told. Which is the right story?"

"I thought it must have been Alfred. He was the only one who could have done such a thing."

"But still, you don't know for certain. It may have been your—"

"No, no. That could not be for he had not got his knife with him. At home he carries one. It is a habit with him. It was Alfred who found that out and told my father he must not do so in London. It was in his room at our hotel when Captain Hunt was killed."

"What about Hartford and this man Miller?"

"I know nothing of them."

Maurice ran his fingers through his hair, and there was a puzzled frown on his face when he spoke.

"If the police weren't after me as well I'd go to them now and tell them Alfred is here, but as it is I'll stay on board, for the time being, anyway. I'll see your father later on, and when I get a hold of the true story I'll spring it on Alfred when he thinks he's alone, but I'll arrange to have a couple of the crew listening in."

"Maureece, you may kiss me as much as you like, but you must smile first."

· · · · ·

Alfred woke on Sunday morning with a head which ached and throbbed so that he hardly dared to open his eyes. He had forgotten to open the port-holes before he went to sleep, and as he was struggling with the fastenings the door opened and Kudorfer slipped into the cabin.

"Ah, you are at last awake?" he said.

"Yes, and I wish to hell I wasn't. That stuff of yours has just about finished me."

"You have had too much, perhaps. A little more and you would be dead."

"I wish I was."

Alfred turned from the light and shaded his eyes.

"Another time you must have less. If you die what will become of me?"

He picked up the phial from the table by the bunk and slipped it into his pocket.

"There was trouble last night."

"Trouble? Where?"

"Over there." Kudorfer pointed in the direction of the "Brewery" and then set to work to tidy up the cabin. "I will make you some coffee in one minute and then you will feel better. Black coffee with no sugar."

"Damn the coffee! Tell me what happened last night."

Alfred swung his legs over the side of his bunk and held his aching head in his two hands.

"Myself I saw nothing, but a man came to the wharf running. The tide was out and he went down under the piles. Later he came out and saw me. He was one of the men who was at the office last Thursday. I knew his face. He is tall and thin."

"Dusty Miller?"

"Yes, that was the name. He asked for you and I tell him I do not know where you have gone. Then he swear."

"Good. Then you sent him away?"

"No. He is on board. He would not go."

"You'd better tell him to come up here, then."

"I will bring him before I make the coffee. There is water in the basin if you want to wash."

Dusty Miller was very sorry for himself when he sought sanctuary on board the *Karnoc*. He had slept in his clothes for three nights and had not had a chance of having a wash or shave.

"Good God, what's been happening to you?" Alfred was startled at the apparition framed in the cabin doorway. "Come in, then, and sit down if you want to."

"So this is where you are." Dusty pulled the door to behind him and eyed Alfred suspiciously. "I might have known you'd have some place to run to. You didn't think of me, did you?"

Alfred laughed a little nervously.

"Every man for himself, Dusty," he said. "Besides, I've had a lot to think about."

"Well, it's all right so long as I know. Have you got a 'bine? I'm cleared right out and the Dago has only got some foul black cigars. I tried one last night and it nearly turned me up."

"There's a box on the table. Help yourself. Kudorfer's bringing some coffee along in a minute."

"Yes, and you look as if you could do with something yourself. Did you hear the rozzers last night?"

"No, thank God, I was asleep."

"More than I was. I was standing up to my knees in mud alongside this old hooker. I'd lost all feeling in my legs when I got on board, and look at these trousers! Fair ruined they are. They cost me thirty bob."

"Tell me what happened last night."

Dusty lay back in his chair and blew out a cloud of blue smoke.

"Last night," he said, "I thought my number was up. When I left you on Thursday I came along to the 'Brewery' as being the safest place I knew of to lay up. Old Smoky Joe fixed me with a doss and I gave him a couple of bob to hang round and keep his weather eye lifting. Nick Wheeler came along on the Friday. He said the busies were after him but he didn't stay. He said it wasn't safe, but it was good enough for me. Last night Smoky came and shook me. I was asleep at the time, dreaming I was manager at Selfridges. He told me there was a dozen busies coming in and that if I didn't want to be seen I'd better run for it. It was too late to make for the street side, so I made over towards the river and struck this wharf. At first I thought of coming on board right away, but then I saw a bloke messing about in the galley, so I slipped down a ladder on to the mud."

"Yes, I know the rest," Alfred interrupted. "You'll have to stop here now till the coast's clear."

"Sure I am," replied Dusty. "Now I've found you, Alfred, I'm sticking to you closer than a clam to a rock. You got me into this jam and you've got to get me out."

"Well, you can stop on board," Alfred replied.

Kudorfer appeared with two mugs of coffee and set them down on the table.

"I have been thinking," he said. "Yesterday I told you that the ship could not float for ten days because of the tide."

Alfred, sipping his coffee, grunted.

"Yes, I know. What's the good of going over all that again?"

Kudorfer produced a folded newspaper.

"It say here that north-westerly gales are expected and that will make the tide rise higher. Maybe one or two tugs could then pull us out astern. It is a chance."

"I wish to hell I could believe that."

Kudorfer tapped the paper.

"It is written here clearly about the wind. Read it."

"We couldn't wait for a cargo," said Alfred. "It would be too risky."

"What does it matter for a cargo? You have the policy? Yes? Let me see. Insured against total loss. That is all right." Kudorfer lit one of his black cigars. "Well, what do you think? Shall we make the try?"

"When'll this high tide be?" asked Alfred.

"Who knows? Tomorrow perhaps, but more likely Tuesday."

"Good. That'll give us time to get a crew on board, but only just."

· · · · ·

Blacker was a man who would do practically anything if he was paid well enough. Alfred had given him £100 when the purchase of the *Karnoc* was put through, with a strict injunction that the cash paid over should not be paid into a bank. Alfred knew that if the theft from the house in Graves Crescent was brought to the notice of the police the numbers of the notes would be circulated without delay. When Kudorfer and Dusty had retired he set down to write a letter to Blacker. He enclosed £200 in notes in the envelope, and when it was dark ventured ashore to the "Brewery". Smoky Joe was at his post sheltering from a light drizzling rain under a tarpaulin stretched over three posts. He started up at the sound of Alfred's footsteps.

"Oh, it's you, is it?" he wheezed. "How long is this going on for?"

"What do you mean?"

"Me sitting here. I don't fancy it much, after last night. The rozzers were round about the place till close on one o'clock. None of the boys could get a wink o' sleep."

"I've paid you well, haven't I?"

"Yes, yes," the old man answered hurriedly. "I'm not complaining about that."

"Anyway, here's half a quid. It won't be for more than a couple of days if you do what I tell you."

"What's that?"

"Take this letter to the address I've put on it. You'll find the place easy enough. It's not more than a tuppenny bus ride."

Smoky looked at the letter.

"I'll walk," he announced. "I haven't lost the use of me legs yet, but what about while I'm gone? I mean you'll want someone to keep a lookout, won't you?"

"I'll chance that," replied Alfred. "Now hook it."

· · · · ·

On receiving the letter, Blacker lost no time in carrying out the instructions it contained. In the course of his employment as a shipping clerk he had met a number of Merchant Service officers, and before he finished buttoning up his overcoat he had decided on which one he would first call.

Captain Lampeter's landlady sniffed when Blacker inquired for her lodger.

"He's not in," she said. "He never is in as long as they're open and he's got the price of a double gin. You'll find him at the 'Castle' down the street." She glanced at the clock in the passage. "He'll be screwed by now most likely. I don't know why you want to see an old soak like that I'm sure."

"Just a matter of a little business, that's all," Blacker murmured and hurried away down to the "Castle".

He found Captain Lampeter more or less conscious.

"I've got a job for you, Captain. £30 a month and all found."

Captain Lampeter clawed at Blacker's arm.

"Thirty pound?" he hiccuped. "Gawd, I'd do anything for that. What's the job?"

"Take a ship out to the Mediterranean and back."

"That's easy, me boy! Do it on me head. There's some think I couldn't, but they're wrong. Why, do you know what I did once—"

"You can tell me another time," Blacker interrupted. "You've got to be ready to sail by Tuesday morning."

"Well, today's only Saturday, ain't it? What's the hurry?"

"Today's Sunday."

"Good God, I can't have bin home last night. That's what it is. It's Sunday, is it? Well, well, fancy that now."

"And tomorrow you've got to get a crew together and sign 'em on before four o'clock."

"Can't be done," said Captain Lampeter firmly. "Why, I'll want a mate and a bosun and—by the way, what's the size of the hooker?"

"Five thousand tons."

"Well, I'll want seven seamen, and then there's a chief engineer and his crowd to be got."

"You know as well as I do, Captain, you can do the job in a couple of hours. There's hundreds of good men out of a job."

"Yes, yes, that's true enough, but to do it all in one day, that's asking too much of one man."

"I'll give you a hand," replied Blacker. "And it'll mean an extra ten pound in your pocket if the ship sails on the morning tide on Tuesday."

"That's all right. But what's all the hurry?"

"The ship's on a charter to load at an island in the Eastern Mediterranean and her cancelling date is fourteen days from tomorrow."

"What's the name of the ship?"

"The *Karnoc*."

"God! That lousy old box o' trouble. I knew there was a catch in it somewhere."

"You haven't got the wind up, Captain, have you?"

"Wind up? I'd navigate anything, anywhere, specially when the pay's £30 a month. You did say thirty, didn't you?"

"Yes, and plenty of good grub."

Blacker spent the busiest day of his life on the Monday following his interview with Captain Lampeter. At times he almost despaired of carrying through the job, but by dint of alternate threats and blandishments, he finally shepherded a complete crew on board the *Karnoc* at eight o'clock on Monday evening. The stores he had ordered were delivered in due course, and by the time three tugs arrived off the ship on the next morning everything was in order. The engines were warmed through and the boilers had all the pressure of steam they could be reasonably expected to stand. As the last rope was cast off Blacker stood by the rail waiting to jump ashore. Alfred was by his side.

"I don't know how to thank you, Blacker," he said, "for all you've done. I don't know who else could have done it in the time."

"That's all right, old scout. I'm afraid the Captain's not up to much, though."

"That doesn't matter. The pilot'll see us out, and after that Kudorfer'll do all that's necessary, and of course there's the mate."

"I'm afraid he's a soak, too. For the love of Mike lock up the booze."

"That's all right," said Alfred. "And now I think we'd better say good-bye. The tugs have made fast. Kudorfer says they'll pull us out all right. There was an extra three feet on this morning's tide."

The pilot on the bridge blew a succession of short blasts on his whistle. The screws of the tugs churned the muddy water of the river into a yellow froth. The hawsers tautened and shivered with the strain. Alfred gripped the rail and tried to smile at Blacker who was standing looking across the river and tapping impatiently with his foot. Alfred shifted his gaze to a scar in the wharf planking opposite to where he stood. He could hear the beat of the tugs' engines and feel the tremor which ran through the ship in answer to their pull. Water rushed and gurgled through the piles and then, as it appeared to Alfred, after hours of waiting, the ship began to move. At first so slowly that he hardly dared to believe that it was true, and then quicker, quicker, until Blacker had to stride out to keep up with the moving vessel. At last!

"So long, Blacker, and thanks. I'll let you know when we arrive."

The stern of the *Karnoc* was swung up-stream, and when she was straightened out the tugs ceased their towing and the hawsers dipped in the water.

"Let go aft."

"All gone aft, sir."

As the heaving-ropes splashed into the water, Alfred heard the ting-ting of the telegraphs in the engine-room and the deck began to quiver and vibrate. They were off!

At Gravesend pilots were exchanged and later, as the Mouse Lightship disappeared in the haze astern the *Karnoc* began to lift and heave to the swell which was rolling in from the northward. Alfred retired to the cabin which he was to share with Dusty, and lay down on his bunk. He knew his own limitations. Dusty, who was smoking a cigarette and reading an evening paper, looked up.

"Well, we're off."

"God! Don't I know it? I hate the sea. I'm going to lie down and try to forget it."

At Ramsgate the pilot was dropped, and the *Karnoc* turned southward and westward towards the Downs where a blanketing fog rolled up and the night became hideous with the sound of wailing foghorns.

• • • • •

When Alfred had told Blacker to carry through the sale of the *Karnoc* in the name of Uncle Thomas, he made a bad mistake. If the old man's name had been more commonplace than "Honeypenny" it would not have mattered, but the name stuck in the mind of a certain detective engaged in the case, and when a paragraph in a shipping paper containing that name caught this said detective's eye he began to wonder. He went farther and verified the fact that the owner of No. 96 Graves Crescent bore the Christian name of Thomas, and thereupon reported his discovery to his immediate superior. Thompson, receiving this information at noon on Tuesday, had despatched Lomax to the City to investigate the matter. Blacker, on being run to earth in the office of the late owners of the *Karnoc*, was disposed to be uncommunicative, but admitted that it was he who had arranged the sale.

"Your boss tells me you paid over the purchase money in banknotes. Was that so?" Lomax asked.

"Yes, that's right," Blacker replied. "It was a cash transaction."

"That was a bit unusual, wasn't it?"

"I suppose it was in a way, but I received the money in that form and I handed it over to the cashier right away."

"When did you receive this payment?"

"On Saturday, some time before lunch."

"Would you mind describing the man who paid it you?"

"I don't see what that has got to do with you," Blacker replied quickly. "This was an ordinary business transaction."

"Then there can be no reason why you shouldn't tell me all about it."

"I'm afraid I'm not quite a free agent. Mr. Honeypenny asked me not to reveal his identity. It is quite common for the purchaser in a deal of this sort to remain anonymous."

"That may be so," said Lomax. "We'll leave that for the moment while I have a talk to your cashier."

As soon as Lomax had left his room Blacker reached for his hat and made for the door. A policeman by the lift barred his passage. It was then that Blacker lost his head. Alfred had told him not to pass the notes through the bank, and he had asked the cashier to hold them in the safe for a day or two. It had not entered the calculations of either Alfred or Blacker that the police would come to the office and make inquiries there.

It did not take Lomax many minutes to discover that the money paid for *the Karnoc* was made up of the notes stolen from No. 96 Graves Crescent, and before returning to his examination of Blacker, he put through a call to Thompson.

On his return to the Yard Lomax found his Chief as excited as a schoolboy.

"Lomax!" he shouted. "That was a damn' lucky shot. They can't get away from us now!"

"But the ship's sailed. She was cleared early this morning."

"Yes, I know that, but you've forgotten the Navy. I've just been over to the Admiralty with the Commissioner, and they're going to help us all they can with every destroyer available."

"But what the devil's at the back of it all?" queried Lomax.

"I don't know," Thompson replied. "But if I'm certain of anything it is that the man who did the murders is now on the high seas."

"Alfred Brown put through the deal," said Lomax. "I managed to put the wind up that man Blacker, and I think he told me all he knew. Alfred first thought of buying the ship about a fortnight ago. He saw Blacker on Friday and told him he couldn't go on with it as the man he had been relying on to put up the money had failed him. However, he was back again at Blacker's office on the Saturday morning with the whole amount in notes."

"Yes, that all fits in," said Thompson. "That was the day after the burglary of the house in Graves Crescent. Alfred seems to have been the moving spirit. It was his thumb-print on that piece of Sheffield plate. The knife was sent to him. He assisted in getting rid of Hunt's body after he had been killed. He put the knife in the dust cart, and now he fixes up as good a getaway as I've ever known."

"What about the others?"

"They're probably on board too. Dusty Miller and Mr. X."

"And Maurice Crane?"

"I suppose he must be, but what's the use of guessing? In any case, he's clear of suspicion. When the ship is stopped one of them at least'll talk and we'll be able to put the whole jig-saw together."

•••••

Meanwhile the *Karnoc* chugged her way through the fog. Once the lee of the North Foreland was reached the swell began to go down and Alfred, bemused with brandy and ciga-rette-smoke, climbed up on the bridge for a breath of air. The fog had closed in around the ship, enveloping her as in a yellow shroud. Alfred glanced at the telegraph which was standing at 'full speed ahead'.

"Bit risky, isn't it, skipper?" he said. "Going at full speed in this weather."

"Risk be damned," replied Captain Lampeter thickly. "I know my way down Channel blindfolded." He let go his grasp of the rail and, staggering slightly, made his way aft to the chartroom. Then from out of the fog ahead came the wailing note of a syren. The Captain poked his head out of the doorway.

"That's a damn' warship," he said.

Alfred took a step towards the telegraph, but the Captain was there before him.

"Get to hell out of that! I'm skipper of this ship."

Again came the syren's shriek, this time finer on the star-board bow.

"He's crossing ahead," muttered the Captain. "He'll clear us all right."

Maurice, seated in a lifeboat smoking a cigarette, started up at the first sound of the syren.

"That's a destroyer," he said to himself. "And too damn' close to be pleasant." He looked out from under the canvas cover. "And we're going full speed." There was no one on deck within sight and he dropped down from the boat and ran along to Le-na's cabin. She was lying on her bunk reading a novel.

"Maureece! You fool! Go back at once!"

He stepped in and closed the door behind him.

"It's all right, no one saw me, and it doesn't much matter if they did."

"But why? What do you mean?"

"Well, we're going full bat in the thickest fog I've ever seen. There's a ship close to us now." He listened for a moment at the open port-hole. "We seem to have missed her, but why we did, I don't know. I reckon we're about entering the Downs and there's every chance of a pretty crashing collision. I came down to warn you to get your lifebelt out and stand by to make for a boat. If anything hits us we'll sink like lead. I say, what's that?"

There was a tapping on the wooden bulkhead and Lena whispered:

"It must be the wireless operator. This is his cabin, as you know. And he's next door now. Wait here while I see what he wants."

A moment later Lena was back in the cabin with a flimsy scrap of paper in her hand.

"He gave me this and asked me to take it to the Captain. He is very busy."

Maurice quickly scanned the message.

"My sainted aunt! They're on our trail! This is a message to all warships, from the Admiralty.

"*Intercept and stop S.S.* Karnoc *stop armed guard to be put on board her stop place every one on board under arrest stop escort to British port.*"

Maurice folded the message and slipped it into his pocket.

"And now what are we going to do? Personally, I've no desire to go swimming in the Channel in this fog. I don't know about you."

"I can't swim," said Lena.

"That settles it. I'm going to stop the ship. Have you got a gun?"

"A gun?"

"Yes, a revolver."

"Of course, yes. Wait a little minute." Lena burrowed in a drawer and produced an automatic.

"Will this do?"

"The very thing. And now . . ." The scream of a destroyer's syren rent the air. "Another of 'em, by Jove! I must run."

The first person Maurice saw as he reached the bridge was Alfred, and he almost laughed at the expression of blank dismay which came over that gentleman's face. A straight left sent him staggering backwards on to the man at the wheel who, taken by surprise, let go his grasp of the spokes and the two fell backwards, kicking and sprawling. The Captain, who had been holding on to the rail, vainly trying to peer into the fog, looked round into the muzzle of Maurice's automatic. He loosed his grip and lurched forward, but Maurice sidestepped in time and with a short arm jab knocked him up against the binnacle. Again a destroyer's syren sounded. Nearer this time and more ahead. Maurice leapt for the telegraph, but the Captain reached it a split second before him.

"What's this? Mutiny?" the Captain muttered. "I'm not scared of a gun, you lousy . . ."

Maurice let drive with all his strength and the Captain fell like a sack at his feet. He reached for the handle of the telegraph, but he was too late. The helmsman rushed him from behind and pinned his arms to his side. At that moment there was a shout from the look-out on the forecastle.

"For God's sake go astern!" A shape loomed out of the fog on the starboard bow. It was a destroyer, with a plume of foam at her knife-edge stem. The helmsman let go of Maurice, jumped to the wheel and started to pull it over. Maurice rang full astern. He could hear the gong clang in the engine-room, but before the engineer on watch had time to raise his hand to the reversing-gear the bow of H.M.S. *Scorpion* had cut into the side of the *Karnoc*, smashing and buckling her plates down to the waterline.

Like rats bolting from their hole before a ferret, the crew dashed up on to the forecastle deck to find the destroyer looming over them. Ropes and ladders were thrown over from the bows of the destroyer, and they clambered up with an energy born of fear. The Captain, still dazed from Maurice's blow, pulled himself to his feet and leaned over the rail and swore. Maurice rushed down the ladder to Lena's cabin. She was standing on deck calmly tying the tapes of her life-belt.

"You were a true prophet, my Maureece, and I was not unprepared."

He took her by the arm.

"Run, for the love of Mike."

The Captain of the destroyer, realizing that the damage to the *Karnoc* was extensive, kept his engines going full speed ahead in an attempt to plug the hole until the crew of the doomed ship had been saved. Water was pouring in, however, into the foremost hold and the *Karnoc* was well down by the head when Maurice and Lena gained the forecastle. A rope-ladder dangled within their grasp.

"Jump for it," urged Maurice, and when he saw her being pulled up he leapt for a rope and swarmed up it hand over hand.

Deeper and deeper sank the bows of the *Karnoc*. From the bridge could be heard the drunken voice of Captain Lampeter raised in hot dispute with someone.

"No, you don't, you lily-livered skunk! You're going to stop up here along with me. The ship won't sink. She's a good ship, that's what I says—"

"You crazy devil! Let me go, can't you?"

It was Alfred's voice, shrill and despairing. Then a third figure joined the two men on the *Karnoc*'s bridge. It was Kudorfer, just aroused from his sleep.

"What is all this . . . ?" But his words were drowned, as, with a roar, the watertight bulkhead collapsed. The engines of the destroyer were rung full astern. The *Karnoc*, rolling first to port and then to starboard, sank in an eddying swirl of water as the destroyer drew clear. Maurice drew Lena to him, trying to hide her head against his shoulder.

"I'm afraid—I'm terribly sorry, but your father . . ." She was sobbing in his arms.

"I know. I know, but—I'm glad. Some day I will tell you why."

THE END

www.ingramcontent.com/pod-product-compliance
Lightning Source LLC
Chambersburg PA
CBHW070928190726
48292CB00004B/1150